<u>Praise for *Witching Moon*</u>

"When a lunar eclipse occurs on a winter solstice, immortals are born. K.E. Bonner has written a story that's hard to put down. With compelling characters and a quick-paced plot, readers are swept into a world that spins the ordinary with the fantastical so cleverly it's difficult to separate the two. Protagonist Anne always knew she was different, that something was missing in the quiet life she led with Mama Jane and her patchwork quilt of a family. There were too many memories she could only catch the edges of, and there was something potent and curative inside her that Mama Jane called her 'shine.' Anne is happy on Cusabo Island, but from the moment she finds half-drowned Phillip and passes her healing cure into him, it's clear things are going to change. Weaving the mythical with the biblical, the common with the magical, the mortal with the eternal, Bonner tells a tale of mystery, dangerous conflict, and more than a hint of romance. As immortal Anne begins a quest to reunite with her sister and bring the powerful forces of prophecy and healing together again, we lucky readers can sit back and enjoy the ride."

—Sandy Coomer, author of *Available Light* and
director of Rockvale Writers' Colony

"With a magical mixture of romance and historical adventure, *Witching Moon* brings heroic characters and an action-packed plot together in a book that will keep the pages turning and the imagination churning."

—Rebecca Wells, author of *Divine Secrets of the Ya-Ya Sisterhood*,
The Crowning Glory of Calla Lily Ponder, and other novels

"The action-packed *Witching Moon* grabs you by the throat and never lets you go as the magically gifted Anne sweeps you along on a heart-stopping, heart-tugging journey to find her true home and her true love. *Witching Moon* is a fantasy, but the emotions are as real as they come. Treat yourself to this unforgettable heroine and this unforgettable book."

—Kimberly Elkins, author of *What Is Visible*

"Young heroine and gifted healer Anne is as tenacious as the boot-sucking marsh mud on the barrier island where she grew up. Readers will cheer her on as she embarks on a perilous journey over land and sea in search of her beloved 'selfsame' sister, Rowan, and her rightful tribe on the magical island of Amaranth. Infused with the ancient vibrations of other worlds, Bonner's first historical fantasy is a heart-thumping odyssey of self-discovery, danger, and most of all, love."

—Leslie Muir, author of *The Little Bitty Bakery*, *Gibbus Moony*,
C.R. Mudgeon, and *Barry B. Wary*

<u>More praise for *Witching Moon*</u>

"'Deep in my bones, I always knew a part of me was missing.' This is how K.E. Bonner begins her debut novel, *Witching Moon*. If you've ever felt lost or alone or out of place; if you love historical fantasy, especially one set during the Civil War; if you like adventure; then this book is for you. I love every description, especially those of the outer banks of South Carolina. This magical novel begs you to savor each page. Congratulations to K. E. Bonner on an exquisitely written and suspenseful book!"

—Katharine Crawford Robey, creative writing instructor
and author of *Cardinal Coat and Other Stories,*
Hare and the Big Green Lawn, Where's the Party?,
and *The Sleeping Bear Wakes Up*

"*Witching Moon* is a rollicking adventure yarn and a hugely impressive debut. It is, at once, intimate and epic and is elevated beyond its genre trappings by a vivid sense of time and place. The exotic and enchanting locales aren't just set pieces: they're authentic-feeling ecosystems, brimming with well-drawn characters whose rich inner lives are every bit as fascinating as their daring, breathless exploits. This is the sort of book you want to pick up and read again as soon as you've finished it."

—Brendan Murphy, writer-director of *Speakeasy,*
game writer of *Republique* and Marvel's *Iron Man VR*

"K.E. Bonner's *Witching Moon* renders the historical American South into a rich and magical land in which ancient immortals of myth confront a real and messy history. From the first engrossing paragraph, the reader is catapulted on a riveting adventure of the familiar and the fantastic with engrossing beings that have much to teach and much to learn."

—Stacey Margaret Jones, author of *Mr. Catherine*

WITCHING
MOON

K.E. BONNER

BELLE ISLE BOOKS
www.belleislebooks.com

ISBN: 978-1-947860-92-6
LCCN: 2020923839

Designed by Michael Hardison
Production managed by Christina Kann

Cover photo ©jorisfavraud / Adobe Stock #320262222

Printed in the United States of America

Published by
Belle Isle Books (an imprint of Brandylane Publishers, Inc.)
5 S. 1st Street
Richmond, Virginia 23219

BELLE ISLE BOOKS
www.belleislebooks.com

belleislebooks.com | brandylanepublishers.com

For Danny, now and always

1

March 1865
Cusabo Island, South Carolina

Deep in my bones, I always knew that a part of me was missing. Not an arm or a leg, but something that ran deep. When I was a young'un, it was hard to set my mind on just what wasn't right, but then as I grew older, visions of another girl began to seep into my thoughts. Sometimes I caught a glimpse of her out of the corner of my eye, but when I turned to see if she was really there, she never was; it made me feel like a person who's had their foot cut off but still feels the pangs and tingles of where that foot used to be.

From the frayed ends of sleep, that girl called out to me. In the mist, I followed her to the edge of a cliff, where the sea stretched out turquoise green below us. A ruby, big as the fleshy pad of my thumb, hung from a leather rope around her neck. She took my hand, and we jumped, but before we hit the water, I flapped my arms and flew away.

There ought to be a law against waking somebody up in the middle of a dream, especially one where the dreamer is flying. Ruth, my sister, wouldn't abide by any such rule. That morning, she'd roused me out of bed to get up and go check on the crab traps we'd set the day before. It was molting season, and a soft-shelled crab made for easy picking and a tasty supper. Ruth was an early riser; she leapt from our straw-stuffed pallet every morning to go wake up her luck. I, on the other hand, was fine with laying in till the light filtered through the slats of our cabin just to teach luck a lesson: it could wait on me.

The morning air was crisp, so I wrapped my shawl around my shoulders and followed Ruth down the porch stairs. Wrens were chirping their high-pitched calls while frogs croaked in return as we plodded along the dirt trail that ran through the marsh. The sun was just peeking through the clouds, lighting the path under our feet and coloring the fronds of sweetgrass gold. I would've given a hot buttered biscuit for just a few more winks of sleep.

"Anne." Ruth turned and snapped her fingers at me. "You awake?" She'd stopped in front of me, and I almost plodded into her.

"Not quite." I yawned and breathed in the salty air. "Dreamed I was chasing that girl again last night." In truth, the girl had been coming to me often in my dreams. I even imagined she was smiling down on me as I went about my daily chores. Thoughts of her were weaving their way into my days like strands of sweetgrass lacing around each other to make a winnowing basket.

"The one that looks like you?" she asked, and I nodded.

"You're just dreaming about yourself and what needs doing." The basket Ruth held rustled as she shifted it from one hip to the other. "I'm surprised you could sleep at all with that storm raging." She started off down the trail toward the river. "Thought the walls were gonna blow in."

A gust of wind yowled over the sand dunes, whipping my hair across my face. "You smell that?" I cocked my head toward the beach.

"What?" Ruth sniffed at the air.

"That woody smell," I said. "Or maybe it's burnt clove."

"Don't smell nothing but spring rain." Ruth inhaled again.

Without thinking, I stepped off the path. "There's a hitch in the wind." The cordgrass that led to the beach crumpled under my weight.

"We got chores and sick folk to tend to." Ruth snatched my homespun blouse by the sleeve and tugged me back. "We get done in time, we can chase the wild ponies." She was doing her level best to reel me in.

"Something's there." I shook myself free of her grasp and tramped closer to the chest-high dunes.

Ruth's basket landed in the dirt with a soft thunk. She brushed by me, and even in the dim morning light, I could see her jaw was set firm. She was out to prove me wrong. The black braid that hung to her hips swayed as she crawled up the tallest dune. Ruth drew her breath in sharp as she cleared the top of the mound. I pulled myself up beside her.

The sun's rays seeped through the clouds and shimmered on the ocean, where five hogshead barrels rolled in the waves. Sandpipers darted between the water and splinters of wood strewn along the beach, marking where high tide had been. Further down the shore, a broken mast with a tattered sail jutted out of the sand.

Ruth gasped. "Shipwreck." We exchanged a glance; we could use, barter, or sell whatever we could salvage from those barrels. Lifting our skirts, we skidded down the loose sand. The sandpipers scattered, then flapped away.

"Get that barrel!" Ruth gestured to the surf as she ran.

Cold water splashed into my eyes and my skirt flowered

around me as I charged against the incoming waves. I swam out to the bobbing cask, positioned myself behind it, and prodded it toward shore. The barrel towered over me, big as a boar. The water stung my skin, and my clothes weighed me down. It took all my strength to keep myself afloat and push against the keg. A wave washed over me, and something took hold of my hem. I glimpsed back, expecting to be tangled in a clump of seaweed.

I let out a shriek. A pale hand with a thick gold ring had latched onto my skirt. Whether on purpose or because of the rolling waves, the hand tugged me backward. I kicked out, and my legs flailed against a solid body, which was attached to the hand.

Heaving forward with my arms swinging, I tried to climb onto the barrel but only managed to make it bob further away. Another wave crashed, towing me under and carrying the barrel out of my reach. Salt water filled my mouth and nose. I thrashed in the current until I was free and crawling in the surf.

"Land sakes!" Ruth cried, drenched and stumbling my way, waving a shard of wood in the air like a sword.

"Man!" I jabbed my finger at the limp body tossing face-down in the waves, then scooched on my bottom further up to dry land.

"He dead?" Ruth asked.

The wind cut through me, sending a ripple of shivers through my body. "Grabbed me," I sputtered.

Ruth's eyes went from wide to narrow. I knew just what she was thinking: If this man was alive, there might be a reward for saving him, and if he was dead, he wouldn't miss that gold ring.

"Get his leg," Ruth commanded. She waded out, flipped him over, and grabbed hold of his boot.

I didn't much care to touch a drowned man, but I didn't want Ruth to take all the glory of saving him either, so I gathered myself and took hold of his other boot. Together, we heaved him onto the beach and rolled him on his side. He had a long sword in a leather scabbard, and a silver pistol in a holster. Brown hair was matted to his face. Ruth started slapping his back, and his limp body swayed. A faint yellow glow shone around him; although his spirit was weak, it was still bound to his body.

"Do something," Ruth said. "He don't seem dead yet."

I slipped one hand under his head and pressed my other hand against his cheek. Everything went hazy, and the sun seemed to flash. My heart fluttered and gave a thump, and my arms and legs tingled like they had been pricked by a thousand needles. My soul overflowed, much the same way a wave swells before it crests and turns to whitewater. I flattened out as my cure passed into him.

The stranger retched, coughing up at least a pint of salt water, then collapsed on his back, gulping in air. He didn't look much older than me, maybe seventeen or eighteen. I couldn't make up my mind whether to call him a man or a boy. His skin was smooth, but his body was muscular and his shoulders wide, like a man's.

"He's alive!" Ruth threw up her arms.

A whirl went through my head, and I slumped back, dizzy and exhausted.

"Lay down." Ruth nudged me. "Last thing we need is you swooning." She understood how weak I got after I laid hands on someone. "You reckon he's the only survivor?" She ran her eyes back to the waves. "I don't see anybody else."

The sand was soft as talc under my head, and for a moment I thought the earth would open up and swallow me. The sun's rays soaked into my skin, making me whole again.

"You all right?" Ruth asked, but she didn't give me a chance to answer. "Go fetch Abel and Noah." She prodded me with her toe.

"You fetch them." I pushed myself up to sitting. "I'll stay with him."

The stranger gave a low moan, his cheek and nose pressed into the sand. He had a shine about him. His clothes were finely made with tiny, even stitches. A scar cut through his left eyebrow.

"You can't be alone with no buckruh." Ruth shot me a look that asked if my brains had rattled loose. "What'll Mama say?"

"Same as she'll say to you." I held the back of my hand next to the stranger's. His skin was pale as Sea Island cotton, just like mine.

Ruth puffed herself up. "I'll watch over the barrels and him. You get home; time's a wasting."

I'd just about had enough of her lording over me, so I rooted myself to the beach and pretended I hadn't heard a word she'd said. For a moment I thought she was going to pitch a fit.

"Fine." She stomped away.

The stranger turned on his back, and I noticed his sword was crusted over with a mixture of broken shells and sand. Something glinted on the handle of the blade.

I brushed the grit off the pommel. My thumb brushed a ruby—just like the girl's necklace in my dream. Sunlight bounced off the stone, then slanted and broke into a hundred streams of crimson. The world became still, and I felt my jaw go slack. A lightness rose from under my breast bone and expanded through my entire body like I'd been lit up with a blessing.

2

Folks don't have to share the same blood to have a strong bond. Out of us children, Ruth was Mama Jane's only true kin. Mama took me in after my real mother died in childbirth, and she adopted the twins, Abel and Noah, when their parents, runaway slaves, died of fever. We were a patchwork quilt of a family.

When I was little, Mama Jane used to smear mud on my skin to keep the mosquitos at bay and to shield me from the sun, but I liked to think it colored me copper, just like her and Ruth, and the other Cusabo Indians that called our island home. The Cusabo were on this land long before the Spanish showed up and laid claim to the low country.

Getting the barrels from the beach to our farm was no easy task.

"Gator's got your skirt," Abel sang. The wooden slats of the barrel he rolled creaked behind me, and every third roll he gave it just enough muscle to nip at my heels. He and Noah were a good two years younger than me, but they stood tall and pounced on every chance to remind me that they could give me a walloping if they aimed to.

"Stop pecking at me," I said. Turned on its side, my keg was much wider than the path. It took all the strength I could muster to keep it from teetering off into the marsh reeds.

"What d'you think's in these heads?" Abel asked. He could go from troublesome to angelic in a snap.

"Cotton?" I shrugged. "Tea?" Secretly, I was praying for tea leaves. I'd only ever tasted real tea once, and it was a far cry better than the roots that Mama brewed.

The clouds had burned off, and the sun was warming my back. I stopped to catch my breath, and Abel halted behind me. Over his shoulder I could see the stranger limping between Ruth and Noah, his arms draped over their shoulders for support. His hair fell in front of his face, hiding his eyes. Noah seemed to be reassuring him, probably telling him our mama could cure what ailed him.

Ruth wagged her wrist for us to press on. "Don't dally!"

It took a while to get to where the marsh gave way to the field behind our garden. A plume of smoke rose up over the cook shed just beyond the rows of spring turnips. Chickens scratched at the ground, and the scents of sassafras root and birch bark wafted through the air.

Noah and Ruth toted the man to the cook fire, which Mama Jane was hunched over. Her silver hair was in a braid, and she wore her apron with the deep pockets. Mama motioned to lay the man on a bed of palmetto fronds.

The stranger groaned, and his fingers clasped the hilt of his sword. Ruth and Noah lay him down on the fronds. The boys and I hovered close to Mama, but Ruth went straight to the fire to stir the cauldron.

"You're safe." Mama Jane pulled the man's lids back to examine his eyes. "You with Crow Jane now." She undid the buttons on his shirt, and I felt myself lean in. Several scars puckered the skin of his torso, some long and straight and others jagged. The man winced as Mama put her ear to his chest and thumped her pointer-finger along his ribs, making clucking sounds. "He's cold as hoarfrost. You boys get him in the cabin. Anne!" Mama Jane snapped, and my stare jumped from the stranger's body to mama.

"I'm gonna need some thistle root and a crock full of pluff mud." She dug in her apron pocket, pulled out a boar's tusk spoon, and handed it to me.

"Yes'm," I said. "Is he gonna be all right?"

"Nothing a root poultice and some shut-eye won't cure." Mama Jane unbuckled the man's scabbard and holster.

The man whimpered as Abel and Noah lifted him from the ground.

"Wait a minute." Mama Jane pushed his hair up and examined the scruff of his neck. Her eyes widened. Out of the corner of my eye, I saw Ruth shoot Mama a glance, and Mama gave a small shake of her head.

"You boys take his wet clothes off and get a fire going," Mama said as the twins carried him around the back to the cabin. "Ruth, get the soup started, and send Abel to fetch your crabs." Wrinkles furrowed into Mama Jane's forehead as she gave the sword a going-over. "And send Noah out to the settlement road to stop any sick folk from coming to see us. He can tell them we got a case of the pox." She started walking toward the cabin. "And bring our buckruh some birch bark tea."

"Yes'm." Ruth said. She took down the yellow glazed mug from the cook shed's upper shelf. It was the one Mama used for sickly folks. She handed me an earthen jar from the basket where Mama kept her hoodoo supplies.

"Get on." Mama Jane shooed me away and slung the stranger's holster and gun over her shoulder, then followed the boys to the cabin.

3

Folks from the mainland don't cross the Cusabo River unless they have a good reason to visit our island. Maybe it's because the river is wide and the current swift enough to sweep a boat clear out to sea, or maybe it's the carefully placed hinder charms and osprey skeletons high in the oak trees gazing down on the riverbank. The handful of souls who live on the island only come out to our farm when they are in need of healing, a tonic, or a hex.

I mulled over the glance that Mama Jane and Ruth had shared as I made my way to the clearing in the woods. They had a bond that went bone deep, and truth be told, it wasn't the first time I had seen such a going-over pass between them. They held secrets only true Cusabo root doctors could know.

Grabbing a handful of thistle leaves, I used my spoon to dig out the root, then shook the dirt free and lifted the tuber to my nose. It had an earthy, honeycomb smell. I slipped the thistle in my pocket and continued to dig.

There was a rustling overhead. A covey of quail lighted in the tree limbs above me. My thoughts kept going back to the stranger. There was something in him that stirred something in me, but I shrugged it off as nonsense. Still, Mama claimed that I had the sight and advised me to mind my inklings. Brushing my hair out of my face, I gave a huff. An animal in the brush behind me huffed back. Slowly, I turned.

I was face-to-tusk with a wild boar. Relaxing my shoulders, I settled back on my haunches and waited while the huge sow snorted at the seeds scattered on the ground. She plopped herself down, and two striped piglets scurried from behind her and nestled themselves over her teats. The sow blinked at me and turned her snout to the side, showing the scar that remained from a snare she'd been caught in last year. I'd managed to free her from the trap and lay my healing hands on her. She leaned into my palm as I gave her ear a scratch.

I headed to the oyster rake on the north side of the island. The river lapped at the muddy banks scattered with sharp clusters of gray and white shells. Abel was chest-deep in the current, wading toward the shore with a reed trap balanced on his shoulder. I hooped my skirt through my arm, stepped in the mire and sank down to my ankles. The pluff mud was warm and smelled sickly-sweet with decay.

"Did you see that man's sword and pistol?" Abel shook himself off and wrung out his shirt tails. He lowered the trap to show off the catch. About two bushels of crabs crawled over each other, clacking and trying to escape.

"I did." I spooned slimy sludge into the crock.

"He didn't look like no soldier to me," Abel said. We'd seen Union soldiers scouting the riverbanks of the mainland in December. Those men had been rag-tag and hollow-eyed with hunger. "That man's wiry, like a field hand. And somebody tried to gut him." Abel traced his side belly with his finger, showing me where the stranger had a scar. "He's got nips and scars all over."

Abel strolled ahead of me, jabbering on about cracking open the barrels, but I barely heard him. All I could think about was where this stranger had come from, and why the wind had carried him to our island.

4

Ruth was hunkered over the worktable, mincing dried seaweed. Little mounds of berries, barks, and herbs wobbled from the motion of her knife. She had situated the bench close to the cauldron, and when she turned to stir the pot, I could see she was vexed. I placed the crock and thistle roots next to the herbs.

"That buckruh. . . ." Ruth shook her knife at the back of the cabin. "His coming here wasn't no accident." She laid a long rag on the table, then turned to the simmering soup. Using a ladle, she splashed enough broth over the cloth to soak it through.

Deep down something told me Ruth was right, but I wasn't about to agree with her just yet.

Ruth scooped a handful of the mud and smeared it on top of the wet rag. "He's a wandering spirit." She picked up the stranger's drained teacup with her clean hand. "There's something here I've never seen before." Ruth lowered the mug so we both could see the loose stems and leaves that swirled in the bottom. "What'd you spy?"

Careful not to jiggle the leaves, I took the yellow mug and gently blew into it. A longish clover stem crossed two thicker stems that bent upward. "Is that a double cross?" I asked.

"It is." Ruth gave a half smile. "I reckon he's on a crusade of sorts, and we're in his way." She broke off a piece of thistle root, popped it in her mouth for a chew, then spit it on the poultice.

Eyeballing what was left of the tea stems, I breathed on them once more. The stems shifted into the shape of a bird with outstretched wings. My heart sputtered, and the mug slipped through my hands. I quickly caught it before it hit the dirt and placed it on the table.

Ruth twisted the poultice in the rag and gave it to me. "Mama wants this." The wrap was heavy in my hands. "Be watchful," Ruth warned.

Careful not to step on any twigs, I walked around to the side of the cabin and paused next to the wood plank that had a knot-hole in it about the size of a pecan. Mama Jane was speaking in a low voice. I crouched down and pressed my eye against the peephole.

The cabin was only one room with a loft where Abel and Noah slept. The stranger was wearing Abel's loose nightshirt and sitting on the hearth, facing Mama Jane, who rocked back and forth on her three-legged stool. The stranger's clothes were hanging on hooks by the fire. His sword lay at his feet.

Mama's eyes narrowed, and she stopped swaying. She sat up, her back straight as an arrow. The stranger's silver pistol rested in her lap. "How'd I know there's any truth to what you say?"

The man turned his head and lifted his hair so Mama could see the back of his neck. "I've been searching for the healer since the last witching moon."

Mama gave a chuckle, then asked in a raised whisper, "What d'you know about any witching moon?"

"The last one was just over fifteen years ago, on the winter solstice." He spoke in an accent I had never heard before. "The one before that was the winter solstice of 1567, when I was born."

I wasn't too handy with ciphering numbers, but I reckoned anybody born that long ago should've been dry bones by now.

Mama ran her fingers along the barrel of the gun.

"And the one before that was—"

"1019." Mama finished his sentence. "Long before the white man came and took our lands."

They sat in silence for some time, studying each other.

"I reckoned one of your kind would come calling," Mama said finally. "Just wasn't expecting it to be so soon." My heart pinched at the sadness in her voice.

"What does Anne know?" My name sounded softer, almost foreign coming from the stranger's mouth.

"Not a thing." Mama seemed defeated, her shoulders slumped and the corners of her lips turned down. "Figured there was no need to speak of such till there was just cause."

The stranger gave a nod and leaned forward. "Has she always been able to heal?"

"Anne's had a fire in her belly from day one," Mama said. "But it's gotten powerful strong since she started to bleed." My face burned at her sharing something so private.

"Who else knows about her?" the stranger asked.

Mama dropped her head. "Just the Cusabo people. She stays in the cabin when strangers come. She's only laid hands on animals and my people."

The man rubbed the scar that cut through his eyebrow with the tip of his thumb. "You know I have to take her away from here."

His words stung like a red wasp bite.

"There are others, like me, searching for the healer, others who will kill to have her, or kill her to keep her from reaching her rightful sept."

Mama Jane's forehead wrinkled.

"A sept is a tribe," he explained.

"I know a fair bit about your tribes." Mama's voice was steely. "But tell me this: how do I know that you're the one I've been saving her for?"

The man shrugged. "By rights, I could walk away with her

right now, but we have a long journey ahead. I need you to trust me." He sighed. "I need Anne to trust me."

Trust him? I almost laughed, but instead squeezed the poultice so drops of broth dribbled in the dirt. Nothing of what Mama Jane or the buckruh said made sense.

Wood splinters from the cabin wall were plastered to the side of my face. As I brushed them off, I realized how hot my skin was. A huff escaped my lips. What did all this mean? Septs and rightful tribes and witching moons? And how could Mama calmly sit there and agree to handing me over to some buckruh? None of what they said made a lick of sense. Every step I took back to Ruth made my head swim.

"What's the matter?" Ruth asked when she saw me.

My skin felt tight as I shook my head. "I got to go." I needed to be alone, to chew on what I'd heard, so I dropped the poultice at Ruth's feet and cut a path toward the garden.

"Anne," Ruth said behind me. "Where you off to?"

Running was the only thing I could think to do. My feet sank down in the earth between the garden rows.

"Anne!" Ruth hollered, but I didn't turn back. My legs carried me away, across the field and down the path to the water.

Halfway to the beach, the mottled pony I called Sugar Foot stood on the path. He took a step toward me and stilled as I stroked his shaggy mane, then turned to his side. I bounced myself up and onto his back. The pony trotted down the trail, through the dunes, then took off at a gallop down the beach.

5

The moon was hanging low in the sky when I decided to head back home.

My heart drummed, and I could feel that Mama Jane was close. Where the path opened up, I saw the outline of her shadow at the edge of the garden. She was wobbling on her stool and gazing up at the moon.

"Hey." Mama's voice was scratchy, like she'd been crying.

All the fear and hurt that I had run from earlier came flooding back, and my temples started to throb. I sank to my knees and leaned against her legs. "I don't want to leave you."

"There now." Mama Jane rested her palm on my head. "Who says you're going anywhere?" Her fingers snagged on the tangles in my hair.

"And I don't want to be killed by some sept either." The word "sept" felt strange on my lips.

"D'you think I'd let anything bad happen to you?"

I opened my mouth to speak but thought better of it.

"Reckon I should tell you about the night you were born," she said.

"You already have, a bunch of times."

"You don't know all." Mama Jane craned her neck to search the sky as she gathered her words. "It was warm for December.

That night, the moon started off full and ripe as a peach. Then, little by little, it was bit away by darkness, until it shone again in a fresh light." She paused to take a breath. "I was visiting with the mainland Cusabo. I got word that there was a widow woman up the way who was having a hard labor, so I went to her. She was bad off, and the smell of death hung over her."

I knew that acidic tang. Lots of folks came to see Mama Jane too late, with their flesh festering. Sometimes, if Mama trusted them, I laid hands on them and they got better; sometimes they didn't.

"She was too far along." Mama shook her head. "I didn't ask no questions about why a woman so old was having a young'un; I just gave her some yarrow tea to calm her nerves and stop the bleeding, but it didn't do no good. When she pushed you out, she breathed your name with her last breath." Mama's voice trailed off.

I knew the rest of the story; my mother didn't have any living kin, and the neighbors were too poor to take me in, so Mama Jane took me with her.

"I'd never seen a baby with eyes so bright," Mama said. "That little stork bite shined like a ruby and was feverish." Her fingertips outlined the birthmark on the back of my neck. "Wasn't until the woman's neighbor carted me back to my people, and I saw the moon glowing like your mark that I realized what had happened." She let out a sigh. "My grandmama taught me everything she knew about midwifery and root doctoring, just as her mama and grandmama had taught her, and theirs before them, all the way back to Bible times. There are vows that midwives keep. Vows that most of us never reckon to hold to, but we promise just the same. In olden times, midwives were set afire or put in pits and stoned for witchery. Most went into hiding or refused to pass on their knowledge. Our kind nearly died out. But there came a tribe of people who offered the midwives protection."

"That was good," I said, hoping to coax more out of her.

"This man you saved, this Phillip of Amaranth—he is from that tribe," Mama said. "And he's been searching for his people."

"I'm not his people." The words came out like a hiccup.

"My grandmama said his kind outlived Methuselah," Mama said. "Phillip's almost three hundred years old, and he knows our ancient ways." She sounded like she was trying to convince herself.

"This doesn't make any sense." I stood up and started to pace in a circle. "I never would have pulled him from the water if I knew—" I flat-out refused to say he was going to take me away.

"You don't have to go anywhere," Mama said, reading my mind.

"Does Ruth know about this?" There was no way Ruth would keep this kind of secret from me.

"She does."

This news was like a kick to my stomach. My lips pressed together. Ruth and I kept secrets from other people, not from one another. I stared at the light flickering through the cabin wall slats, wondering what else was being kept from me. "Is Ruth tending to him now?"

"She told him to leave and not come back," Mama Jane said.

"So he's gone?" A pang of disappointment shot through me, though I wasn't sure why.

Mama held out her hand for me to help her up off her stool. "I imagine he'll be back after he gathers his self, then we'll see if he's made of ash or stone."

"Don't make no sense," I said as we made our way past the garden. "He looked too young to be so old."

"His kind ages slowly." Mama Jane stressed the word his, and I wondered if she was lumping me in there too.

The back of our cabin glowed from the fire within, and as we got closer, I saw the two salvaged barrels were now upright on the front stoop.

"What's inside?" I asked.

"Cotton," Mama said. "It'll need brushing and spinning."

Ruth stood on the porch in her nightgown, glaring out into the darkness, daring anything to come into the clearing that surrounded our house.

"Where are the boys?" Mama asked.

"Bed," Ruth said as she wrapped her fingers around my arm and squeezed hard. "Don't you run off like that again." She was glad to see me.

My nightgown was laid out on the pallet next to the fire. I undid my blouse and skirt and let them puddle at my feet before I slipped my arms through my nightgown. Ruth hung my clothes over the spinning wheel, and we settled on the straw mattress.

"Maybe we can stuff some of that cotton in with the straw, make this mattress less lumpy," I said, beating the pallet down.

"Maybe so." Ruth snuggled in next to me.

"Night," I whispered and turned my back to her. Ruth grumbled something under her breath. I could tell she had things to say, but I was too scared to talk. Sometimes, if words are said out loud, they become truth, and right then I wanted to keep any understanding that I felt to myself.

"I don't care about no sacred vow," Ruth whispered as she nudged her forehead against my shoulder. "Nobody's taking you anywhere."

6

Abel and Noah rambled ahead of me on the path to the water well that was situated halfway between our farm and the settlement at the other end of the island. It had been two days since the stranger had come and gone, and this was the first time Ruth had let me out of her sight. I suppose she was expecting the buck-ruh to jump from behind a cabbage palm and carry me off at any moment. With the way Ruth had been smothering me with her constant companionship, I half-wished he would.

The sun streamed through the trees, and my mind was busy sifting through what Mama Jane had told me about the ancient tribes who protected midwives. I had more questions than she had answers, but that was nothing new. What she did know was that without their protection, there would be no midwives.

Abel and Noah were carrying on, arguing about who had caught the biggest trout and taking swipes at each other with their empty pails. Abel took off running and hopped up a low piece of old tabby wall that ran along the trail.

"King of the well!" Abel shouted as he spun around, jutting his pail in the air. He danced a little jig on the crumbling oyster shell and mud barrier. Noah cut a path for the well, and Abel jumped down to chase him.

I dallied, knowing it would be a spell till I could have a turn at filling my bucket. The bushes beside me rustled, and a hand slipped out from the leaves and placed a brace of limp quail atop the wall. A gold ring flashed as the hand retreated into the underbrush. I stood still, blinking as the realization washed over me that Phillip was close by, was showing himself only to me, and was giving us a gift.

Cold water splashed on my toes, and I gave a little jump.

"What's the matter?" Abel plopped his bucket down, then followed my eyes to the birds. "They weren't there before."

Noah dropped his bucket down the well and craned his neck our way. "What?"

"Did you see these?" Abel held the quail up.

Noah stomped over, grabbed the brace, and inspected the speckled fowl. "They were got with a spear."

"Lemme see." Abel ran his hand over a bird's breast. "Who uses a spear?"

Noah shrugged. The men on Cusabo hunted with bow and arrow or set snares.

"Maybe they were left as payment to Mama Jane," I reasoned. "Nobody wants to come out to the farm cause of the pox, remember?" It was rare for folks to pay with coin for Mama Jane's services. Running my eyes to the underbrush, I was alert for any movement in the woods as I stepped to the well.

"They're fresh, and we haven't had quail in a coon's age, so I'm taking them." Abel slung the brace over his shoulder, lifted his pail, and started back home.

Noah tugged his bucket up from the well, then I lowered mine. I stuck my face into the cool darkness and sang, "Hello." Hello, hello, hello, my voice echoed back.

Even though my pail was heavy, I high-stepped it on the walk back home. Ruth hadn't run Phillip off after all.

"I'd wager it was Phillip that left those fowl," Noah said.

"Phillip?" My toes curled into the dirt. My brother's eyes met mine and challenged me to not know who he was talking about.

"He's been camped down by the river since Ruth chased him off." This news slid out like it was a common fact: Shrimp run in spring. It's best to harvest on a full moon. Phillip's at the riverbank.

Water sloshed over the sides of my bucket as I set it down.

"Gave him some fishing line yesterday." Noah's voice trailed off like he was already regretting saying anything.

Did he ask about me? was the first question that popped into my mind, but instead I said, "Ruth'll skin you alive if she finds out."

Noah sucked in his cheeks.

"I won't tell her," I promised. "What's he like?" It just slipped out.

"All right." Noah said in his thoughtful way. "Waves his sword around a good bit."

"How so?"

"Holds it over his head till his arms shake. Jumps around with it like he's dancing a reel. It's heavy as a gopher tortoise."

"You held it?" My voice rose up.

Noah bobbed his head, then dug deep in the pocket of his britches, pulled out a gold piece, and held it up so it glinted in the sun.

"Let me see." I grabbed at the coin, but Noah jerked it out of my reach and held it over his head with a grin. Pawing at his arm, I jumped for it twice before he decided to let me have it.

The coin was wafer thin and smooth on one side. I turned it over and studied the side of a woman's face that had been stamped into the metal. She had a hint of a smile and a dainty nose. Soft curls cascaded around her face and over her shoulders.

"She kinda looks like you." Noah glanced from me to the coin. "Who?"

"Her." He pointed to the woman's silhouette.

I barely heard what Noah was saying. The coin stirred a memory that I could only catch the edges of. Calmness washed over me as my fingertips circled the smooth surface of the disc.

"You all right?" Noah's voice hovered over me.

"Umm," I murmured. Somewhere, in a distant place, I'd held a thin gold wafer like this coin without the etching. The girl from my dreams bubbled up in my thoughts. She pressed a gold piece into my palm and closed my fingers around it. Her ruby necklace blazed in the sun.

"Better get back." Noah tucked the coin back in his pocket and lifted his pail.

I trudged silently beside him, absorbed in a feeling that I was pleasantly swirling in an eddy. Could I have dreamed this gold piece? Because that's what it felt like; the coin had spurred a memory of a long-past dream.

Ruth was leaning against one of the salvaged barrels on the porch, eyes peeled in our direction. "This cotton's not gonna spin itself!" She lifted a handful of white fluff.

Noah cut his eyes to me. I set my bucket down and stretched my back just to show that I hadn't been dawdling.

"Shouldn't take all morning to fetch water," Ruth said as we passed.

"You fetch it next time and see how long it takes," I muttered.

I dumped my bucket into the large pot that Mama Jane was stirring our soiled clothes in and caught a whiff of lye and vinegar.

"These'll be ready to wring out and hang in a bit." Mama churned the clothes with a long stick.

Ruth was hauling the spinning wheel out the cabin door.

"What needs doing?" I asked.

"Comb out those bolls." She nodded to the barrel. We had all speculated on how many shirts, trousers, and skirts could be made out of the cotton we had found. But first it needed to be seeded, combed, spun, and then loomed into fabric.

"Who you reckon left those quail Abel found?" Ruth settled herself behind the spinning wheel, but I could feel her eyes on me.

Trying to act unmoved, I shrugged. Ruth prattled on about what needed to be done now that warm weather was upon us, while I pondered how I could sneak down to the riverbank.

After a while, Noah and Abel took off with their fishing poles.

"You want to go see if the ponies are on the beach?" Ruth asked. She was trying her best to get us back on the same familiar footing we'd been on before Phillip had washed ashore, but I wasn't ready for that to happen.

"No." I rose and brushed my hands off on my skirt. "I've got to hang clothes out to dry, then I expect it'll be time to get supper ready."

"I suppose you're right." Ruth stood. "After supper then."

"Maybe." I started down the steps.

"When you going to let go of that grudge you've been holding onto?" The corners of her mouth turned down as she fiddled with the spindle on the spinning wheel.

"I think I'll keep it in my pocket and take it out to polish it up when I want to remember that you keep secrets from me," I muttered.

Ruth followed me down the steps. "I've done told you, I don't have any more secrets from you. You know everything!" She tugged on my blouse, and I spun around.

"Why'd you run Phillip off?" I asked.

"He can't just come up in here and lay claim to you." Red blotches were rising up her neck and fanning out over her cheeks.

My mouth popped open then sealed shut. I wished I was good with words the way Ruth was. I wanted to say he wasn't laying claim to me anymore than she was, but squabbling with Ruth was like teaching a wild boar to fly: useless. "I don't want to argue with you," I said.

"'Cause you know I'm right." Ruth always had to get the last word.

We laid the wet clothes atop a layer of palmetto fronds. Ruth hated tending to the wash, but I didn't mind it so much. I wrung out a pair of trousers and draped them over a low branch, then cloaked a cabbage palm with a blouse. Maybe I could work my way into the woods, dangling clothes as I went, then sneak down to the river and take a peek at whatever Phillip was up to. I had a bushelful of questions to ask him.

As I wrung out a shawl, I got the feeling that I was being watched. I whipped around and saw Ruth peeking around the cook shed.

"Could use some help," I called, and she ducked her head back. I twisted her calico skirt free of water, then walked it to a weeping willow in the woods and slung it on a low-hanging limb.

Something glinted at the base of the tree, and I bent low to suss it out. A ring was perched on the knob of a root. I snatched it up, then glanced around and over my shoulder. The gold was nubby, like it had been hammered with a teeny mallet. A ruby, redder than a blood moon, was set into the ring. All of a sudden I felt like I was sleepwalking.

"This ruby will protect thee," I whispered as I rubbed my thumb over the stone that was about the size of my pinkie nail, then slipped the ring over the knuckle of my finger. The weight of it was just right, like it had been made for me. My hand rose to my throat. "The necklace," I murmured.

"Your sister has the necklace." A man's voice spoke low. "She had faith that I would find you."

The ground beneath me felt unsteady. The muscles in my legs twitched while I tried to decide if I should run or stay. I searched the trees and bushes but saw no one. Although part of me was thrilled to speak to the stranger, I was wary. "My sister?" The only sister I knew was Ruth.

"Rowan," he said.

Rowan. The name pinched my heart. "Show yourself," I said.

The stranger stepped from behind a cluster of red cedar with his arms at his side. His sword hung on his left hip. "I mean you no harm." He showed me his empty palms. He approached me cautiously, like I was a wild animal. "I am Phillip of Amaranth." He stayed still, glancing at me but not meeting my eyes.

"I remember wearing this." I held my hand out, examining the ring, but also keeping him in view.

"Memories are buried deep in your soul." Phillip spoke gently. "You're calling to mind experiences from another life."

"What?" I took a step back.

"You lived before, a long time ago. You were a healer." He rubbed his chest. "You still are." Then he turned and lifted his hair off his collar. There was a raised mark at the nape of his neck. It was the color of port wine.

"You've got a stork bite." As I said this, my own mark burned with a fever, and I thought I might swoon.

"Just like you," Phillip said. "We're from the same immortal tribe."

Panic surged through me, like when I had been caught in a riptide as a child. A surface part of me had wanted to flail against the current, but something deep-rooted kept me calm. I remember letting that animal part of myself take over, and I drifted until I was able to swim again. Now, that inner part of me was whirring faster than a hummingbird's wings.

"What does that mean?" I asked.

Phillip rubbed the scar over his eyebrow and gave a shy grin. "I had it all worked out—what I would say to you if I ever found you—but now, words escape me."

"Start with Rowan." Her name felt heavy on my lips.

"You look just like her." Phillip cocked his head to the side. "But younger, of course." He reached inside his jacket, pulled out a tube the length of my forearm, and passed it to me. It was leather, with two stoppers made of animal bone. "It's a scroll." He motioned for me to remove the end cap.

I unrolled the paper and felt my eyes widen at the painted crest and symbols underneath. A smaller piece of paper fell from the scroll. I didn't recognize the lettering. "What does it say?" I asked.

"It's written in Latin." Phillip took the paper and glanced down at it, then back at me. "'I pray thee come home. Rowan.'"

7

My hands trembled, shaking the papyrus as I unrolled it on the worktable. Mama and Ruth stood close on either side of me, eyeing the scroll. The crest was half blue and half red on the diagonal. In the center was a gold phoenix, its head turned in profile. Two silver tusks curved on either side of the phoenix with small acorns scattered around them.

"I painted this." I felt the hint of a wooden stem in my fingers. The memory of crushing red berries between two rocks to get their pigment wafted through me.

"It's the crest of our tribe." Phillip stood an arm's length away. "The phoenix symbolizes resurrection and life. The tusks indicate longevity and strength, and the acorns antiquity."

Mama Jane gave a polite nod, but Ruth pretended she hadn't heard a word Phillip said.

"The shield is blue for truth and loyalty, red for bravery, gold for generosity, and silver for peace." Phillip's voice faded under the whooshing of my heart.

The canvas seemed to ripple and sink into the table. My fingertips prickled as they traced the brushstrokes.

"You all right?" Mama Jane caught me as I wobbled.

"This is hoodoo," Ruth said. "He's got you tangled in a spell."

"Ruth." Mama Jane's tone was comforting, but underneath

there was a warning to behave. "This isn't about you."

Ruth waved her hand. "So we're just gonna let some buckruh make pretty offerings and take Anne away?"

"Mind yourself," Mama said. "Let's fix supper. Things will be easier to sort out on a full belly."

Ruth pressed her hip against mine as I rolled up the scroll.

"Anne, you and Phillip dig up a mess of turnips to roast with these fine quail." Mama handed me a basket.

"Yes'm," I replied, avoiding Ruth's eyes.

Phillip followed me to the garden. "I have no gift for sorcery," he said once we were alone.

"That's too bad." I peered out over the leafy stalks. "Ruth could make use of a charm for a sweeter temperament."

A dimple dented Phillip's cheek. "You two are close."

"Maybe too close." I tugged on a bunch of turnip greens, loosening them from the soil. It was fine with me if Ruth wanted to grit her teeth and eke out a hardscrabble life on Cusabo, but it was downright spiteful to insist I do the same. "She's the only sister I've had," I said, then added, "till now." A ripple of shame ran through me for speaking ill of Ruth.

"There's no shame in wanting something more," Phillip said.

"I've dreamed about her, you know."

Phillip tilted his head.

"Rowan," I said. "She was wearing a necklace with a ruby big as the one on your sword, only it wasn't as shiny."

"This stone has been cut." He fingered the jewel on his sword's pommel. "Rowan's stone is unhewn."

"Like mine." The sunlight sank into my ruby, making it glow. "Tell me about her."

Phillip inched closer. "What do you care to know?"

"Everything," I said. "What's she like?"

"Honest and kind." The corner of his mouth twitched up, and he added, "But she can be fierce too, you know, especially if she sees an injustice being done." He used the outside of his knee to bounce his sword. "She taught me how to handle a blade." He thought for a moment. "When you speak to her, she listens like you're the only person in the world that matters." He brightened like someone had lit him up from the inside.

"Sounds like you love her."

"I do," Phillip said. "Everyone does. Rowan is a mother to all those she has saved."

"A mother?"

"Well, she's older than you." His voice softened. "When you perished, she mourned deeply. Helping others was the only way she was able to overcome her grief."

"I thought being immortal meant you can't die," I said.

Phillip cleared his throat. "If your head becomes separated from your body, you will die."

A chill shimmied up my spine.

"But then, you will be reborn on a witching moon, making you immortal again."

"How is that decided?" I rubbed the side of my neck.

"Who aligns the stars?" Phillip asked. "Who decides who is born and who is not?"

I knew enough to know there were countless mysteries between heaven and earth that no one could explain. A few years back, Noah found in the marsh a baby gator that had two heads. He wanted to keep it, but Mama made him set it free, saying that God made that gator special and it wasn't our place to question God's plan.

"Once Rowan understood that our kind could be reborn, she began searching for others like us," Phillip went on. "She found me in Marseilles, in the slave market. I was six. I was the only immortal. Once we were in the hills outside of the town, she freed everyone, and promised shelter, food, and work to anyone willing to return with her to Amaranth."

Pride welled inside of me as I pictured the scene. "What'd she do with all the people?"

"She found homes for them in stables or on farms along the way to Amaranth." Phillip had a far-off look in his eyes. "You can go out to the countryside to this day and find shrines to Saint Rowan, breaker of chains. Slavery was abolished in France because of her."

"France?"

"Oui, France," Phillip said. "That's where Amaranth is, where your sister waits for you."

"Amaranth," I whispered, trying out the word for myself. "France."

"It's that way." He pointed out past the marsh reeds in the direction of the beach. "Across the ocean."

"How do I get there?"

"Our sept, our tribe, has a ship in Charleston harbor. If we leave tonight, we can set sail in two days' time." Phillip seemed excited by this prospect.

"Tonight?" My fingers clenched the handle of the basket.

"It's best to travel in darkness. The fewer mortals we encounter the better, for their safety as well as ours."

○))) ❭ ❭ ● ● ❬ ❬ ((○

Ruth didn't say a word during supper and flat-out refused to touch the roasted quail. My stomach seized up, and I could barely eat a thing. The boys ate mine and Ruth's share, then pelted Phillip with question after question about where he came from and what it was like there.

After supper, Mama Jane dragged her stool out to the porch and sat, picking at her teeth with a reed. Ruth and I dangled our legs over the cabin porch and watched the shadows of Abel and

Noah have a go at each other with wooden swords that Phillip had fashioned out of sticks. The boys thrusted and swiped while Phillip offered pointers on how to lunge and retreat.

"You don't have to leave," Ruth said, so low I could barely hear her.

"I know." I pondered a way to explain to her what I was feeling. My heart was towing me in two different directions. "Haven't you ever wondered what's on the other side of the river?"

"I know what's on the other side—war." Ruth glanced back at Mama. Her face glowed bronze in the lantern-shine. Mama never spoke much about what she had seen on the mainland, but we gathered it was grim. "This man is gonna march you right into the battle's path."

"Phillip says the Confederate army is weak; they'll be surrendering any day now, and the war will be over."

Phillip turned at the mention of his name.

"You trust him?" Ruth's voice rose up. "You've only known him a day."

"I know what he says is true." I rubbed the ring on my finger. "I have all these recollections I can't explain."

"Be careful." Her jaw was set hard. "If you sow the wind, you will reap a whirlwind."

It was useless to argue. "I'm sorry," I whispered.

"The Union army is marching north to Virginia," Phillip interrupted, stepping closer. "Our path to Charleston should be clear."

I turned from Ruth and realized that Noah and Abel had lowered their wooden sticks and were gawking at us.

Phillip leaned against his sword. "Our only problem will be staying ahead of the other tribes."

"You speak of these other tribes," Ruth said. "We haven't seen hide nor hair of any other strangers."

"They'll come soon enough for the healer." Phillip bowed his head toward me as he spoke. "All the septs know of the prophecy."

"What're you talking about?" Ruth swung her head back to Mama, but Mama just rocked on her stool, listening to Phillip.

"Long ago, it was foretold that the healer would be reborn in the new world and found during a time of war."

Abel and Noah gathered close behind Phillip, hanging on his every word. Ruth's eyes narrowed into slits.

"Every sept has had venators scouring the Americas since the last witching moon. It's a miracle I found Anne first."

"Venators?" Ruth asked.

"Hunters," I said, surprised that I knew what the word meant.

"It's only a matter of time until another venator locates Anne and takes her by force," Phillip said.

"How many tribes are there?" Noah asked.

"Are they Indian like Mama Jane?" Abel blurted.

"Nine," Phillip answered Noah. "There is an Indian sept, but it's in India," he said to Abel.

"Diddly-squat." Ruth pushed herself off the porch. I followed her around the back of the cabin to what was left of the cook fire.

"I don't like him," Ruth said. "He's got a snap-answer for everything." She spat on the glowing embers. I hooked my arm in the crook of her elbow, and we stood there for some time not saying a word, just watching two moths flutter above the coals.

"I want to stay here," I said finally, and Ruth breathed out. "But I want to go to Amaranth too. It's like a string has been tied around my heart, and it's pulling me there."

Ruth crossed her arms over her chest.

"I have a sister there, and she's been searching for me."

"You got a sister here," Ruth said.

"Rowan is my real sister." I pressed my hand against my chest. "My blood."

Ruth jerked back like I had slapped her. "You gonna leave just like that? What about Mama? What about Noah and Abel?"

"It's safer for you if I'm gone," I said. "You heard what Phillip said about the other tribes. Besides, once things have settled down, I'll come back."

    Ruth let out a bitter laugh. "You been yearning for the mainland since I can remember. You step off this island, you know you ain't coming back."

8

The inside of the cabin was dark, peaceful even. Ruth's leg twitched beside mine on our pallet, and Mama snored softly in her bed. I lay still and closed my eyes, trying to make myself go back to sleep, but I kept thinking about Phillip sleeping out on the front porch. Was he comfortable out there? I'd offered him my pillow, which was just an old flour sack stuffed with grass and feathers, but he'd refused to take it from me. He said at Amaranth, pillows were stuffed with the down of geese; I guess that must be like laying your head on a cloud. You'd think that having him close by would be a comfort, but instead it flustered me and scattered my thoughts in a hundred different directions. I wanted to go with him, to see Amaranth and meet Rowan, but it terrified me to leave Mama, Ruth, and the boys. How would they manage without me? A sinking sensation had come over me, and the more I tried to push it out of my mind, the more it persisted. Fear was swelling inside of me, making my stomach roil like cream turning in a butter churn. The wood slats on the porch creaked, and I sat bolt upright, fumbling around in the darkness for the fire poker.

"It's me," Phillip crouched in the doorway, paused, then crawled inside the cabin. "Someone's out there, just beyond the clearing."

Before I had a chance to say a word, Mama called from her bed, "Who's that?" She sounded half asleep.

"Phillip," he whispered. "There's someone outside."

"Nobody comes calling before dawn," Ruth groaned, and rolled over. But that wasn't so. On occasion, folks came out to our farm past midnight to ask for Mama's help in delivering a baby or if somebody was awful sick.

Mama Jane's feet scuffed the floor. "It's probably somebody bad off."

"If it was someone seeking help, they wouldn't be hiding in the woods," Phillip whispered. He was right, but Mama had already shuffled to the doorway.

"Who's there?" she called out in a voice that sounded like she wasn't afeared of things she couldn't see. Mama was of the mind that most people spent all their lives being afraid of matters that only God could control. Best to put your faith in him and leave the fretting to weaker men. She stepped further out onto the porch.

"What's goin' on?" Abel climbed down from the loft, followed by Noah.

"Shh," Ruth hissed. "Stay back." The boys tended to charge ahead without thinking.

"I hear you threshing about out there!" Mama called out to the darkness. "What do you want?"

There was a sharp thud against the cabin wall.

"Don't you go shooting no arrows at me lest you want me to come out there and put a hurting on you!" Fire rose in her voice. "Shoot an arrow at me, you'd better aim better than that." She was talking to herself now. Dry wood splintered, then Mama stepped back inside. "I got their arrow. It's long. Light the lantern."

"No," Phillip whispered. "Don't help their aim."

"Sit here." Noah set Mama's stool next to the pallet, and we all gathered round.

"There's at least two of 'em mumbling out there." Mama kept her voice low. "What do you think they want?"

"Anne," Phillip said flatly.

I scooted closer to Mama, and she put her arm around my shoulder. "They're from those other immortal tribes?" Her question hung in the air. Noah and Abel scooched up close behind me, and Ruth closed in on the other side, making a protective nest with their bodies.

"May I hold the arrow?" Phillip asked, and Mama passed it to him. "Feels weighted, like it has a silver tip." He took my hand and placed it on the arrow.

"It's as long as my arm," I said. The arrowhead had tiny spikes on it.

"It's a samurai arrow," he said softly. "They're the only venators I know who uses arrows this long. This was a warning shot. Samurai are skilled huntsmen; they don't miss."

"How dare they come to our house and attack Mama when we've done nothing to them!" Ruth's voice rose up.

"They're not trying to offend you; they're just letting you know they are out there and could harm you if they chose," Phillip said. "They've put you on notice."

"Well, I'm gonna put that notice right back on them," Ruth said, and I knew she was arching her back like she did when she got riled.

"What's the samurai?" Noah asked.

"The sept of Japan," Phillip said. "Japan is an island on the other side of the world."

"Like Cusabo?" Abel asked.

"Much, much larger," Phillip said.

"What are we gonna do?" Ruth asked. "There could be a whole army out there." She was never one to back down from a fight, but this was different.

"I will fight them," Phillip said. "We'll need to lure them into the yard." I wished I could see his face to measure what he was thinking; all I had to go on was the sound of his voice, which had a hard edge.

"What if they have three men?" Abel asked.

"Or more?" I chimed in.

"I'll fight however many men they have," Phillip said.

"I'll get my bow," Noah said as he turned to climb up to the loft.

"Bring mine down too," Abel said.

"Go fetch my hexes," Mama Jane said. Ruth crawled over to Mama's bed and felt around for the little wooden box that she kept her dried crow's feet and poisonous herbs in. Water hemlock and deadly nightshades grew along the creeks deep in the marsh, and they'd been known to kill any animals that fed on them.

"How do they know Anne is here?" Abel asked.

"Immortals are perceptive. The samurai will have a strong feeling that another immortal is close by without actually seeing them," Phillip said. I thought about the morning of the shipwreck, when I'd had a notion that something was happening at the beach, and wondered if I knew Phillip was there before I ever saw him.

"Then why don't you go out there and show them that you're here?" Abel said. Mama and Ruth mumbled that it seemed like a fair idea. "Let them think it's you they got the scent on."

Phillip was quiet for a moment. "That's actually a good idea," he said. "But we should wait till it's light. If it comes down to it, I'll have to fight them while everyone takes cover." He placed his hand on my arm. "If you can get away, is there somewhere you can hide? A hole you can burrow into and cover yourself up?"

"Yes," I said. If all was lost and I could get out of the cabin, there were hundreds of hollows and sloughs in the marsh I could hide in.

Everyone huddled in together, waiting for dawn. Phillip and Mama murmured to each other, setting out their plan, but other than that, no one spoke. When the marsh wrens began to chirrup morning song, Mama leaned her mouth to my ear. "Go curl up in the back of the loft under the blankets, and don't make a peep."

Phillip stood and shuffled his boots on the floor to mask my footsteps. Ruth boosted me up to the sleeping loft, where I burrowed under quilts.

9

Shortly after sunrise streamed into the cabin, the hens under the house began to peck and scratch. Pressed against the back wall of the loft, I couldn't see a thing, but my ears perked to every sound.

Phillip stepped out to the porch, let out a yawn, and from what I could hear, just stood there for a long while. Just when I wondered if whoever had shot that arrow had decided to move on, I heard the crunch of coquina shells under boots.

"Phillip?" a man's voice called from a ways off.

"Hattori!" Phillip shouted back with surprise in his voice. The front steps creaked under his weight as he stepped off the porch. "I knew I recognized that arrow."

Then, to my surprise, Phillip began speaking in a strange tongue. In the yard just off the front porch, Phillip and the man spoke in short bursts, saying words I couldn't decipher. A third person chimed in, and there was more squawking. The voices rose and fell like seagulls grappling over a fiddler crab. It was impossible to tell if they were friends or foes, but I didn't hear any fighting, so I assumed they were friends. I had the urge to peek over the ledge of the loft, but if I did, I might give myself away, so I kept still and silent as the grave.

"What's Phillip saying?" Abel asked below me. "Is he speaking in tongues?"

"Noah, help me up," Mama said. Her skirts rustled as she stood.

"Don't go outside," Ruth said. From their shuffling, I guessed they were standing in the doorway.

"After the shipwreck, this family took me in," Phillip called. I imagined him gesturing from the yard to Mama, Ruth, and the boys.

"I would like to meet them," Hattori said. He was closer now, and although his accent was strong, he spoke our language well.

"Crow Jane, I present to you Hattori from the immortal samurai sept, and his apprentice, Momo," Phillip said. "Hattori, Momo, I present to you Crow Jane, root doctor of the Cusabo tribe, and her children Ruth, Abel, and Noah."

"It is my pleasure to meet you, Crow Jane," Hattori said.

"Ma'am, it is an honor," a soft, feminine voice said. Momo was a girl! I don't know why this surprised me, but it did, in a pleasant way.

"It was my understanding that the Cusabo had moved inland years ago," Hattori said.

"Not all of us," Mama Jane said.

"My apologies for the arrow," Hattori said. "I was not aiming to kill."

"I don't usually offer hospitality to intruders, but since you are friends with Phillip, we'll make an exception. Abel, take Noah and fetch some fresh water for tea."

"Yes'm," Abel said.

"Ruth and I will get a cookfire going," Mama said. She and Ruth went to the back of the cabin.

"Crow Jane is a midwife," Hattori said. The porch steps creaked.

"Yes," Phillip said. "But she has no knowledge of any witching children. It was the first thing I asked."

"I imagine if she did know something, you would no longer be here," Hattori said. "Still, I would like to question her. One never knows what secrets a midwife keeps."

"True," Phillip said. Their boots scuffed the floor in the cabin.

"How long have you been here?" Hattori asked. His voice came from the corner where the spinning wheel was kept.

"A few days," Phillip said.

"And your boat that sank, where was it headed?" Hattori asked.

"Saint Augustine," Phillip said.

"How many venators do you have there?" Hattori's voice continued to move around the room. I had the odd sensation of my skin burning, like I'd stayed in the sun for too long, and I hoped that Hattori wasn't feeling the same.

"Three," Phillip said. "Where are you coming from?"

"Savannah," Hattori said. "An herbalist there told me about a midwife in these parts. I thought I'd search her out."

I could hear Mama or Ruth setting up the pot over the fire. They were mumbling to each other, but I couldn't make out what they were saying.

"What is up there?" Hattori asked.

"Sleeping loft," Phillip said.

"Momo, take a look," Hattori said.

Momo made a light grunting sound as she lifted herself up. I lay stock-still and held my breath. There was a light slapping sound on pallet, then the blanket was jerked off of my head. I clenched my jaw as Momo's dark eyes met mine. I was done for, but I was too terrified to move. Her face was stony, without expression. I only had a moment to notice her delicate, high cheekbones before she blinked, then threw the blanket back over my head as if she'd not seen me.

"No one's there," Momo said as her boots hit the wood planks.

My whole body was tensed like a taut rope. Momo was lying. I knew, for sure, that she had stared me straight in the face. What game was she playing? Why would she lie? A hundred questions swirled in my head as I decided to lie still and see what happened next.

"Are the samurai still in New Bern?" Phillip asked.

"We have a few venators there," Hattori said. "The future lies west. With the building of the railroad, we are going to be able to cover more ground in a swift manner." He paused, then asked, "What is this?" There was a little squeak from a hinge as the wooden box was opened. I bit my lip and prayed that Mama Jane had taken out any poison roots and seeds.

"Crow Jane's herbs," Phillip said. "Have you found any witching children?"

"Not the precise one I'm looking for," Hattori said. "Have you?" The box's lid closed.

"No," said Phillip. There was nothing in his tone to suggest he was lying. "I've spoken to every midwife and witch doctor on these sea islands. When I return to Charleston, I'm going to suggest heading west."

"The healer will be reborn in the new world and found during a time of war," Hattori said, as if he were a preacher quoting scripture. "Let's hope the oracle was speaking of this civil war and not some other war to come."

"Conflict is always brewing somewhere," Phillip said.

"We're back!" Abel called. Water sloshed in a barrel.

Boots scraped on the porch, and I guessed that the men and Momo had left the cabin, but I couldn't be sure. I could hear Mama chopping roots and wondered if she would steep any water hemlock into the samurai's tea. It grew in the marsh, and mama tried to harvest as much as she could, saying that you never knew when it would come in handy.

Everyone gathered around the fire at back of the cabin, but I didn't dare peek at them. Was Momo waiting to tell Hattori where I was? I didn't have a choice but to wait it out.

"Y'all came at the right time," Mama said. "We harvested crabs yesterday." She would be sure to dredge them in corn meal and fry them in a little hog fat. "Ruth, see if the hens laid any eggs for our guests."

"I've been teaching the boys here a bit of swordplay," Phillip said. "Boys, go get your wasters."

Noah and Abel let out whoops as they ran off, and I could hear the distinct clatter of them grabbing their sticks that had been fashioned into practice swords. The samurai laughed as Phillip directed the boys to lunge, retreat, and parry. Far as I could tell, everyone was acting as normal as could be, even Ruth, who was always quiet around newcomers.

Slowly, I turned my head so I could see outside through the slats in the wood wall. Momo had pulled out her long sword and play-battled with Abel and Noah. Her hair was as black and straight as any Cusabo Indian, and she wore a dark blue jacket that was cinched at the waist with a belt. Hattori was dressed similar to Momo and stood with his shoulders squared and his hands behind his back. His eyes ran over the garden, the cook shed, Mama's hoodoo supplies, then back to the cabin. I shrank back, but I couldn't help but wonder if Hattori suspected that some sort of trickery was afoot.

Ruth mashed a few turnips, some flour, and an egg together in a bowl, then patted the batter between her palms to shape a cake and dipped it in corn meal. Turnips grew plentiful in our garden; when they were in season, that's about all we ate.

"Food's ready," Mama said. She reminded Abel and Noah, "Eggs are for our guests." The boys gathered next to Ruth, who was frying turnip cakes on the skillet.

"Can I offer you a bit of honeycomb for your tea?" Mama asked.

"Please," Hattori said. Honeycomb plopped into three teacups.

"Will you not eat with us?" Hattori asked.

"The women and children eat after the guests are finished," Mama said.

"What if there is nothing left?" Hattori asked.

"Then we'll go without," Mama said. "My people are known for being hospitable."

"My people are known for their wisdom," Hattori said slowly. "Do you mind taking a bite of this crab?"

"All right," Mama said, then after a moment added, "Needs a little salt."

"Have a sip of my tea," Hattori said.

Mama slurped loudly. "I'm sorry I only got sassafras and birch bark to offer. Ruth, get a spoon to stir the honeycomb around with." Through the slats, I watched as Mama handed him back his mug, and he took a long swig of tea.

Hattori and Phillip began to eat, and Momo gobbled up the food like she'd missed several meals.

"Are these the only children you have?" Hattori asked. He pushed up his sleeves, bearing muscular forearms, as he sat up straight with his chin lifted. Had I met him in the street, I might have been charmed.

"Yes," Mama said.

"What is it you do here?" he asked.

"Grow food, catch fish, tend to the sick," Mama said. "Deliver a baby every now and then."

"Any witching babies?" Hattori took a bite of crab and tilted his head toward Mama. Momo glanced up to the back of the cabin where I huddled, and I drew my head back from the slat in the wall.

"No," Mama said. "Thought that was an old wives' tale till Phillip asked about them."

"The honeycomb is lovely." Hattori took a long slurp from his mug.

"It's aster honey," Mama said. "Helps to settle the stomach."

Ruth offered the guests more tea and turnip cakes.

"Get down the last of that sorghum syrup." Mama pointed to the top shelf of her hoodoo supplies. "Syrup makes the corn meal and turnips go down easier." Turnips were naturally a touch bitter, as were most poisonous roots. I supposed that was why Mama was being so generous with the honey and syrup.

"You may not know it to look at me, but I have lived over a thousand years," Hattori said. "In my experience, no two midwives are alike. Some are timid; others are thankful to we who have offered them protection; but those who are guarded have the most interesting tales to tell."

"If farming and shrimping strike your fancy, I suppose I can entertain you," Mama said. She poured some tea.

"What do you know of the witching children?" Hattori asked.

"Only what has been passed down," Mama said.

"Entertain me with the story, if you don't mind," Hattori said.

"Every so often, a baby is born on the winter solstice, and if you find one of them babies, you got to keep it safe for the immortal tribe that'll be searching for it," Mama said. "And when they come for the baby, they're supposed to give you a sack of gold."

Abel and Noah muttered together at the mention of gold.

"How do you know which sept to give the child to?" Hattori asked.

Mama chuckled. "Before I met you, I thought all immortals were together, one sept." She sipped her tea.

"How did you mark the last witching moon?" Hattori asked.

"There was no celebration, if that's what you mean," Mama said. "My grandmother spoke of her grandmother building a pyre and sacrificing a goat, but we don't do that. We need all our animals."

"The witching moon is not celebrated as it once was," Phillip said.

"The old ways are being forgotten." Hattori took a long slurp of his tea and sighed. "This syrup is delicious."

"Thank you," Mama said.

"Your daughter doesn't speak much," Hattori said.

"Nothing wrong with being quiet," Mama said. I wondered how long Momo would be quiet about me hiding in the loft.

"People who have secrets come in two varietals: the ones that are mute, and the ones that can't stop talking," Hattori said. "Which are you, Ruth?"

"I don't have nothing to hide," Ruth said.

"That's good," Hattori said. "Because if you were hiding something, I would find it."

The tiny hairs on my arms stood straight up. Every instinct in my body told me he was staring at the back of the cabin.

"I've already questioned Crow Jane." Phillip sounded annoyed. "If she was hiding anything, I would have seen it."

"Then why do I feel a—a—presence?" Hattori took a deep breath and let out slowly. "A soothing aura."

"It's my pneuma," Phillip said.

"I don't think so." Hattori laughed. "This is a gentle one, fresh with ancient vibrations."

"You describe me to a tee," Phillip said.

"No; your pneuma is vibrant but rough," Hattori said. I could hear his boots or belt buckle jangle as he stood. He sniffed the air as if he were a bloodhound on a trail. "The aura I perceive is unique." Coquina shells that were mixed into the dirt crunched under his boots.

Momo uttered something, then coughed, like a chicken bone was stuck in her gullet.

"You all right?" Mama asked.

Momo made a muffled sound, then a dish thunked in the dirt.

"Here, drink some tea. You just swallowed the wrong way," Mama said.

Momo retched loudly.

"Pat her back," Mama said.

Momo hacked to the rhythm of someone beating against her backside.

"She's turning purple!" Abel cried.

A body thudded in the dirt.

"She's not breathing!" Phillip yelled.

"Poison," Hattori said in a voice so low I barely heard him. He cleared his throat. "What did you give us?"

No one said a word. Hattori gagged as if he were sticking his fingers in his mouth, trying to force back up what he'd eaten and drank.

"Stay back," Phillip said.

Carefully, and quietly as I could, I pressed my eye against the crack between the wooden boards. Hattori was bent over, hacking and spitting on the ground. Momo was pale, sprawled out in the sand, her tongue sticking out the side of her mouth. Phillip approached Hattori slowly as the samurai dropped to his knees, gasping for air.

"How much did you give us?" Phillip asked as he clawed at his neck and sank next to Hattori.

"Enough to kill a horse," Mama Jane said.

10

Mama had poisoned them all, even herself.

"Anne!" Ruth hollered. "Come quick!"

By the time I made it to the back of the cabin, Phillip was on his hands and knees. Noah patted him on his back as he gagged and spat on the grass. A grimace spread across my face when I laid my hands on Phillip's bare neck. Bile rose in the back of my throat, and my muscles got all twitchy and weak. The color came back into Phillip's face, and he puffed up as my cure passed into him. Noah caught me before I swooned.

"Now do Mama," Ruth said. Mama had gone limp, and Ruth was holding her up by her waist while Abel fanned her with a palm frond.

Phillip helped me to her. Mama wasn't as bad off as he'd been; there was some dizziness and a dull ache when I laid hands on her, but within a breath, she was standing tall. She raised her face to the sky and took a deep sigh. I gripped her skirt as I sank to my knees. Mama settled on the ground with me and guided my head to her lap. Shivers tensed my muscles, and I took shallow breaths because it hurt to breathe. I was spent.

"Shh." Mama brushed my hair out of my eyes. "Take in the sunlight."

"Here's some water," Ruth said. Abel and Noah drew close, and someone's shadow fell over me, blocking the light.

"What's happened? Phillip asked. "Is she ill?"

"Get back," Mama said. "Give her space to breathe."

"Does this happen a lot?" Phillip sounded far away.

"When Anne lays hands on folks, she gives them a part of herself, it takes time for her to recover," Ruth said.

The sun took its sweet time to soak into my skin and pass to my spirit, plumping me up like a flower after a hard rain. Several moments passed before I squinted my eyes and asked for water. Phillip was staring at me, rubbing the scar that cut through his eyebrow with his thumb. For some reason, it troubled me that Phillip had seen me out of sorts, so I pushed myself up and ran my fingers through my hair to shake the dirt out.

"You steady enough to stand?" Mama asked.

"Why on earth did you drink the tea?" I asked her as I shook my legs out.

"To get them to drink it."

I offered Mama my hand and pulled her to standing. Her eyes rested on Momo, who was softly moaning on the ground. "Don't take an ounce of pleasure in doing harm to no one," Mama said.

Hattori was lying on his side, his body twitching with spasms. His eyes locked on mine, and I moved behind Mama for protection. I didn't want him to see me, to know what I looked like, just in case we ever met again.

"I know you don't." I squeezed Mama's hand. She turned and held my eyes; without her saying a word, I knew that everything she'd done was for my sake.

"Momo saw me in the loft," I whispered in Phillip's ear.

"You sure?" he mouthed, and his eyebrows knitted together. I nodded.

He brought his finger to his lips, instructing me to keep quiet.

"What're we gonna do now?" Noah asked, shaking his head slowly. The matter of what to do with two poisoned samurai was a predicament we'd never faced before.

"Do you have any rope?" Phillip asked. He bent over and removed Hattori's boots.

"Got a bit of braided hemp," Abel said, and ran off to fetch it.

Phillip rolled Hattori over, unbuckled his scabbard, and removed the samurai's great sword, dagger, and bow. "Forgive me, old friend, I am only relieving you of your weapons momentarily." Phillip handed Hattori's things to Noah.

"Can we keep these?" Noah asked.

"Only if you wish to incur a curse," Phillip said as he relieved Momo of her boots and weaponry.

"I don't," Noah said.

"We'll hide them for safekeeping. When they recover, they'll have to free themselves and find their swords before they can start after us."

"I know just the place," Abel said, dropping a length of rope on the ground.

"It has to be close," Phillip said to Abel, then turned to Mama. "You're going to need to leave the farm for a while."

"I'm not leaving our home," Ruth said with her chest puffed out.

"Hattori and Momo will be themselves again by nightfall. Do you want to be here with two venators you poisoned?" Phillip tried to take Ruth's arm, but she shook him away. "The farther away you are the safer you will be." He turned to Mama. "Is there someone you can stay with for a fortnight or so? Just until things settle down?"

Mama nodded.

"Pack what you need. The boys and I will be back in a bit."

We didn't own a trunk or a traveling bag because we never went anywhere, so Ruth cinched the waist of a calico skirt together with a belt and began to stuff the makeshift bag with clothes. Mama gathered her herb box and Bible. I picked up

Ruth's sewing basket, but my hands were shaking so bad that I dropped it. Needles, thimbles, and spools of thread scattered at my feet.

"This don't seem real," I muttered as I picked up a spool.

Ruth hunkered beside me. "It's going to be all right. I'm afeared too, but it's gonna be all right."

"How d'you know?" I asked. I'd pictured myself leaving Cusabo many times, but never like this.

"Because it has to be."

"What about the chickens? The spinning wheel? The butter churn?" There were too many things we couldn't take with us.

"It'll all be here when we get back," Mama said.

"How d'you know that?" I stumbled around the room picking up things—a shard of mirror, an arrowhead—and putting them back down. I weighed each item in my hand, deciding if it was worth carrying.

"Who's gonna come take it?" Mama asked, exasperated.

"Three days ago I would have said no one, but now, it seems like anything is possible," I said. "What other immortal sept is gonna show up on our doorstep?"

"Don't worry about what might happen; just concern yourself with right now," Mama said. "Ruth, make another skirt-satchel for my hoodoo supplies."

"All this is my fault." Tears were burning my eyes.

"Hush now," Mama said. "I suppose I knew this time was at hand, even if it stayed out of my mind. And before you say another word, you've always been a blessing and never once a curse." She wrapped me in her arms and squeezed me till I hardly had any breath left in me. "God ain't gonna send nothing my way that's too big to conquer."

Behind the cabin, both samurai had been stripped down to their underclothes and were lying face down and hog-tied with rope and their own belts. Hattori's eyes rolled into the back of his head; he was gurgling, and little bubbles escaped his lips. It was disquieting to look at them, yet hard to turn away. They were like exotic plants that had sprung up in the garden.

"How long you think they'll be this way?" I asked.

"It's hard to say." Mama wrapped jars in pieces of cloth and stuffed them in the makeshift sack. "Never poisoned anyone that couldn't be killed before."

"You've poisoned others?" I asked.

"If need be. There are bad people in the world, and sometimes you gotta do whatever it takes to survive."

"Have everything you need?" Phillip asked, and Mama nodded. His mouth was a hard line, but his eyes held concern. "I'm sorry to put you out of your own home."

"I've survived worse," Mama said.

"We should go," Phillip said. The wind picked up, and thunder rolled from a ways off. A storm was brewing.

With their bows strapped to their backs, Abel and Noah each carried a sack as they walked on either side of Phillip. Mama, Ruth, and I followed, each carrying a squirming chicken. I couldn't help myself; I turned to take one last look at our cabin, which now stood empty as an abandoned bird's nest.

"Come on." Ruth tugged at my skirt. "You don't want to end up like Lot's wife, turned into a pillar of salt."

"It's so hollow, like a cast-off shell of a sea snail, ready for some animal to come in and take it over." Tears welled in my eyes.

"Cry all you want later; we need to be long gone when those samurai regain themselves." Ruth pulled me away.

"Do you have somewhere you can go?" Phillip asked Mama as we walked.

"I got family on the mainland," Mama said; upcountry cousins I had only heard her talk about.

"You're gonna need to stay there for a while, possibly a month," Phillip said.

"You think these samurai gonna come looking for us?" Mama asked.

"No, they'll be too busy trying to find Anne." Phillip said. He reached into his jacket pocket, pulled out a leather pouch, and held it out.

Mama's eyes widened.

"Take it," Phillip said. "It's all the gold I have. It should get you settled wherever you're going and get you back home with plenty to spare. I'll take Anne to Charleston."

"Why can't we all go to Charleston?" Noah asked with the corners of his mouth turned down. I suppose he was feeling left out and wanted to follow Phillip on to adventure.

"Soon as the other septs find out I have Anne, they are all going to try to take her for themselves," Phillip said. "Anne and I won't be there for very long, anyway."

"We ever gonna see y'all again?" Abel lowered his eyes and kicked at the dirt.

"Not for a long while," Phillip said. "But I promise, when things settle down, when Anne is safe at Amaranth, I'll be in touch." He then turned to Mama. "When other immortals find their way to you, be honest. Tell them I came and took her. That way, they'll leave you alone."

"Take care of my girl." Mama's voice cracked. Her eyes became shiny, and the corners of her mouth turned down. I didn't think I'd ever seen her so sad.

"I will," Phillip said.

"I know there's goodness in you."

"I see it in you as well." Phillip touched her shoulder.

For the rest of the walk, I stayed close to Mama's side, trying to soak up as much of her as I could. Abel and Noah were quieter than usual, taking turns brushing up against my arm and ladling out bits of advice as drops of rain splatted in the dirt path.

"Stay clear of any soldiers," Abel said. "I hear tell they can be mighty ornery."

"I will," I said.

Noah pressed a hook and some fishing line in my hand before he ran ahead to walk with Phillip.

"Guess it wasn't right to keep things from you," Ruth said. "I suppose I figured you were meant to be part of our tribe."

"I'm always gonna be part of your tribe." I bumped against her hip.

Soon as the trees thinned, I could see that the sky toward the mainland was dark. Phillip took stock of the storm clouds but didn't break his step. A gaggle of Guinea hens squawked, and a farmer leaned against his hoe.

Mama held her head steady, nodded to the men who tipped their hats, and smiled to the women who stepped out of their shanty houses. Past the blacksmith and the store was the dock where the ferry waited. Rain drizzled, and a haze settled over the river.

"Do you mind if we take the first ferry?" Phillip asked.

"Not one bit," Mama said. "We can say our farewells here."

I gave my chicken to Noah and gave him a hug. "I love you, brother," I said.

"I love you, sister." He squeezed me tight with one arm and held the chicken with the other.

"I'll be fine," I said as I hugged Ruth, but I wasn't sure if I was trying to calm her or myself. I kissed her slick cheek. Her eyes were shiny. "Don't cry. You'll make me cry, then we'll all be standing here boohooing."

"I'm never going to stop praying that you're safe," Ruth said between sniffles.

"Write and tell us where you are," Abel said. "Noah and me want to come visit."

Mama pulled me to her. "Wish I had something special to give you." She smelled like crepe myrtle and lye soap.

"You've given me heaps." I held her close.

"Don't forget about where you came from." Mama gave me a kiss, then let me go.

Phillip held out his hand and helped me into the flat-bottomed, wooden boat. There was no seat, just an empty hull. I struggled to keep my balance and hold my family in my sight for as long as I could. Mama gave me a tight-lipped smile and a nod, and Ruth, Abel, and Noah waved.

The grizzled ferryman dipped his head to Mama as he balanced on the square-cut bow. He pushed off with a long pole, guiding us into the mist. My eyes welled up as the only family I had ever known faded from sight.

11

Rain pelted the boat's hull as it cut through the choppy water. Waves crested and spilled over the side walls while my belly pitched and rolled. Part of me wanted to tell the ferryman to turn us around, that I'd made a mistake, but I couldn't bring myself to speak.

The ferryman struggled against the swift current as the rain came down in sheets, like we were standing under a waterfall. The boat bobbed to and fro, and whooshed right past the dock on the far side of the river.

"Wasn't that our landing?" I asked, and Phillip shot me a nervous glance. The river had a mind of its own, and we were headed straight for the ocean. Lightning crackled overhead. We rounded a narrow bend, and the river widened. The ferryman used his pole to nudge us toward a shoal. The rain was letting up.

Shells scraped the hull as we ran aground near the mouth of the inlet where the ocean swelled the river. Phillip slipped a coin into the ferryman's palm, leapt to the riverbank, and landed with a crunch, then extended both his arms to me.

"Jump." His boots dug into the sharp edges of an oyster rake.

Sopping wet, I teetered on the bow of the boat, my toes slipping on the wood. "You'd better catch me."

"Trust me." Phillip pushed the hair out of his eyes.

I leapt before I could think twice. Phillip caught me, and I flung my arms around his neck and wrapped my legs around his torso like a small child clings to an adult in the ocean waves. Phillip wobbled, and we fell back with a splat. Shells cracked, and he let out a yowl. My thighs pressed into his chest as I crawled over him and up the muddy riverbank, where I managed to stand.

"You all right?" I wiped the mud off my face as my feet sunk down in the mire.

Phillip winced and rolled over onto his belly. A mess of jagged oyster shells lay snapped and broken where he had fallen. My legs were trembly, but I offered him my hand anyway. I was used to avoiding the perils of the salt marsh, and he clearly was not.

"Think so." Phillip reached for me, and I tugged him to his feet.

"Turn around," I said. "Let me see where you're cut." My sight was blurry, so I rubbed my eyes, but that only made it worse.

Phillip shrugged his jacket off, then reached into an inner pocket and presented me with a square of linen about the size of the kerchief Mama Jane tied her hair back with. "You have mud on your eye."

I dabbed at my eyes until I could see clearly. The cloth smelled like leather and him. I folded it over and saw that it had a thick streak of muck on it. "Sorry." I offered the handkerchief back to him.

"Keep it," he said, and I stuffed it deep in my pocket. He untucked his shirttail so I could examine his back. I lifted his shirt and lightly ran my hand over his skin, feeling for any cuts or scrapes that could cause infection. The well-formed muscles that ran along either side of his spine quivered.

"You got lucky." I pulled his shirt down. "Your jacket saved you from getting all cut up."

The ferryman used his pole to shove off from the oyster bed. Phillip stood and waved to the ferryman, who tipped his hat in return.

Phillip ran his eyes over the horizon. The great salt marsh lay before us, bleak in the rain. "The sun is breaking through just over those palms." He pointed inland and started to pick his way through the maze of ridges and sloughs.

"D'you think Mama, Ruth, and the boys will cross the river okay before those samurai get loose?"

"It'll take a bit for the ferryman to get back to them, but I think they'll be fine." Phillip stood at the edge of a slough, examining the best way to proceed. Minnows darted between sprouting cattails in the murky water. "How do you suppose we cross?"

I stepped back a few paces, hitched up my skirt, took a running start, and leapt over the tidal creek, landing in a thicket of spartina grass. Phillip grinned as he rubbed the scar above his eye, then backed up to follow my lead. He had a good start, but his sword weighed him down. He landed on the bank just short of the ridge and sank down in the pluff mud. A water moccasin reared its head and hissed.

"Snake," I said. "Kick it!"

"I can't." Phillip struggled to wiggle free but sank knee-deep into the mire.

"Then splash at it!" I glanced around for a stick or something to haul him out. A clump of cattails came out at their roots when I tugged on them. I tossed Phillip the wet stalks and braced myself as he struggled to get his footing.

"My boot." Phillip scrabbled up the slippery bank and plopped down. His stockinged right foot and britches leg were covered in muck. "Do you see it?"

Only the inner pull strap of the boot stuck out of the water. The snake reared back and struck the top of the leather tab. The rain was slowing to a drizzle.

"I'd let that boot be."

"Perhaps you should lead the way." Phillip stood and shook his leg, trying to get the mud off. I didn't bother telling him it was no use.

"You okay?" I asked.

"I'm fine."

Dripping wet and covered in mire, Phillip seemed far from fine, but I knew better than to poke at someone when things weren't going their way. I led him across the tideland, away from the river. There was no trail, so we slogged along, feeling our way and trying to stay on firm ground. Far as I could tell, the mainland wasn't much different from Cusabo Island. Truth be told, if I wasn't so beside myself with fear and worry, I probably would have been a mite disappointed.

It was slow going, footslogging through the marsh. Once the rain stopped and the sun came out, mosquitos and horseflies swarmed our heads, so we had to pick fronds of spartina to swat at the pesky critters.

"Rub this on your neck and face," I said, scooping up a handful of pluff mud and dabbing it under my eyes, around my ears, and under my chin.

"You can't be serious." Phillip's chin tucked in, and his face twisted in disgust for just a moment; then he composed himself quickly and said, "This mud stinks worse than a dead fish on a hot day."

"Smells like the salt marsh to me." I shrugged. He dipped his finger into the mud and dabbed it on his neck and face in blotches.

"May I?" I held up my hand, and he gave a quick nod. He closed his eyes as I smoothed out the thick blots into a thin layer with my thumb. His skin was soft, yet sturdy, like the under-belly of a horse. When my thumb traced his lips, he opened his eyes, and I saw they were the color of spring moss. My eyes held his for a moment too long, and I felt the heat rise from my neck to my cheeks. "Once it dries, it won't smell so bad," I said, dropping my eyes and wiping my hand on my skirt.

"We certainly make a motley duo," Phillip said.

"I suppose," I murmured, turning my face from his and taking in the landscape. Touching his face had been thrilling in a strange way. Why had I circled his mouth with my thumb? I was sure that Mama would not have approved of such a thing. Phillip probably thought I was too forward.

"Do you think you can get us back toward the boat landing?" Phillip asked. "The samurai probably left their horses hobbled there."

The sun was peeking through the clouds, coloring the marsh gold with thickets of green sprouting here and there. "It's over that way, I believe." I pointed to the far-off grove of river oaks that lined the Cusabo river.

"Lead the way," Phillip said, holding out his hand for me to go first.

"Momo saw me in the loft and didn't say a thing to Hattori," I said again, passing in front of him.

"That you know of," Phillip said. "She may have let him know some other way. After all, he was headed back into the cabin when he succumbed to the poison."

"If she'd wanted him to know I was there she would have said something, but instead she lied to him," I insisted. "She told him no one was in the loft, but she saw me there, clear as day."

"Are you sure?"

"She looked me straight in the eye."

"She could have had an ulterior motive." Phillip rubbed his thumb across his scarred eyebrow.

"What's that?" I asked.

"Her own reasoning, different from Hattori. Maybe she thought to break away from Hattori and come back for you on her own."

"Maybe, or it could be that she had been protecting me from Hattori." There had been something about Momo's lack of expression, almost like she was guarding herself from any reaction to seeing me so as not to let Hattori know I was there.

"Why do you say that?"

"It's just a feeling I got from her."

"The samurai do not treat their women as they treat their men," Phillip said.

"How so?"

"It is my understanding that the women of the samurai sept have no say in who they mate with." Phillip's face flushed crimson. "In fact, they have little say about anything at all."

"Is that how things are at Amaranth?"

"Not at all. Rowan is a force to be reckoned with," he said. "You'll see."

The sun was sinking, and the sky had cleared when we reached the woods. Despite only having one boot, Phillip stepped lightly through the brush, and when he stopped to rest, he either bent low or leaned against a tree, making his shape part of the land.

Just before dark, we stumbled across a path. Phillip motioned for me to hide under a sea myrtle while he sussed out the trail.

"You think it's safe?" I asked.

"Maybe," Phillip said. "Keep to the side. If you sense danger, hide in the brush."

Not being able to see made my ears perk to any little sound. I followed closely behind Phillip's padding footsteps. The trail ended, and stars winked in the open sky.

"Seems to be a pasture," Phillip said.

"You think we overshot the landing?" I asked.

"It seems so."

"Should we turn around?"

"No, let's move ahead."

We'd only gone a little ways when we came to a split-rail fence. An animal snorted in the darkness. Phillip crouched next to a post, and I hunkered down beside him. We waited for a bit, but we only heard the whinnies of two horses. Phillip slipped through the opening of the wooden fence, and I followed. One of the horses stamped the ground.

"Hey." I held my hands out. A warm nose pressed against my palm. "This is a big yard for just the two of you." I ran my hand along the colt's withers; it wasn't very big, maybe eight hands high. A larger horse nosed the top of my head.

"I'd bet my left boot the army has been through here," Phillip said. "The farmer must have hidden these horses or else the soldiers would have taken them."

"That's not right," I said.

"It's survival." Phillip got real quiet. "Listen. We need these horses."

"You think the farmer will sell them?"

"No, I don't." He spoke gently. "We're gonna have to steal them."

"Horse thieves get hanged."

"Only if they get caught."

"Scripture says you reap what you sow." I sounded like Mama Jane, doling out wisdom. On the far side of the field, firelight seeped through a cabin's walls.

"It'll take three days to walk to Charleston, and we'll have the samurai on our trail, but these two can get us there tonight."

"Isn't there something we could leave as payment?" I asked. "Don't you have any more of those gold pieces?"

"No." Phillip moved quietly in the grass ahead of me.

My pockets only held knobby roots and a fishing hook with line. Then I felt the ring on my finger. "Here," I said, sliding the band over my knuckle and feeling for Phillip's hand. "Leave it where the farmer can find it."

Phillip turned, and I could feel his breath in my hair. "You would offer a relic of your past to a stranger?"

"I don't want to." There was something about the darkness that made it easy to speak the truth. "But I can't be no thief."

"Give me your hand." Phillip slid the ring back over my knuckle and gave the tips of my fingers a slight squeeze. "Keep your ring. I'll leave mine. It will more than pay for a new horse."

"Then we'll just take one of them," I said as he turned toward the barn.

"Fine," Phillip said over his shoulder. "Choose the stronger one."

I stroked the larger horse's nose, and he snorted, then I ran my hands over the colt. I reasoned that it'd be better to leave the farmer with a younger animal, so I coaxed the bigger one along the fence while I felt for a gate latch.

Phillip returned with a bridle and reins, slipped them over the horse's nose, and led him through the gate.

"Where'd you leave your ring?" I asked as I tied my hair back with the linen kerchief he had given me

"On the hook where the reins were," he said. "There was only one saddle, so I left it. I hope you're all right to ride bareback."

I liked the way he thought. "I've never used a saddle anyway."

Phillip led our mount out to the road, then bounced me up onto its back. I hitched up my skirt and tucked it around my legs. Phillip climbed on behind me and made a soft clicking sound. The horse began to trot. Phillip wrapped his arm around my waist, and I leaned into him. As we rode, it occurred to me that we were molded together; his legs pressing against mine, my hips shifting with his, his chest thumping against my back. All of these things happening together made me feel that I was caught in an undertow, and I had no idea where I was being pulled.

12

There comes a time in the wee dark hours when nearly all living things lie down and silence falls; Mama Jane called it the dead of night. It is when spirits rise up to see to any unsettled dealings and inner sight is the strongest.

Even though I was on horseback, I had drifted off to that muddled place between waking and sleep, where dreams seem real, when I felt a shadow pass. Out of the darkness, an eagle swooped down, its talons spread as if to pluck me from the horse. My arm shot up as I bobbed down, then I opened my eyes and realized I'd been asleep.

"What is it?" Phillip tightened his arms around my waist.

"A dream." I shook my head.

It wasn't until we slowed to a trot and I heard the gurgle of water that I realized just how still everything had gotten. Phillip stopped the horse and slid off, and I was right behind him, stumbling to the stream and dropping to my knees to cup water to my mouth. We had been riding for hours, and my legs and back ached.

"How much longer?" I asked between gulps.

Phillip lapped water into his mouth, and for a moment I wasn't sure if he had heard me. "If we keep riding hard, maybe we can be there before the sunrise; if not, we'll hide in the woods and make our way in after nightfall."

"Why?"

"There's another sept quartered in the city. It could be dangerous if they know you're there."

The tiny hairs on the back of my neck stood up. "What if they find out?"

Phillip was quiet for a moment, then said, "There's no need to worry about things that haven't happened yet."

He was right. Mama Jane liked to say that fretting over things that hadn't happened yet made up most of a person's misery in life.

Nothing about this night felt true. I was sure that at any minute, I'd wake up with Ruth's knee wedged in my back. We kept riding through the trees that gradually thinned and gave way to starry sky. Just before daybreak, the marsh trail merged with a dusty road. We crossed a wide wooden bridge, and in the first rays of light, I gasped at the sight of buildings with steep pointed roofs rising up in the distance.

"Church spires," Phillip said.

"Is this Charleston?"

"Yes."

Jasmine scented the air. I craned my neck at houses with wide covered porches and gardens behind iron gates.

We turned a corner, and I startled at the clip-clop of hooves. The dirt road had turned into cobblestones. Phillip tensed and wrapped his arm tight around my waist. It took me a moment to realize that our horse had stopped.

A goliath of a man sat on a mottled stallion, his horse situated so he blocked the narrow street. The sight of him, lean and strong, stole my breath. He lifted his chin and shook his black hair out of his face, then his dark eyes held mine. In that moment, it occurred to me that this was the kind of man who was used to having his way.

"Rex," Phillip hissed. He twisted the reins in his hand, and his legs gripped our horse.

Rex's face broke into a grin, the same kind a hunter gets when he spots his prey. He gripped the pommel of his saddle, and his fist was clad in a black leather glove.

Our horse turned and took off like a shot, causing my head and shoulders to jerk sideways. Hair flew into my face, and the handkerchief that I'd tied my hair back with floated to the ground.

"Hold on!" Phillip yelled. I squeezed my legs tight and laced my fingers into the horse's mane, but the horse's speed slid me to the side. I would have fallen off had Phillip not grabbed me by my waist. Everything was happening so fast that it didn't seem real. My heart was pounding, and it was all I could do to hold on. We veered right and bounded over a low wall, landing in a clump of flowers. Cats screeched and scattered out of our way. The horse charged through the garden, past a fountain, over another wall, and landed smack in a boneyard.

Crosses were aligned in rows, and a stone angel lifted her arms to the heavens. Behind us, the stallion's hooves plowed into the dirt, and Rex laughed. His laughter was more mocking than happy, and it sent a hailstone-cold shiver up my backbone.

Our horse cut a line through the grave markers and jumped an iron fence, then crossed a street and ducked down an alley that narrowed the further we went, until our legs were brushing against the sides of the walls. We galloped into a courtyard that was closed on all side by houses. I looked around wildly, trying to see what was going on.

Phillip slipped off the horse behind me and reached for a rope that hung next to the alley wall. An iron gate crashed down with a clang, barring entry to the yard. Phillip drew his sword and held it out, ready to cut down whatever came through the gate.

My fingernails dug into my palms. "Who was that?" I huffed, struggling to catch my breath.

"Doesn't matter." With his tensed back to me, Phillip peered through the gate back down the alleyway. "He can't bother us now."

"It matters to me!" My voice rose high, and my fists shook as they gripped the reins. I tried to unclench my fists, but they had a mind of their own and remained clamped.

The lathered horse trotted in a wide arc around the courtyard, which gave me a moment to breathe deeply and calm myself. "Why was that man chasing us?" I asked.

"I told you there was another sept in the city." Phillip said, as if that explained everything. He pivoted to face me; his face was flushed pink, and he was breathing hard.

"That doesn't account for—for—whoever that was!" I slid off the horse and realized, too late, that my legs had turned to jelly. My behind hit the stones with a painful splat, and my eyes started to sting with tears that I struggled to keep inside.

Still holding his sword, Phillip rushed to my side and slipped his free arm under mine. "Are you hurt?" He helped me to my feet.

"Don't." I wriggled away from him and shook my legs out. I was embarrassed that he'd seen me so helpless and flustered. Here I was in a strange city, being chased by a madman, with only Phillip for protection. For the first time I found myself questioning if Phillip really knew what he was doing.

"We're here now; were safe," Phillip said, gesturing to a set of stairs that led to the nearest townhouse. A door creaked open, and a bald man appeared at the top of the stairs where Phillip had pointed. The man caught sight of Phillip, then me, and his whole face lit up as he rushed down the steps.

Phillip slipped his sword in his scabbard, and then he and the man embraced.

"Brother," the man said in a thick accent. A tiny ruby glinted in his earlobe. He wore leather pants and a tunic, and a sword dangled from the scabbard fastened around his waist.

"Where are the guards?" Phillip asked.

"On the ship." The man ran his gaze to me, and his eyes went wide. "The healer." He bowed low to me. Unsure of what to do,

I bowed in return, which increased his smile to the point that his eyes sparkled. I'd never witnessed such obvious pleasure in anyone who had met me. The collar of his shirt was open, showing inky markings on his chest. I'd never seen anyone as exotic as he was with his dark oval eyes and thick eyebrows, but his smile and friendliness seemed genuine.

"Anne, I'd like you to meet Ram-An of Amaranth," Phillip said.

"Hey," I said.

"I am at your service." Ram-An gave another bow. This time, I just dipped my head in return.

"Where did you find her?" Ram-An asked Phillip as he rattled the chain on the gate to check that it was secure.

"Cusabo Island." Phillip held his hand out to me, and I took it reluctantly, reminding myself that he'd gotten us this far and he said we were safe now, even though I felt more flustered than anything.

"It is my greatest honor to welcome you to our sept." Ram-An gestured to the back stairs of the house.

"Who is Rex?" My legs were still shaking.

"He's from the tribe of Valen." Phillip led me to the back steps of the house.

"Valen." The name flowed easily from my mouth, but at the same time my innards seized up. An image of a man with hawk-like eyes bubbled up in my mind.

"Let him be of no concern to you." Ram-An urged me up the stairs and into the house. "Rex cannot enter our sept's domain without an invitation, which we shan't be offering."

13

The aroma of bread filled the small room that Ram-An ushered us into. Bricks lined the floor, and scabbards, capes, and hats hung on wall hooks. Phillip plopped down on the lowest step of a staircase and set to tugging off his solitary boot and mud-crusted sock.

"You're shaking." Ram-An removed a shawl from a peg and covered my shoulders with it. "Come, warm yourself by the stove fire in the kitchen." He ushered me from the cloak room through a door to our left.

Mama Jane had told me that kitchens on the mainland were indoors or attached to houses, but even in my dreams I'd never imagined anything like the cook room I now stood in. Shelves filled with crockery lined the wall over the wash basin, and a black cast-iron stove stood in the corner pumping out heat. Ruth and Mama would've had themselves a time in a place like this. Two stools were pushed under a wooden block table. Beyond that, a square hole in the brick wall was rigged with ropes and some sort of contraption that seemed to raise and lower things.

"What's that?" I pointed to the ropes and pulls.

"This is a dumbwaiter," Ram-Am said. He tugged on a rope, and the wooden shelf inside the hole in the wall rose. "You can deliver food or tea to another floor in the house through a set of ropes and pullies."

"Who all lives here?" I asked.

"Venators and guards," Ram-An answered. "We are an outpost of the Amaranthine sept."

"Phillip!" A woman's voice rose up in surprise outside the kitchen.

"I found her," Phillip called in reply.

A young woman stepped into the doorway. She wore a yellow dress with a thin belt from which a dagger hung in a sheath. Her lips parted in surprise when her wide eyes landed on me.

"Marie-Hélène, this is Anne," Ram-An said.

Marie-Hélène lowered her head and bobbed at the knees. She was smaller than me, with wheat-colored hair tied back in a knot. "It is a pleasure to meet you, Anne." She stared openly for a moment before she said, "You are so like Rowan."

"You know my sister?" I asked, and she nodded. "How am I like her?"

"Your hair, your eyes, your shine." Marie-Hélène ran her eyes from my head to my toes and back again, then she blinked and her cheeks grew pink. "Where are my manners?" She pulled out a stool. "Please, sit."

"I'm fine stretching my legs, if that's all right," I said.

"Can I offer you some water? Tea?" Marie-Hélène didn't wait for me to answer. "I'll put a kettle on." She brushed past me and made herself busy at the basin. A pale half moon was tinged pink on the nape of her neck.

"You've got a stork bite," I said. "I've got one too." Twisting my hair, I bared my neck and felt the heat of Marie-Hélène's fingertips hovering over my mark.

"Yours is raised, just like Rowan's," she said softly. "And you're wearing your ring. What has Phillip told you about us?"

Phillip squeezed into the cook room in his bare feet. "There's been no time for history lessons."

"How did you find her?" Marie-Hélène put the kettle on the

cooker. She wrapped a cloth over her hands and bent down, then pulled a pan of biscuits from the oven.

"It's a long story," Phillip said. "Are you hungry?" he asked me, and I shook my head. He grabbed a hot biscuit, then dropped it on the counter and blew on his hand before he tried to pick it up again.

"Rex saw them," Ram-An said to Marie-Hélène, whose cheeks went pale.

"Chased us." Steam rose from the biscuit as Phillip broke it in two. "He was waiting for us in the middle of Dock Street."

"Waiting?" Worry creased Marie-Hélène's forehead.

"It seemed like it," Phillip said. "It could have been happenstance, or Rex felt Anne's presence."

"You have a strong pneuma," Ram-An said to me.

"A what?" I asked.

"Spirit." Ram-An lifted his palms to my torso but did not actually touch me, as if to show that something was floating around me.

"Oh." Mama liked to say that my soul shined like a harvest moon.

"The spirit has many names," Ram-An said. "With a bit of practice, you will be able to pick up on our pneumas as well. Soon, you will be able to feel our pneuma vibrations before you see us." He held his palms out to me. "Hold your hands to mine, but don't touch."

I did as he said. "I don't feel anything."

"Don't you?" Ram-An asked. "Close your eyes. Breathe in through your mouth, and blow out as much air as you can. Do this slowly three times."

I did as he said. Sure enough, my hands began to pulse. Something whooshed between our palms, like the ebb and flow of tide.

"Strange." My hands tingled numb, like I'd fallen asleep with all my weight on top of them.

"We are like lodestones attracting iron," Ram-An said.

I supposed he could see on my face that I didn't understand.

"Come," Ram-An said. "I'll show you." We walked back through the cloak room, then through a corridor toward the front of the house. A woven rug lay over shined hardwood floors. Etched windows surrounded the front door, which was barred with a thick iron rod. Phillip and Marie-Hélène followed us through an archway to a room lined with shelves of books. Ram-An stepped behind a desk and pulled the draperies shut while Marie-Hélène struck a match and lit a lantern. Fancy swords and jeweled daggers hung on the wall closest to me.

A map was spread out on the desk. Several pewter ships had been placed on the blue areas of the chart, and figurines of men were scattered across the brown sections.

Ram-An opened a desk drawer and held up a rock about the size of my fist. "Take it," he said.

When I accepted the stone, it was smooth and shaped like a bean.

"Watch." Ram-An opened a tiny sac and sprinkled what looked like specs of dirt onto the desk. "Hold it over these iron shards."

Doubtful, I hovered the stone where he gestured. The iron bits leapt from the desk and planted themselves on the underside of the rock. Startled, I let out a gasp. "It's magic!"

"Actually, it's magnetism," Ram-An said.

"A natural attraction." Marie-Hélène took a pin from her hair and stood it on end, so it was pointing at an odd angle against the underside of the rock.

"I sensed you and Phillip when you entered our courtyard," Ram-An said. "Rex is much older and more attuned than I. It's possible he felt your magnetism when you crossed the Ashley River."

"How is that?" I set the rock on the desk and held my hand out to Ram-An. His hand hovered over mine, and the unseen power pushed and pulled between us. "I didn't feel this with Phillip."

"Didn't you?" Phillip's mouth curved down and his brow furrowed.

"Not like this." My hands felt swollen.

"You may have sensed him without knowing what you were feeling," Ram-An said. "Besides, Phillip's spirit is young. His pneuma is weak."

"It is not," Phillip said. He held his hands up, and I turned to him. It was true: I didn't feel the same pulse from him that I did with Ram-An.

"Your pneuma is strong to me." Marie-Hélène scrunched up her nose at Phillip. "You need a change of clothes and a bath."

"What we need is to devise a plan to safely board our ship." Phillip shrugged his jacket off and slung it over the back of a chair. "Rex is, no doubt, gathering his sept right now."

"He only has a handful of men in the city," Ram-An said. "He sent two venators west several days ago."

"Who do we have?" Phillip asked.

"Three guards," Ram-An said. "They're provisioning the ship."

"That's it?" Phillip swallowed hard and rubbed the scar on his eyebrow.

"I'm afraid so," Ram-An said. "We sent two guards to Wilmington and two to New Orleans. I'm afraid our defenses are limited at the moment." He raised one eyebrow and cocked his head toward the entry hall. A second later, a loud banging erupted from the front hall as if someone was hammering against the front door with a mallet.

"Stay with Anne," Phillip said to Marie-Hélène. He and Ram-An rushed to the entry hall.

Marie-Hélène dashed behind the desk, and I followed. She drew the window's curtain back and gasped. A gaggle of fierce-looking men were gathered on the street. A few wore vests or hats made of animal fur, and one man had an odd, familiar mark on his forearm of three interlocking horns.

"Vikings," I said, even though I had never uttered the word before and wasn't sure what it meant.

"That's right." Marie-Hélène met my eyes.

"That man." I pointed to the Viking holding a lit torch. "He bears the sign of Odin." Memories swarmed me, and I recalled that Valen wore the mark of Odin on his chest. I had seen a flash of it through his tunic as he'd knelt before me, asking for my hand, proposing an alliance between the northern and southern tribes. Fury had blazed in his eyes when I denied him.

"They're Rex's men," Marie-Hélène said.

"You mean Valen's men."

"Same thing. Rex is Valen's right hand."

"What are those strange bows?" I asked. Several of the men held carved wooden contraptions.

"Crossbows."

The archers held their arrows to the torch until they were flaming, then set their bows. One of the Vikings pointed my way, and they all started hollering. Marie-Hélène shut the drapes and nudged me away from the desk.

The hammering on the door began again, and Ram-An shouted, "Who goes there?"

"Release the healer to me!" commanded a voice.

"It's Rex," Marie-Hélène said.

"He's come for me," I said. There was no doubt in my mind that I spoke the truth.

14

A long-past memory had bewitched me. The bygone time spooled out in front of me like freshly spun flax. A ruby, big as a conch shell, glowed in Rowan's hands. Her fingertips traced a split in the stone as she spoke. "Valen will never give up his quest for your hand."

"I will not bind myself to someone I do not love," I said.

"He is full of wrath and vengeance," Rowan said.

"Let him choke on it." I stood in the doorway of our sunbaked clay and stone house and gazed up at the orchard in the hills. In the late twilight, I could barely make out the silhouettes of my tribesmen descending into our valley. A broad-shouldered shadow trailed behind the others, and the closer he came the more his pneuma glowed a brilliant green. He raised his hand in a wave, and my heart fluttered.

Rowan was speaking again.

"What?" I turned to her.

"I will watch for any signs of Valen's return." She cradled the rough stone.

"I know." I smiled at my sister.

"Ego protector tuus," she whispered. I will protect you.

The spell broke when something was placed in my hand. I twitched and returned to the present. It took me a moment to realize I had been in another place and time, and now I was standing in the room with the desk and books. I looked down, and Marie-Hélène closed my fingers around a dagger.

"I don't know how—"

"Jab anyone who comes near you." She buckled a scabbard that held a curved sword around her waist. "They're going to burn us out."

"You're outnumbered!" Rex's voice thundered through the door. "Hand the healer over now, and you can keep your head!"

Marie-Hélène moved to the front hall, and I followed her. She held up her hand to catch Phillip's eye. "He's got eleven men," she said. "They're lighting arrows."

"You dare to break our sept's armistice?" Ram-An yelled, but there was no answer.

Fire exploded over the door. Shards of the window rained down on Ram-An as he stumbled back. A blazing arrow dropped to the floor. Phillip grabbed a rug and threw it over the flames. Another fiery arrow shot through the window and quivered on the far wall. Upstairs, glass was breaking. My mouth popped open, and my first instinct was to run, but where? Instead, I clutched my dagger and bounced from one foot to another.

"Get to the kitchen!" Phillip turned to me. "Now!" His eyes were wild with panic or fury, I wasn't sure which.

"Yes!" The kitchen—that was the safest place; we could barricade ourselves in there. I caught a whiff of smoke as Marie-Hélène rushed me past the back stairs and into the cook room.

"The tunnel!" Phillip barged in behind us.

"It's flooded." Marie-Hélène grabbed some rags from a shelf and dunked them in the wash basin.

"Are you sure?" Phillip asked.

"Ram-An was down there last month. It's infested with rats."

A shudder swept through me. I hated rats.

Marie-Hélène coughed and thrust a wet cloth at me. "Hold this over your mouth and breathe through it."

"Rex's men are raising the gate in the alley." Ram-An burst into the room with a singed rug in his arms.

"Our neighbor's homes," Marie-Hélène said to Ram-An. "We can't let them burn." Fire crackled somewhere above us.

"The only way out is through the tunnel." Ram-An pushed past me to the square hole in the brick wall. "Help me with the dumbwaiter." He reached into the hole and tugged a rope. A wooden tray with a copper base rose up. Phillip leaned into the shaft and wedged his dagger between the brick edge and a flat grate. He lifted the copper tray and handed it off to Ram-An, who placed the grate on the floor.

"Marie-Hélène and I will hold Rex off to give you enough time to escape," Ram-An said.

"Come with us," Phillip said to Ram-An.

"We must stay to seal off the passage," Ram-An said. "Two will travel faster than four."

A plume of smoke swirled across the ceiling. I coughed into my wet rag.

"Where will we meet?" Phillip asked.

Ram-An's eyes rested on me for a moment. "Rex will assume you've fled to Wilmington or to Saint Augustine." He narrowed his eyes and bit his lower hip; he seemed to be ciphering things in his head.

"What makes you say that?" I asked.

"We have venators there," Marie-Hélène said.

"Can you get to Norfolk in a fortnight?" Ram-An asked Phillip.

"I think so." Phillip patted down his britches pockets. "I need gold."

On tiptoes, Marie-Hélène reached for an earthen crock. She shook gold discs out onto the counter, then swept the coins into her palm and passed them to Phillip. Ram-An lit a small lantern.

"How will you—" I began.

"Don't worry about us." Ram-An urged me to the square hole in the wall. "We'll see you in Norfolk."

Phillip flung his legs into the dumbwaiter shaft, shimmied forward, then disappeared.

"There's not much room," Phillip said as he looked up. I sat on the edge of the ledge and slung my legs over.

"Wait!" Marie-Hélène said. "Take my slippers." She toed off her dainty shoes with bows at the toes and gave them to me. I slipped them on my feet, and they were a perfect fit. I'd never owned shoes so pretty. On Cusabo I either went barefoot or wore Mama's old deerskin moccasins.

There was a crash above me and the hiss of flames. I glanced up and saw that a patch of ceiling was melting away. Phillip stood in the pit with his arms stretched up. My feet dangled at his shoulders.

"It's bigger than it looks." Phillip pressed his back against the wall.

"I'll help you down." Marie-Hélène slid her arms under mine. "Get her feet," she said to Phillip, and he wrapped his hands around my ankles.

"I trust Phillip with my life, so should you." Marie-Hélène nudged me forward. I slid down against Phillip as his hands outlined my body. My feet hit packed dirt, and I looked up from the pit to see Marie-Hélène's concerned expression and flames licking the hole in the ceiling.

"Watch out!" I cried as smoldering bits of plaster and horsehair rained down on Marie-Hélène. She swatted at the flyaway, smoldering dust.

"Can you turn around?" Phillip asked. His chest brushed against mine as he breathed out. For a moment, I thought I might swoon. My head felt swimmy, like it was filled with sloshy salt water.

"I think so." I swiveled until my back was to him.

"See that opening in the wall?" Two bricks lengths were missing, creating a narrow entry.

"Yes."

"Squeeze through. It's wider on the other side."

I pressed my face into the opening and saw nothing but pitch darkness. Mold and decay filled the air.

"Go on." Phillip's voice echoed off the dank walls.

"Take this," Ram-An said from overhead. A light loomed up behind me.

"I'm with you." Phillip's whisper sank into the tunnel.

Edging forward, I stretched my arms out and stumbled into the abyss.

15

Phillip passed me the lantern, then squeezed through the entry and pressed himself against the opposite wall. I could see his pulse thumping in the hollow of his neck. He held my eyes for several heartbeats, then turned his head up and called, "We're in!"

"Safe travels." Marie-Hélène's voice echoed off the walls.

A heavy rasp was followed by a clang that vibrated through me and into the passage. We had been sealed in a tomb. Phillip reached over and brushed the tips of his fingers against my ear and flicked something from my hair. From the corner of my eye I caught a blur flying into the shadows. I glanced behind me, where a spider's web glimmered in the light.

Phillip pried the lantern from my hand. "There's only one way out." He held the oil lamp high and stared down the tunnel into nothingness as I gripped the tail of his shirt. The last thing I wanted was to lose him down here.

Phillip hunched forward so as not to scrape his head against the ceiling and stepped into the dim tunnel.

"Won't Rex follow us?" Mire squished under my shoes. Hundreds of cockroaches darted out of the lanternlight and into the shadows.

"No one knows of this tunnel," Phillip said. The nubby marl walls and mud floor soaked up the light. Drops of water dribbled from the curved ceiling.

"How long does it go for?" A beetle the size of a small yam clamped its pinchers shut as I skimmed past it.

"Not quite a mile."

"Where does it lead?"

"The crypts under the chapel of Saint Blaise."

"No good comes of disturbing the dead." I repeated words that I had heard Mama Jane say a hundred times.

"I don't plan on waking them." Phillip stopped and shook out his leg. "I should have asked Ram-An for his boots."

The tunnel narrowed and sloped down. With every step, we sank further into water and muck. Phillip turned his body to the side and the walls pressed against my shoulders. Something splashed up ahead.

"What's that?" I jerked on Phillip's shirt tail as he sloshed forward. There was another splash followed by a high-pitched screech. "What's that sound?" I was shaking.

"Rats, I assume." Phillip's voice was calm.

I wheezed. "They carry sickness." I couldn't remember the last time I was so afeared.

"I don't suppose you'll be wanting one for a pet, then." Phillip trudged forward, pulling me with him.

"Not funny." The water was above my ankles, and the mud sucked at my heels, trying its best to tug Marie-Hélène's slippers off my feet. "I don't like this." It was hard to breathe, and my chest was as heavy as if a full-grown alligator was sitting on it. "Alligator," I mumbled.

"What?" Phillip had stopped.

"What if there's a gator down here?" I squeezed my eyes shut and pressed my back against the wall. Blood was whooshing in my ears.

Phillip was real quiet for a moment, then said gently, "There is no alligator down here; if there was, there would be no rats."

"That makes sense." I took in short, flustered breaths.

"You're panicking."

"I think we should go back." The muscle under my eye started to twitch.

"We can't," Phillip said calmly. "The house is burning, and as soon as it cools, Rex will sift through the rubble for any clues as to where you've gone."

I thought long and hard about that. If I went back, I'd have to face Rex. If I went forward, I'd have to deal with heaven knows what. I wasn't sure which scared me more, Rex or the unknown.

Phillip reached out and tangled his fingers up with mine. "We'll take it step by step."

"Can I keep my back against the wall?"

"Yes, as long as we keep moving forward."

It was slow going, and soon we were wading in water up to our knees. Silt squished between my toes. Phillip gripped my hand, and I pushed away any notion of snakes and rats. On Cusabo, critters didn't have a chance to get too big on account of them getting eaten by something bigger, but down here I reckoned a snake could grow into a dragon. With every step the murky water rose until it lapped against my hips. I tilted my head up and forced myself to breathe through my mouth.

"Does the water get any higher?" The idea of having to dunk my head and swim in this foul-smelling slough made me twitchy.

"I hope not," Phillip said.

The path began to slope upward, and my breath came easier. The water ebbed, and after a while we were sloshing through shin-deep mud again. "Almost there," he said. Black bugs darted between crannies in the wall.

"Good," I said between clenched teeth. My toes wiggled free, and I knew that the mud had taken my shoes.

The tunnel widened, then opened to a cavern. Cat-sized shadows moved along the floor in the dim light, chittering and hissing.

"What are those?" My voice quivered.

"Rats," Phillip said. "Stomp your feet and they'll stay away from you."

The soles of my feet slapped the dirt floor, and I waved my arms around, making myself seem big and menacing. I even let out some howls and growls.

"This way." Phillip led me to the far side of the cavern, where elevated tombs filled the cramped space. Angels and crosses carved out of stone decorated the raised crypts. I hummed the tune to Mama Jane's boneyard chant to keep the spirits at rest as we walked between tombs to a set of stairs.

"Up there." Phillip nodded to a wooden door at the top of a landing. I quickly climbed the steps and waited for him. He took out his dagger and jiggled the tip of the blade into the door's keyhole. He fumbled with the latch, but the door didn't budge. "I don't suppose you have a hairpin," he said. The lantern's light was growing faint.

"Let's knock." I raised my fist, but before I had the chance to do anything, the lock clicked and the door opened. A lanky man in a brown monk's robe stood before us, holding a candle. He gave Phillip and me a blank stare with eyes that were sunk into deep hollows under bushy eyebrows, making his pointed nose resemble a beak. Without a word, the monk swung the door wide and stepped aside. The curved corridor led to a chapel, where he used the flame of his candle to light two more candles on an altar.

"Stay here." Phillip motioned to a wooden pew. I checked under the bench to make sure there weren't any rats, then sat down. "I'll be right back." He followed the monk.

16

There were no windows and only four rows of benches all facing a wooden cross that looked about as old as the earth itself. It seemed unholy to be dripping wet and mud-bogged in such a sacred place, but there wasn't anything I could do about it, so I just kept quiet and said a prayer for Mama Jane, Ruth, Abel, and Noah. I wondered if they missed me half as much as I missed them. I felt inside my pocket for the hook and fishing line that Noah had given me. It was the only thing I had left of my family. My eyes started to burn as I thought about the last time things were simple. It was probably right before Ruth and I had stumbled upon the shipwreck.

I'd been alone for a good spell when Phillip slid in next to me.

"Brother Barnabas is going to help us get out of the city." He glanced my way. "What's the matter?"

"I've made a mistake." I dabbed my face with my wet blouse sleeve. "I want to go back home."

"Have you gone feebleminded?"

"I suppose I have." I sniffled. "I've had nothing but trouble since I left."

Phillip crossed, then uncrossed his arms. "You can't go back to Cusabo." He turned to face me. "I can't protect you there."

"You can't protect me here." Soon as I said those words, I wished I could take them back.

Phillip's head hung down like a kicked dog. "Things haven't turned out the way I wanted them to. I had this whole plan of what would happen if, and when, I found you, but nothing has been like how I imagined it would be. It's been one disaster after another."

"I'm sorry," I muttered.

"I do know two things: you're better off with me than with Rex or the samurai, and they will never stop hunting you."

"Why?" I choked. "Why can't I just live normal? What's so special about me?"

"No other immortal has the power to heal the way you do. And as far as I know, you and Rowan are the only immortal twins on the whole earth."

"Twins?" This news caught me by surprise and took my breath away. Of course we were twins. I closed my eyes and recalled Rowan and I standing face to face, mimicking each other. Her hand moving with mine, my nose twitching with hers, our toes tapping together; it was our mirror game.

"Twins." Phillip nodded.

The girl from my dream hovered in my mind's eye. She looked like me, as much as I could tell what I looked like. On Cusabo, we only had a shard of a broken mirror that was about the size of my foot, and you had to hold it up at just the right angle to take yourself in. Ruth had always assured me that the girl I dreamed about was, in fact, me; that I was dreaming about myself. I couldn't help but smile at the fact that I'd never argued with her about this, and now I knew for sure that Ruth had been mistaken. How I wished Ruth was with me so I could tell her to her face that she was wrong. God, I missed Ruth. "Why didn't you tell me this before?"

"I assumed you knew." Phillip slumped back. "That was stupid of me. I should have said something."

"So when you say I look like Rowan, I really do look like her." I traced the underside of my jaw with my fingers.

"Only younger. She lived on after you were killed."

What would it be like when Rowan and I came face to face? Would it be like staring at my future self? Would she see me for who I was, or would she feel that she needed to guide my every move, like Ruth did?

I twisted a strand of my dark hair around my finger and thought about Rowan's blue eyes. "I dream of her."

"She told Ram-An that after you died, she never felt whole again."

I swallowed the lump that had grown in my throat. "Who killed me?"

"Valen," Phillip said, then added, "Well, he sent his wife to do it."

"What was her name?" I asked.

"Gudrun."

I closed my eyes, remembering the first time I saw Gudrun, her long red hair matted with bits of twigs and leaves. No one was sure how she had made it past the guards and stumbled into our camp. Both her arms had been broken, and her mouth bled where her tongue had been cut out. I laid hands on her and healed her body, but her soul had been damaged, and the only way to restore that was time. Rowan recognized her as a Viking and warned me against her. But I felt pity for her, and I was the only person she seemed to trust.

"Gudrun wouldn't do that." I raised my hand to my neck.

"She took your head, stole a horse, and rode north," Phillip said.

"My head?" My throat went dry.

"I'm sorry to be the one to tell you." His eyes were soft as he spoke. "But Rowan and her guards chased her down. Gudrun confessed, and Rowan killed her."

I bit my lip. "Rowan is peaceful; she doesn't kill."

"She made an exception."

Before I could ask anything else, we heard the sound of

footsteps. It was Brother Barnabas returning. He motioned for Phillip and me to rise, which we did. Then he led us from the chapel to a circular staircase, and we climbed into a sanctum with giant windows. Light filtered through the colored glass, which portrayed stories from the Bible. I'd never seen anything so beautiful, and I craned my neck at the detailed patterns of cut glass.

We stopped at a heavy wooden door. Brother Barnabas inserted a key into the lock and pushed the door open.

We emerged from the church into a graveyard. The morning sun peeked through the clouds. We ducked under moss-covered trees and past headstones to find two stout mules harnessed to a cart. Phillip lifted me into the back of the wagon, then climbed in and pulled back a canvas tarp, exposing two long, wooden rectangles. I caught a sharp whiff of pine.

Phillip lifted the lid of one of the boxes as thunder boomed. "Climb in."

I sputtered. "This is a coffin."

"I know."

Every muscle in my body went rigid.

Phillip placed his hand on my elbow. "It's all right." He dipped his head to the second box. "I have one too. If anyone stops Brother Barnabas, he'll tell them he's taking two bodies out to be buried, plus the pine resin masks our scent."

"Does it mask our pneuma?" I asked.

"No," he said.

Raindrops landed on my shoulder. It was only a matter of moments before the sky opened up. A grinding sound filled my ears, and I realized that it was my teeth gnashing at the choice being forced on me. Rex would be pounding on the church door soon enough, and if I stayed, I doubted there was much the brothers could do to save me or themselves. Phillip's plan was sound; it made sense. We would get out of the city, away from Rex.

"It's not as bad as it seems." Phillip lifted the wooden top of the box for me to climb in. "There is more room than you think, and I'll be right next to you."

"I don't like this one bit." Slowly, I lifted my skirt and settled myself in the casket.

17

There was no air in the box. I couldn't breathe. I lifted my head and pressed my nose and mouth against a crack and whimpered at the sound of nails being pounded into the lid of my coffin.

"Shhh." Phillip's voice was soft through the panel. "Stay quiet."

My eyes were wide open, but they may as well have been shut. All I could make out was pitch-nothingness. A scream was building in the back of my throat; all I had to do was let it out. There was no telling how far away we were from Rex, and if he heard me bawling, there wasn't any doubt he'd come calling. Then we'd all be in a heap of a mess.

"Take deep breaths." Phillip's voice was muffled.

I continued to pant. The tarp made a rasping noise as Brother Barnabas pulled it over my casket. I kept thinking about Marie-Hélène urging me to trust Phillip and wondered if he had ever nailed her into a death box.

The wagon lurched forward, and I was jostled side to side. Drops of rain beat against the tarp in steady plops. The wheel in my head was spinning a mile a minute, but all I could do was lie flat and try my best not to squirm out of my skin. I pressed my hand against the coffin wall and felt a knot in the wood coated with pine gum. My pointer finger traced the knot, and the sticky goo held it there.

Deep breaths, I told myself. Pine coated my tongue and the insides of my nose. I squeezed my eyes shut and willed myself to think of something agreeable. Mama Jane always said to count your blessings when you think you have none.

Okay then, I thought. There are no rats in this coffin. My skirt was soaked through and tarred to my legs. When I wiggled my toes, mud squished between them.

The rain splattered on and on, and I wondered if the cloudburst would make it difficult for Rex to trail us. The wagon groaned as it bumped over uneven road. I smashed against the wall of the coffin as the wheels slipped between ruts and gullies.

At last, the wheels fell into a groove and the ride evened out. My breathing had calmed, and only an occasional drop of rain hit the tarp. I stuck my index finger and thumb together and pulled them apart. The pine gum coated the soft, fleshy parts of my fingertips. I rolled the gum into a little ball, like Ruth and I used to do when we were little. We used to press the little balls together, pretend they were pearls, and make necklaces out of them.

My body swayed back and forth with the rocking of the wagon. I wondered how long it would take to get to where we were going. The road had to be swampy from the storm.

Count your blessings. I heard Mama Jane's voice clear as if she were with me.

"Mama," I said in a voice a little louder than a whisper. "Can you hear me?"

Silence. The wagon wobbled side to side.

I closed my eyes and imagined Mama Jane rocking me when I was a young'un, telling me stories of her growing up on Cusabo. She had eight brothers and sisters, and they had all slept in a one-room cabin, shank to shank. As I drifted off, I pictured myself curled up on the floor of that house with Mama's leg pushed up next to mine.

My eyes fluttered open to the sound of wood snapping.

"Anne," Phillip said, and I blinked at the morning light as he lifted my coffin's lid. "We made it."

I elbowed myself up. "Made it where?" My voice sounded as stiff as my body felt.

"The Hermitage." Phillip extended his hand and helped me out of my box. The scents of manure and fresh cut grass hung in the air. We were in a clearing just deep and wide enough to hold the wagon. Brother Barnabas was nowhere to be seen, and the mules were unharnessed and grazing in the grass.

"This way." We walked through a copse of hemlock trees. "I have a friend who lives here with the brothers." Phillip led me down a path to a stone and wood barn.

"A monk?"

"Not quite. He's a Druid high priest." Phillip opened the door, then stepped aside for me to pass.

"What's that?" I asked.

"The Druids were an ancient immortal sept who were killed off a long time ago. Lugus is the only one left. The brothers here have taken him in. They're quite fond of him."

"They know he's immortal?"

"No, but they realize he's special," Phillip said. "Much like the way your family on Cusabo knew you were special."

The interior of the stable was orderly. The flat stones that made up the floor had been neatly swept. As I walked down the center aisle, I peered over the edges of the stalls at horses who looked proud enough for a king. I glanced down at my mud-crusted toes, wishing I hadn't lost my shoes.

At the end of the aisle was a tack area with pegs holding reins and polished saddles on shelves. Beyond that was an open covered porch, complete with a wooden table and benches, that looked out over the corral and a meadow. A childish figure in a long, woolen monk's robe with a pointy hood pulled over its head was tossing seeds from a burlap sack to a charm of goldfinches. As we approached, the figure turned, and I saw that he was an old man. His blue eyes widened as I came closer. He had a glow, the kind that lights up the sky just before sunset.

"Good morning." His raspy voice had a strange lilt.

There was an air about him that made me wonder if some sort of witchcraft was afoot, so I kept my distance and planted myself a full cart-length away.

"Yes, I'm like you," the man said with a feeble wave. "Closer, so I can see you."

I glanced sideways to Phillip, who dipped his head to me.

"Anne," Phillip said. "May I present Lugus?"

Lugus brushed his hood back and bowed. He was mostly bald with a ring of wispy white hair around the sides of his head.

"Nice to meet you, Mr. Lugus," I said.

He gave a throaty laugh that slipped into a cough. "I am just Lugus."

I spun around in reaction to a movement behind me. Brother Barnabas placed a tray with two bowls and mugs at the end of the wooden table.

"We can acquaint ourselves while you break your fast." Lugus shuffled to the table; he had trouble walking because his back was bent. Brother Barnabas pulled out a wooden stool and bade him to rest. "Please have baths prepared for our guests," Lugus said to Brother Barnabas, who gave a nod and left the porch.

"Please sit," Lugus said. "Eat."

Phillip and I sat across from each other. I examined the glop in my bowl, then lifted a spoonful to my nose and sniffed. The sweet aroma of honey and toasted pecans made my mouth water.

"It's ground oats," Phillip said.

Lugus watched as I tasted the porridge, then turned to Phillip. "Will you be staying the night?"

Phillip shook his head. "There's no time to visit."

Lugus leaned forward as Phillip told of our escape from

Charleston. A thin, cloudy film covered his eyes. Part of me wanted to reach out and lay hands on him, but instead I tightened my grip on my spoon.

"Rex is probably gathering his force as we speak," Phillip said.

"I doubt that," Lugus said. "Rex hunts alone."

"Anne's too valuable." Phillip lifted his gaze to me. "He'll bring scouts at the very least."

"Not if he suspects that you and Anne are traveling alone," Lugus said. "Besides, he'll send some of his tribe to follow Ram-An and Marie-Hélène. Don't you think he'll want to know where they go?"

"I suppose you're right," Phillip said, then looked at me. "Don't worry, Ram-An and Marie-Hélène know how to handle themselves."

"Rex is greedy," Lugus said. "He'll have no desire to share the bounty on Anne's head with his tribesmen. Imagine what Valen will offer if Rex presents the healer to him."

"His own domain." Phillip rubbed the scar that cut across his eyebrow with his thumb.

"At the very least," Lugus said. "Imagine the glory Rex will receive if he brings in Anne singlehanded."

"The honor will be his alone," Phillip said quietly, gripping his spoon as he mulled over the thought.

Lugus smiled at my ring. "Did you have a custodis?"

Custodis, I thought. Guardian. "Mama Jane," I said.

Phillip recounted everything that had happened on Cusabo.

"And the ship you were on, how did it come to sink?" Lugus asked Phillip.

"A squall came up. Lightning struck the mast, sending the ship off course. Anne found me floating in the waves."

Lugus clasped his hands together, and a grin spread across his face. "All this time you've spent searching for the healer, and it was she who found you."

"I suppose so," Phillip said.

"Providence is flowing through you both," Lugus said.

Phillip's eyes met mine, and I quickly dropped my gaze. Something was ribboning through me that I'd never felt before. It was similar to the thrill of catching my first fish, and I kept thinking about the iron flecks holding fast to the lodestone.

Brother Barnabas reappeared, standing silently where the tack area gave way to the porch.

"I think our baths are ready," Phillip said. We followed Brother Barnabas to a walled off horse stall. "I'll bathe in the cloister. You'll have privacy here," Phillip said before he left me.

I entered the stall, then closed and locked the door. Steam rose from a copper tub that sat in the center of the stone floor. A cake of soap and a folded blanket waited on a table next to the tub. I started to unbutton my blouse, then stopped when I remembered the men on the other side of the wall. It didn't strike me as a good idea to strip naked; I would be at a disadvantage if anyone broke through the door. Then I noticed near the top of the door a metal slide bolt, which I slid in place. Maybe I would just wash my hands. I dipped my hands in the water and wiggled them around until they were clean. The water was the perfect temperature: hot, but not scalding. I shook off my hands and paced around the tub. On Cusabo we bathed in a wooden barrel that had been sawed in half and only had enough room to sit cross-legged. Ruth and I counted ourselves blessed if we didn't get a splinter when we bathed. This wasn't like that tub at all, this was a proper tub, sturdy and long enough to stretch your legs out and relax a spell. The walls of the stall were solid; I know because I walked around them making sure that there were no missing boards or holes for prying eyes to peer through. Deciding it was safe, I placed a stool in front of the door before I peeled off my clothes and sank into the water, where I floated weightless as a jellyfish for a long while, amused by how loud my breathing sounded when my ears were under water.

The soap smelled of sweet herbs. I lathered my hair and scrubbed myself clean before I stretched out my legs. Soapsuds blossomed into bubbles that carried the scent of lemon balm and something else—an aroma I had smelled a long, long time ago that brought to mind fields of purple flowers. As I held the cake of soap to my nose, a vision crept up on me. A grove of gray-barked trees, and beyond them, hills rolling into more hills. My hand reaching out to pluck an olive from a branch, feeling the firmness of the ripe fruit, the roundness in my fingers. My laughter. A man's lips curling upward. Solid hands on my hips, pulling me back to rest my head against the hardness of his chest. His breath in my hair. Soft lips on my neck. The beat of his heart. A whisper: My love.

Phillip's and Lugus's voices carried through the wall, and the memory drifted away. Lugus was commenting on Phillip's improved appearance; I could only hear bits and pieces, but it sounded like they were just outside my door. I shivered and closed my eyes, trying to recall the man's touch. My scalp tingled where his face had been buried in my hair. I ran my hands down to my hips and pressed against them as he had. Who was this man? I closed my eyes and willed myself to remember, but the feeling drifted away. It was as if I had been kissed by a ghost. The water had gone cold, and I wondered how long I had been in the tub. The tips of my fingers were wrinkled.

18

Somewhere in the barn Lugus and Phillip were talking, but they were too far away for me to hear what they were saying.

Water sloshed up the sides of the tub as I sat up. It was time to get dressed. After I dried myself, I discovered traveling clothes folded under the blanket. I pulled on the underclothes, then held up the canvas britches to my waist and shrugged. Perhaps the Hermitage only had men's clothes to spare; this was no mind to me, as I'd worn Abel and Noah's pants to ride the wild ponies when I was on Cusabo. I buttoned my shirt before slipping on a wool jacket.

As I unlatched the slide bolt and let the door swing ajar, I heard the sound of something heavy being slid across wood, along with the jangle of metal.

"This saddle will do," Lugus said.

A moment later, I shrank back as Brother Barnabas passed my stall holding a worn leather saddle. He was walking quick and didn't even glance my way.

A new pair of boots had been placed outside of my door. The dark brown leather appeared shiny and stiff. Just as I stepped over them, I heard Lugus speak in a low tone.

"Does she know about—?"

"No." Phillip cut Lugus off.

They had to be talking about me. I was the only "she" around. Their voices came from a stall across and up the hallway towards the entrance, so I tip-toed closer in my stocking feet.

"When the time is right," Phillip said.

"The right time rarely occurs; there is only now," Lugus murmured. "Divine handiwork has brought you both together."

I stopped outside of the stall door, which stood ajar.

"Rowan foresaw that I would find her," Phillip said. My back arched at the mention of Rowan's name, and I touched my ring with the pad of my thumb.

I'd been raised better than to nose in on private conversations, but what they were saying concerned me, and Rowan. I pushed my hair behind my ear and leaned closer.

"Rowan's visions are like my own, spotty and apt to change," Lugus said. "Trust that there is a reason Anne found you. Guard her well. The winds are shifting, and you are favored."

"Can you see what happens once I return her to Amaranth?" Phillip asked eagerly. "Will Ram-An and I be granted a charter to form our own sept in Charleston?"

I inched closer, turning my ear to the door. From where I stood, I could only see long, leather bridles and reins hung on pegs inside the stall where the men spoke.

"Far greater intentions are at work," Lugus said.

"What are they?"

"You must find their purpose." Lugus's hand suddenly appeared on the interior of the door. My heart skipped a beat, but it was too late to pretend I hadn't been snooping. My face grew hot. His eyes met mine as the door widened, and he dipped his head. His expression showed no surprise to find me there; it was like he'd expected me to be on the other side of the door.

"Did you find the boots?" Lugus asked.

"Oh, yes." I quickly rushed back to the stall where I'd taken my bath and lifted the boots, which were heavier than I'd expected.

"Do you need help putting them on?" Lugus asked. Phillip came out to the hallway, cleanshaven.

"I can manage." I tugged the boots on. My toes had plenty of room to wiggle, but the boots were heavy, and I clopped around like a pony that had just been shod.

"Let me tie the laces." Phillip knelt at my feet.

"I'll saddle your horses and send Brother Barnabas to the kitchen for food to take with you," Lugus said, then hobbled in the direction of the paddock.

"He caught me listening to your conversation," I whispered, and Phillip's eyebrows shot up. "I couldn't help it; I heard mine and Rowan's names."

"What did you hear?" he asked.

"Not much." I lowered my head, embarrassed. "How does Lugus know Rowan?"

"He and Rowan have a long history going back to—" He paused to think. "Before I was born." He patted my ankle. "Is that too tight?"

"No," I said as I picked up my feet, attempting to walk like a normal person.

"I need to cut your hair." He nodded to the stall where he and Lugus had been talking. "I have sharpened a pair of shears."

"What for?" I patted my wet curls, which fell halfway down my back.

"Rex will be looking for you and me, not for a man and his young brother." He walked to the stall, and I followed.

"I can tie my hair up with a kerchief or wear it under a hat." I twisted my hair up, showing how easy it would be to disguise.

"That won't do," Phillip said as he led me to the horse stall. "Rex has a keen sense of smell, and much of your scent is carried in your hair." The horse stall was empty save for a bench in the center of the room. Shelves on the wall were lined with brushes, metal picks, and horseshoes.

"But I just washed it. It smells like soap." I wound a long tress around my finger and brought it to my nose. If Mama Jane were here, she'd use a boar bristle brush to comb the tangles out.

"To Rex, it will smell like you." He motioned for me to sit on the bench.

"How is that possible?" I refused his offer and instead tramped around the stall, making an effort to raise the balls of my feet so I wouldn't trip over the toe of my boots.

"You know how animals can follow the scent of their prey?"

I nodded.

"Rex has gotten your scent," he said. "That handkerchief you used to wipe your face in the marsh and tie back your hair. The one that came loose and fell when he chased us. We must assume that he has that, and he will use it to follow you."

"Is he part Indian?" Indian trackers were known for their ability to follow a trail through rain and snow.

"Not that I know of, but he has the same abilities." Phillip picked up the shears and gave them a snap.

"My hair has never been cut." There was a tremor in my voice.

"It will grow back." He gestured for me to sit on the bench, but I stood stock still with my arms crossed over my chest.

"You can cut my hair first." He snipped at his hair, and light brown clippings fell to his shoulder. Then he plopped down on the bench and offered me the scissors. "Chop it all off, if you please."

"I like your hair just the way it is," I muttered, then regretted it because I sounded like a pouty child.

"Me too." Phillip stood to face me. "Like your hair, I mean." He sighed and rubbed the scar above his eye. "This isn't some nefarious plan to steal your power, like Delilah did with Samson. But if you let me cut it, it will be easier for you to pass as a boy, and I can have Brother Barnabas hang it from a tree south of the Ashley river tonight in the hopes that it will throw Rex off our tracks. Your hair will go south as we go north."

As much as I hated agreeing with Phillip, he had a good point. I thought of Rowan and tried to imagine what she would do in this instance: there was no doubt that she would gladly shave her head bald as a plucked chicken if there was a chance of seeing me again. You must be brave, I told myself, then sat on the bench with my back to Phillip. "Be quick about it."

Starting at my forehead, Phillip ran his fingers through my hair, his fingernails grazing my scalp, which sent a ticklish thrill through me. Gathering my hair at the nape of my neck, he snipped the shears. The muscles in my neck tensed. When he was done, I drew my hand up to just below my birthmark and turned around. Phillip grimaced as he held up a long mane that dangled like a horse's tail.

I attempted to smile, tried to pretend that I didn't care, but I couldn't help but feel naked, like a sheep that had just been shorn. Heat rose in my face as I brushed my fingers through the blunt ends. "You cut it all off."

"It's going to grow back."

I wondered if he was reassuring himself, or me. "This is shorter than a trim." I pursed my lips and blinked back tears. I wanted to be strong and not care about how I must look, but instead, I felt as if my heart was bleeding.

"You're going to cry," he said matter-of-factly.

Soon as he said the word "cry," my eyes went cloudy with tears. He put the shears down, and for a moment, I thought he might try to comfort me.

"Quick, stand up and look to the corner of the room," Phillip pointed to the ceiling where walls of the stall joined together.

He was serious, so I did as he commanded.

"Now tighten your girdle muscles, and keep your eye trained on the corner," he said.

"Why are you doing this?" I sniffled.

"Keep your girdle tight." Phillip rubbed his lower stomach

and circled me. "Shoulders straight." He poked his finger between my shoulder blades. "How are you? Do you want to weep?"

"Yes." I had no idea what I had done to deserve such coolness.

"Eyes up there." Phillip pointed to the corner again. "Listen to me carefully: There will be times when you are hurt, emotionally and physically, but you cannot show weakness. Valen, Rex, and others will thrive on your frailty, use it to control you. Never give them the satisfaction of feeding on your tears."

The more I concentrated on keeping my lower stomach muscles tensed, the less I wanted to cry.

"There are rings of muscles in your body called sphincters. They are in your eyes, your stomach, and your lower parts. If you learn to tighten them, squeeze them as hard as you can, it will make it difficult to cry. The corner of the room gives you something to focus on. If you don't have a corner concentrate on a tree, a cloud, or anything tall, but never cast your eyes down. Keep your chin up. You must show defiance against tyrants."

"Is this magic?" I dabbed at my face with the sleeve of my shirt.

"No, it's anatomy. If you tighten one sphincter, you can't help but tighten them all." He placed my hair on the bench. "I'm sorry about your hair, I truly am. But the hard truth is: it will grow back. Rex saw you. He knows what you look like, and he knows what you smell like." He touched my arm. "The most important thing right now is to change your appearance and mask your scent."

My hair lay on the bench. The necessity of cutting it was a hard truth, as Phillip had said. What other hard truths lay in wait for me?

"I'm not trying to be a brute." He extended his hands, pleading with me. "I just want to prepare you for what lies ahead."

"How do you know what lies ahead?"

"Because I know Rex, and I know what he's capable of. I'm just trying to protect you the best way I know how."

"You're right." I wiped my nose. "It's just hair." With my chin up and shoulders squared, I decided to act stronger than I felt.

"You need to pick out a boy's name to go by when we meet strangers. What do you think of Andrew? It has a similar ring to Anne."

"Fine."

"To pass as a boy, you'll need to mind yourself." Phillip hung his arms. "Slouch your shoulders forward."

I wiggled my shoulders and tried to stand loose.

"Slouch more."

I rolled my shoulders forward and let my spine curve.

"When you walk, move with purpose. Shift your eyes to your feet or slightly above." Phillip took a few steps, then stood aside so I could practice my stride.

It wasn't too difficult. All I had to do was picture Noah, then try to move the way he did.

"Don't think too hard about it." Phillip tossed me a wool kepi with a short brim. "You don't want to look constipated."

I relaxed my face and pulled the cap low on my head. "Thank ye, sir," I said in a lower tone than usual.

"You're welcome, young man." Phillip gave me a brotherly pat on the shoulder. "Get yourself together. I'll see you outside."

He left, and I shuffled around the room, dragging my heels like Noah sometimes did when he was cross. I tucked what was left of my hair behind my ears and wondered how long it would take for it to grow down my back again. Probably forever. I stared at the corner of the room and tightened my girdle muscles. It's only hair, I reminded myself, and I stepped from the stall.

Lugus and Phillip stood in the paddock with two of the most graceful animals I'd ever laid eyes on. A chestnut stallion lifted his legs high as he pranced around the enclosure, while a black stallion nuzzled Lugus's neck and swished flies away with his tail. Both steeds were at least sixteen hands tall and well-muscled.

Lugus waved me to join him. "Meet Safeen," he rasped.

I rubbed the bridge of the horse's nose. He sniffed and snorted lightly into my palm.

"Here." Lugus passed me a slice of apple to feed the horse.

"Hello, Safeen," I cooed.

"A good match," Lugus declared. "I've been waiting for a gentle soul to pair Safeen with. It wasn't until I saw you that I knew whom I had been grooming him for."

"Who is that?" I nodded to the chestnut stallion stomping at the dirt.

"Salaa," Lugus said. "I've had him in mind for Phillip for some time now. Salaa is as stubborn as he is strong, but Phillip will know how to quiet him."

Brother Barnabas padded into the corral with two gourds and a bundle wrapped in burlap. He opened Safeen's saddlebag and arranged the contents. Lugus clapped his hands and called Salaa to him.

Lugus winced when he bent over to tighten the saddle belt, then rubbed his knuckles. He tottered like a small child, unsure of his balance. I moved to brush Safeen's mane, and my hand grazed Lugus's arm. For an instant, my vision blurred and my joints ached. I inched my hand out to Lugus.

"Could I—I mean, would you allow me to . . . ?" I stammered.

"Lay hands on me." Lugus finished my sentence. His back stooped, but his eyes lit up at the prospect. "The healer of Amaranth wants to heal me," he murmured to Phillip.

I smiled, and he reached his hand out to mine. I took it, and right away my bones stiffened and my joints dried up. We limped through the corral and up to the open porch. Lugus settled himself on the wooden stool. Standing close behind him so his head was pressed against my belly, I ran my hands over his wisps of hair, forward to his eyes, and cupped his temples with my palms. His skin was dry and flaky. My fingers massaged his closed eyelids.

I shut my eyes, and it was as if I was looking through a dirty windowpane. My heart throbbed in my chest. The vision broke like shattered glass, then fell away, leaving a clear view of the corral. I opened my eyes and pulled my shaking hands away from his face.

"How do you see?" I asked.

Lugus uttered something in a foreign tongue.

I pressed my hands against his shoulders, inhaled deeply, then ran my hands down the spiny lumps of his backbone. A rush of thick fluid entered the tiny pockets of my joints, and they became easier to move. I circled Lugus and stood in front of him. "Your hands."

Lugus laid his knobby hands in mine, and the tingling stopped. He wiggled his fingers in my palm. I backed away, and he mumbled something. When he looked up at me, his wide eyes filled with wonder. He pushed himself to his feet and took two steps to me.

"Thank you." Lugus's voice was tight. "I feel as nimble as a young lad again." He extended his back and stood up tall, but I still stood a good head above him.

"You are pale, my dear," Lugus said. "Please, sit."

My head throbbed like I'd been struck on the forehead by a cannon ball. I plopped down on the wooden stool, my hands clutching its sides and my arms straight, bracing my torso so I wouldn't tumble to the floor.

"Some water," Lugus said, and Brother Barnabas went to fetch a pitcher from the table. "Does this happen every time you heal?" Lugus asked.

My head was swimming. I opened my mouth to answer, but my mouth was so dry, and the porch was growing dark. Someone caught me before I fell over.

When I woke, Phillip, Lugus, and brother Barnabas were hovering over me. I gulped the water Brother Barnabas gave me and held the cup out for more.

"You must learn restraint," Lugus advised. "You give of yourself too freely. It is essential that you retain enough spirit to restore yourself."

"How do I do that?" I asked.

"I find that my sight is strongest when I am full of water and sunshine," Lugus said. "These things will restore you."

"Like a plant," I said.

"Yes. Listen to your body. It will tell you what it needs."

19

The horses had been shod and their saddlebags packed. Brother Barnabas clasped his palms together in a sign of prayer before Phillip. He turned to face me and repeated the gesture, then walked away.

Lugus was murmuring to the horses in what I guessed was Druid-speak. They bent their heads low at his words and rubbed their noses along the top of his head.

"You may want to take your jacket off." Phillip folded his coat, then tied it atop the blanket on the back of his saddle. "It's going to be a warm day."

"What if we meet someone?" Even though I had bound my breasts with a length of cloth, I was afraid that without my jacket on there might be a question that I was a girl.

"We won't be seeing anyone where we're going."

"Where's that?"

"Into the backwood swamps." One side of Phillip's mouth turned up, making his smile mischievous, and my nerves jangled.

"You'll need herbs." Lugus gave Phillip a bunch of sage leaves.

Phillip rubbed a green frond on his neck and in his hair. He unbuckled his saddlebag and placed a handful of sage in the bag, then presented me with a about six crinkled leaves. "Rub these on your clothes and skin. It keeps the mosquitos and ticks at bay."

I wiped the leaves over my shirt and on my neck, then stroked it along Safeen's haunches.

"Put those leaves in your pockets," Phillip said. "Anything to mask your scent."

"Shall I present you with an offering?" Lugus asked me.

Before I could protest, Lugus drew back his outer robe and unclasped a worn leather belt. A narrow silver sword hung from the scabbard. He removed the blade, and with one hand on the ivory pommel and one hand on the tip, presented it to me.

It was beautifully crafted, but I had nothing to offer in return. "I can't take—" I began.

"You must," Lugus insisted. "A lifetime ago, a woman took me in and taught me the importance of kinship. That woman was the Oracle of Amaranth, your sister."

"The Oracle of Amaranth?" The words tugged at my heart.

"Rowan gave me this sword, and now I pass it on to you to use in defense and honorable pursuits." Lugus extended the sword to me, one of his hands under the blade and one under the pommel.

I took it and gave him a light kiss on the cheek, and the old man's entire head flushed red.

I wrapped my fingers around the ivory pommel and held the sword out. It was thin as a spear.

"Phillip will teach you to wield it," Lugus said. He watched as I looped the belt around my waist so the sword hung at my left hip.

Phillip mounted his horse. Lugus helped me onto Safeen. "Take care of each other." He patted my boot.

Phillip leaned forward, and Salaa broke into a trot. Safeen followed. We rode across the meadow and through a break in the trees.

The reins were loose in my hand as Safeen responded to the moves of my body. The weight of my sword felt natural somehow as it bounced against my leg.

We crossed fields of barley and oats, then forged a wide creek and climbed a steep embankment that ended in woods. Birds chirped morning song as we dodged fallen branches and uprooted trees. We popped out of the thicket onto an overgrown path. Vines and fallen leaves covered the ground, but from the break in the trees I could tell we were on a trail. Phillip leaned forward, and his horse broke into a gallop. The wind tasted like honeysuckle as it blew through the loose strands of my short hair, and I felt like I was sailing through the air. Phillip sped up, and Safeen easily kept pace.

The trees thinned and gave way to boggy water and marsh plants. Swarms of mosquitos were hatching in the morning heat. They hung like puffs of black smoke over stagnant pools of water. Phillip seemed to know right where he was going, and I found myself wondering about him. His accent tended to drift depending on who he was speaking to. When he talked to Lugus, he had adopted Lugus's clipped English accent, but with the softer undertones and lilt of a southern gentleman. Other times, like when he was rushed, his cadence had a choppiness to it. There was a worldliness about him. He rode well, shifting his body to command Salaa so he and the stallion moved as one.

"You ever swum a horse?" Phillip leaned back in his saddle.

"Uh, no." My shoulders went stiff.

"We're going to swim the horses across the Cooper River," Phillip explained. "I've picked a narrow point, but it's deep. The horses know what to do. Just hang on!" He flashed a grin, then took off.

Before I could prepare myself for what was about to happen, the trail ended in a bog. Crabs scurried down holes to save themselves. In two strides, we were plunging into the gray water.

I yelped and gripped the front of my saddle as cold spray hit my face. The water was up to Safeen's shoulders. He stretched his neck out as he swam across the current, and my bottom lifted out of the saddle. The horse sank neck-deep, and I was weightless, my feet coming out of the stirrups and my legs floating up. I kicked hard while holding onto the edge of the saddle. Safeen's legs moved under the current, and his hooves grabbed the bottom of the river-bed and spurred us forward. My heart bounded, and I trained my eyes on a lone palm tree on the far side of the riverbank.

"We can make it!" I called. Safeen was no longer swimming, but had found a foothold and was pushing himself along the river-bed. I wrapped my legs around the horse. Two more strides, and we came out of the river and up onto mud mixed with coquina shells.

My fingers locked onto the rim of the saddle as Safeen shook himself. I threw back my head and burst out laughing; although I was soaked to my bones and shivering, I felt as light as a lacewing moth. Standing in my stirrups, I raised my arms over my head and let out a whoop.

Phillip and Salaa emerged from the river several wag-on-lengths up the bank. Phillip pushed his wet hair out of his eyes, and his entire face beamed. His linen shirt clung to his torso, and I could make out the hard lines of his chest and shoulders. His lips curled up and his eyes widened as he regarded me.

I glanced down, and a fire welled up in my chest, spreading to my neck and face. My white shirt was plastered to my torso. Thankfully, my chest was bound, but a bit of bosom still swelled over the top of the binding. I tugged at it, and the linen made a sucking sound as it pulled away from my skin.

Phillip glanced away and quickly turned his horse. "Follow me."

20

Sunlit marsh gave way to swamp as we rode inland. The sun had dried my shirt, but my canvas britches were still damp. Little streams of sweat ran into my eyes, which I dabbed with my shirt sleeve. My tongue had sealed itself to the roof of my mouth, and all I could think about was water.

Safeen raised his head and slowed to a trot.

"There's a spring up ahead," Phillip called back to me. "We can stop and rest the horses."

We had been riding for most of the day, but Phillip was still full of vim and vigor. He leaned back, and Salaa plowed his hooves into the ground. Phillip slid out of his saddle, and his sword jangled as he shook out his legs. He searched the forest with narrowed eyes, then helped me off Safeen. I fumbled at my saddlebag, and with shaking hands brought my gourd to my lips, drinking until only my breath filled the vessel. Phillip retrieved his canteen, then patted Salaa on the rump, and the horses trotted off into the woods.

"How do they know?" I asked.

"Know what?"

"Where to find fresh water." I tugged my kepi from my head.

"Instinct," Phillip said, then added, "And they were trained by Lugus. When we release them, they'll make their way back to the Hermitage just like a homing pigeon." His gourd sloshed as he handed it to me. I shouldn't have taken it—I had made up my mind to be just as tough as he was—but I was so thirsty. I took several swigs, then gave it back to him. We followed the trampled path that the horses had made. There was a gurgling of water and the louder sound of the horses slurping.

Safeen's head was bent down to a clear waterhole no bigger than a rain puddle. The water trickled over a few stones, then into a pond that was almost completely covered with lily pads. Phillip took my vessel and filled it from the spring, then gave it back to me. The cold water stung my lips.

Gnats darted around my head. I swatted them away, walked over to a patch of shade, and slid my sword out. My hand fit perfectly around the ivory grip, and the weight of it was familiar, like I'd held a sword like it before. The blade was honed to a sharp edge, and the tip was pointed. I felt Phillip's eyes on me. With great care, I slipped the sword back into its scabbard.

Safeen snorted at the ground and chomped on sweetgrass.

"The horses don't seem tired." I couldn't help thinking about the shaggy ponies I had grown up knowing. They liked to roll in the sea oats and tended to travel in packs.

Phillip took his hat off, stretched his neck back, and poured spring water over his head. Water ran down the front and back of his shirt, causing the cloth to stick to his skin. I forced myself to look away.

"Arabians are bred for their endurance." He shook his head, and droplets rained out of his hair. "We'll exhaust long before they will."

I fanned myself with my hand.

"There's a creek up the trail. We should be there by nightfall."

By the angle of the sun, that meant several more hours on horseback. Phillip led the horses back to the path.

"You reckon Rex is already searching for us?" I nested my gourd back in my saddlebag.

"If I were him, I would be." Phillip pushed his chestnut hair back and pulled his kepi down. "It wouldn't take long after the fire was put out to see that you and I were missing."

"You think he'd hurt Marie-Hélène or Ram-An?" I twisted my hat in my hands.

"They wouldn't give him the chance, and I don't think he'd take the time for a fight. The moment he realized you were gone, he started his hunt."

"Oh." I hoisted myself up on Safeen.

"Rex is an exceptional tracker. Our best chance is to get a head start and mask our trail."

"How come he's so . . . exceptional?" That last word felt funny in my mouth.

"Experience." Phillip slung his leg over Salaa.

I wrapped the reins around my hand, remembering Rex's hulking form. "He only wears one glove."

"You noticed," Phillip said.

"What happened to him?"

"I've only heard rumors." Phillip tensed his legs, and Salaa began to walk.

"Well?" Safeen trotted next to Salaa.

"Valen had Rex prove his loyalty by holding his hand to the fire. It was burnt to the bone."

I shuddered. "That's horrible."

"Rex serves a cruel master." Phillip spoke plain, like this was a natural fact.

My own thoughts of Valen were misty. When I thought of him, I remembered him as arrogant and brutish, but I couldn't quite recall his physical features.

We rode hard. Phillip sat tall in his saddle, alert to the forest around him. Often we would come to splits in the path, but Phillip never hesitated on which direction to take. We headed northwest.

Just before suppertime, when the forest began to take on

shadows, our path merged with another and the trail widened. The horses walked side by side, swishing their tails to shoo off flies.

"You ride well," Phillip said.

I smiled. "Seems to me you know your way around these parts."

"I've spent some time on these Indian trails."

"Really?" My head twisted around like a hoot owl. I'd not seen any signs of Indians.

"Most people take the main roads between towns, but these old trails were laid out along streams, springs, and hunting grounds. The solitude that this path offers far outweighs a faster route."

"Do you ever see Indians here?" I asked.

"Not in a hundred years."

"You were here a hundred years ago," I said, and Phillip nodded. "How old are you?"

"Two hundred and ninety-eight."

"Why don't you look too much older than me?"

"Immortals mature like every other child until we come of age, then at fourteen or fifteen, everything slows. It seems that for every hundred years, we grow older by a single year. So, although I am close to three-hundred years old, I appear to be eighteen."

"How old do I look?" I took my cap off.

"Fifteen or sixteen," Phillip said. "You will appear so for the next hundred years."

"Really?" It was impossible to fathom: in a hundred years, Mama Jane, Ruth, and the boys would be passed on, and I'd only be another year older.

"It's a cursed blessing," Phillip said. "You'll outlive many of those you love; however, you'll have time to master anything you please."

"I'd like to learn to use a sword," I blurted.

"You will," Phillip said. "Being skilled with a blade is necessary to defend yourself. And if you excel, you can train as a venator and search the world for others like us."

"Like you?"

"Yes. Rowan taught me to fight, then I apprenticed with Ram-An."

"I'd like to be able to read and write." Heat rose in my neck and face. I'd blurted out before I had a chance to think about what I was saying, and immediately I wished I'd kept my mouth shut.

"Can you not?" he asked, surprised.

"A little," I replied. "Bible verses, mainly."

"It's difficult to learn to read if you don't have books, and you can't write if you don't have quills and paper," Phillip said. "I didn't learn to read and write until I went to Amaranth."

"Are there books at Amaranth?"

"Rooms full. Once you can read proficiently, there will be no limit to what you are able to learn. Rowan says that simply teaching a child to read opens up the entire world to them."

"I'd like to understand the stars and the machinations of things."

"You will."

"Like what makes a witching moon?" I asked. I ducked my head to avoid getting snagged by a prickly vine.

"It's when a lunar eclipse coincides with the winter solstice. It hails the births of all immortals."

My eyebrows knotted together.

"I'll explain after we make camp." Phillip's eyes were on a bend in the trail.

21

We didn't have to tramp too far off the trail and into the woods before we found a clearing near a creek to make camp. We unsaddled the horses, and Phillip flung our wet bedrolls over a tree limb to dry while I collected dried moss, bark, and sticks for a fire.

"Should I hobble the horses?" I asked.

"There's no need." He positioned stones in a circle for a fire ring.

"You sure?" I wanted to be helpful. "I'm handy with a rope."

"They won't wander far." Phillip stacked twigs on top of bigger pieces of dry tree limbs. He struck a friction match, held it to the dried moss until it began to smolder, then used that to light the bark and twigs. "You realize they're drawn to you."

"Mama Jane calls that my shine."

"It's more of a warmth." Phillip squatted before the fire, blowing on the smoldering moss, coaxing the fire to catch. "Rowan has it too, this inner flame that draws all of us to her."

I thought about how wild critters calmed and let me near them. How it was always so easy for me to catch the wild ponies, which vexed Ruth.

"Is that why Rex—I mean Valen—wants me?" I picked at the strap of leather that braided the scabbard to my belt.

"It's one of the reasons." Phillip said. "The sept who possesses the healer thrives. Just because we're immortal doesn't mean we don't get sick or injured. Being near you is like bathing in the fountain of youth."

"Is that why your sept wants me?" I asked.

"You and Rowan were part of the tribe of Amaranth before it even had a name." Phillip tapped his chest with his fist. "We are your rightful tribe."

"Sounds like you own me."

"I didn't mean it like that. No one owns you."

"What if I get to Amaranth and don't like it?"

"That has never happened to anyone." Phillip laughed at the thought. "It's an honor to belong to our sept."

I took my sword out and swatted at the reeds that grew close to the creek's bank. The blade sliced through the plants like they were nothing. I held my sword at hip's height and thrust it out, like I'd seen Phillip show Noah and Abel. I plunged it into a birch tree, and the blade bent into a curve, but when I released, it sprang back to its true form. Rowan had given this to Lugus. She had once held this sword and maybe even tested its strength, just like me. This sword connected us.

"Let's have a look." Phillip held out his hand, and I passed him my weapon. "Nimble." He ran his fingers over the pommel and guard. "Dolomite steel." He held the grip close to his nose so his eye was level with the blade.

"It's puny next to yours," I said.

"Doesn't matter." Phillip thrust the sword and whipped it through the air. "It's the skill of the swordsman—or woman, as the case may be. I've seen Ram-An relieve a samurai of his blade, then bring him to his to his knees with a mere dagger."

"Really?"

"Did Lugus say if your sword had a name?" Phillip passed it to his left hand and jabbed at the sky.

"Does it need one?"

"Important swords should have a name. You don't need to

name it now. Get a feel for it first, find out what it has to teach you." Phillip slashed at a cluster of cattails, and the velvet bulbs went flying. "Would you like a lesson?"

"Yes."

He arranged his feet so one was forward and the other backward, then motioned for me to do the same. "Find your point of balance, and root your feet to the ground."

I positioned myself like him.

"Thrust forward." Phillip stepped and plunged my sword in front of him, then returned to his original stance. "Block." He drew the blade across his body. "You try it."

He passed the weapon to me. I planted my back foot at a bracing angle and my front foot pointed forward.

"Arm closer to your side and bent," Phillip corrected. "Turn sideways. Always give your enemy a narrow target."

There were too many directions to remember. I shifted to the side and drew my arm close, then hopped forward and gave a thrust. Teetering off balance, I stretched my arm too far, then fell onto my face. Pine needles pressed against my cheek. "It's more difficult than it looks," I muttered into the leaves. Phillip made swordplay look so easy; what was I doing wrong?

Phillip offered me his hand. "I still miss my footing sometimes." He tugged me to my feet. "If you aren't stumbling, you aren't pushing yourself."

I brushed myself off and picked the twigs out of my hair.

"You're working on several things here, and the hardest to master is balance." Phillip motioned for me to stand tall. "Try again."

You can do this, I told myself and positioned my feet. Struggling to find my balance, I bent my knees slightly and swayed for a moment. I sprang forward and plunged my sword into the air. The sword slipped from my hand and flew in an arc, its point finally stabbing into the ground. The handle of the sword quivered, like it was mocking me. Phillip snickered, then coughed to cover the fact that he had giggled. My ears grew hot with humiliation.

"Useless," I mumbled.

"What was that?" Phillip asked.

"This is useless." My fingernails dug into the soft pad of my palm.

"I disagree," Phillip said. "Trial and error. You are learning what works and what does not. Now, try again."

I grabbed the sword handle and jerked the tip from the dirt.

"Take a moment to re-center yourself," he suggested.

"And how do I do that?" I snapped.

"Regular stance." Phillip stood tall with his hands pressing against his bellybutton, ignoring my frustration. "Breathe."

I did as he showed me, planting my feet firmly and holding the sword so the flat edge faced me.

"Take five deep breaths, and let your mind wander wherever it wants."

Breath one: This is silly. This isn't helping. Exhale.

Breath two: I'm hungry. I wonder if there any berries around here. Exhale.

Breath three: This was Rowan's sword, and now it's my sword. Exhale.

Breath four: I wonder if Phillip is watching me. I'm going to breathe extra deep. Exhale.

Breath five: My breath is my life. My breath connects me with all living things. Exhale.

Breath six. I am one with my sword. Exhale.

Phillip began to speak over my breathing, "You are capable of great things. You are strong. You are brave." The better I forced my posture, the stronger I felt. "If you find your thoughts are drifting to the negative, you have the power to shift them to the positive. You control your thoughts."

"I'm ready," I stood tall.

"Slowly." Phillip motioned for me to try again. "Focus on your stance and position. Speed comes later."

I practiced while Phillip dug an oat cake out of his saddlebag and ate.

One foot back and turned out, the front pointed. Elbow in, wrist firm and straight. Shuffle forward, shuffle forward. Lunge and stab, then step back. The more I practiced, the better I got, until the sword felt like it was part of my hand. "I think I'll call her Soror."

"Your sword?" Phillip asked, and I nodded. "Do you know what that means?"

"Sister." I slid Soror back into my scabbard.

"That's a fitting name. It was once Rowan's, and now it's yours."

"Soror," I whispered under my breath as I ran my fingers over the ivory hilt.

"You'd better eat too," Phillip said. "There should be an oat cake in your saddlebag." He shook out the two bedrolls and laid one out on each side of the fire circle, then pulled his saddle close to him and propped his head against it like a pillow.

My hands were tight as I unbuckled my sword belt and laid Soror next to me. I gazed up at the moonlight filtering through the leaves and Spanish moss. "Why don't I remember anything about the witching moon?" Out of the corner of my eye, the fire's ashes glowed orange.

"No one understood about the witching moon until the middle ages, which was years after your death," Phillip responded. "How could you remember something that you didn't know about?"

"How does it happen?" I asked.

"Do you know what the winter's solstice is?"

"The first day of winter."

"The shortest day of the year. In Pagan times, the winter solstice was celebrated as the rebirth of the sun, a time when darkness gave way to light."

"Okay," I said.

"How much do you understand about the orbits of the moon and earth?" Phillip sat up and stared over the fire.

"I know to sow seeds on a new moon, and crabbing is best done when the moon is full."

Phillip balled up his hands and held them up over the shimmering coals. "Imagine that the fire is the sun. This is the earth." He shook his right fist. "This is the moon." He shook his left fist. "Both the earth and moon get all of their light from the sun. The earth circles around the sun, and the moon circles around the earth." He demonstrated with his hands. "A lunar eclipse happens when the earth comes between the moon and the sun, and blocks out the rays of the sun so the moon becomes dark."

"All right."

"A witching moon is when the winter solstice and a full lunar eclipse happen on the same night. In pagan times, it was believed that the joining of the winter solstice and lunar eclipse allowed the masculine energy of the sun to couple with the feminine energy of the moon. This only happens once every two hundred to five hundred years." He paused and looked at me. "It's when immortals are born."

I had leaned forward when the word "pagan" had crossed his lips. Somewhere, in the back of my mind, I saw a figure in a long cloak holding its arms up to the moon.

"We all have the same birthday?" I asked.

"Yes," he said. "December twenty-first."

I was quiet for a minute, letting this information settle. It was an odd feeling, knowing I shared a connection with Phillip and with Rex, with Rowan and with Valen. On Cusabo, birthdays weren't really celebrated, maybe there would be a bit of something sweet, like a stack cake if we had the fixings. I'd wager there would be a shindig at Amaranth on December twenty-first with cakes and punch and maybe even dancing.

"There's one more thing," Phillip went on. "We are carried in our mother's womb three months longer than mortal children. This is, no doubt, why our mothers don't survive our births."

I closed my eyes and thought of the woman who had died birthing me. Mama Jane couldn't remember her name, or at least that's what she had told me, but one thing she'd made clear was the amount of blood my mother had spilled bringing me into the world.

22

We set out before dawn, putting as much distance between us and Charleston as we could. Phillip rode with a fierceness, as if his whole life depended on us making it to Norfolk. I wondered if he sensed Rex was close and didn't want to frighten me with the news.

By midday, we'd made it out of the swamps and into the upcountry. My mother kept drifting into my thoughts—not Mama Jane, but my real mother. Who was she, why had she been picked to birth me, and how come no one had ever mentioned my father?

Night was falling, and my entire body ached. Relief swept over me when, at last, Phillip leaned back, and the horses slowed to a walk.

"The trail ends up ahead." Phillip dipped his head to a bend farther up the road. "Let's camp here tonight."

Thorns snagged my britches as we guided the horses up a ridge and through the brush. Phillip led me deep into the woods until we came upon a break in the trees. I heard the babble and splash of water, and suddenly we were standing in a clearing with the last rays of sun coloring everything gold. Tall grass mingled with wildflowers, bordered by stream and dense forest. I dropped the reins, slid out of the saddle, and took three long strides out into the grass, stretched my arms out and twirled. Dandelions dotted the field. I dropped to my knees, plucked one, and blew. The puffy seeds scattered, and I made a secret wish.

Phillip gave a cheerful laugh.

"What?" I squinted up at him.

"Nothing." He scratched at the stubble on his neck.

I started to push myself to my feet.

"Oh, don't get up," Phillip insisted. "Bask in nature's glory." He walked past me. "It's rare to see such unbridled joy." He glanced over his shoulder. "I'll make camp."

I dug my heels into the earth and stretched my shins, then plucked a handful of tender grass and whistled. Safeen trotted over and chomped the grass I held for him. I drew my sword and practiced my stance and thrusts while Phillip gathered stones from the stream for a fire ring.

"I'm going to set a few snares," he said as he took a length of rope from his saddlebag. He disappeared into the thick woods.

The sun was fading. I unsaddled the horses and dropped our bedrolls in a patch of grass, then gathered dry moss, twigs, and limbs for the fire. As I worked, I began to hum, and then I realized that something was humming inside of me. It wasn't a voice, but more of a beautiful vibration.

I stood very still, closed my eyes, and listened. The thrumming was like that of a stringed instrument; a full, rich sound echoing every beat of my heart. It grew more lively, as if I were the instrument being played. Suddenly, I felt Phillip's presence. It welled up inside of me like the heat of a hot brick at the foot of my bed. My eyes landed on a copse of trees.

Phillip appeared and raised his hand to me. "I just wanted to make sure you were still here."

The thrumming washed over me in an unexpected wave.

"You all right?" he asked.

"I felt you approaching," I said, skipping toward him. "Even before I saw you, I sensed you. I knew you would appear right there."

"That's amazing." He grinned. "How do you feel?"

"As if I don't weigh a thing and I'm floating up, up, up," I said.

"I've found a rabbit run in the woods and have a few more snares to set."

"Go, go." I shooed him away and tried to decide what needed to be done. The fishing line and hook were still in my pocket, so I decided to try my luck at catching supper in the stream. Smiling as I dug in the soft dirt for worms, I imagined Phillip's reaction when he returned and saw what I had caught.

When Phillip finally made his way back to our camp, I was sitting cross-legged, holding two skewered speckled trout over the fire.

"You've been busy." Phillip spread the limbs and sticks he'd gathered on the ground. There was a tin mug in his other hand.

"Used a match from your bag to start the fire."

"Good thinking." Phillip tilted the cup to me. It was filled with tiny wild strawberries that smelled warm, like summer. "The wee ones are the sweetest." He pushed his hair out of his eyes.

"But they're all tiny."

"I ate the bigger ones and saved these for you." Phillip took the two roasting sticks and turned the fish while I ate the berries. He was right: the tiny ones were sweet as jam.

The moon glowed in the sky, and fireflies flitted above the wildflowers in the meadow.

"It's beautiful," I said, leaning back against my saddle. "Don't think I've ever seen lightning bugs this early in spring."

Phillip appeared more at ease than he had been that morning, and yet there was still an alertness to him. "They remind me of the sky lanterns that are used during festivals in China," he said.

"Sky lanterns?"

"Little lamps made with bamboo frames and rice paper. You put a tiny candle in the lantern, and the heat makes it float up."

"What happens when the candle burns out?" I asked.

"It floats back down," Phillip said. "The Chinese have used them for centuries to signal one another."

"How d'you know so much about China?" All I knew was that if you dug a hole deep enough, you were liable to end up there.

"Ram-An and I lived with the Imperial sept for a few years, training with their guards."

"What was that like?"

"Cold in the winter, hot and dusty in the summer. It's hard to describe. China is charming and peculiar all at the same time."

"Where else have you been?" Ruth and I used to put ourselves to sleep talking about all the places we'd like to visit someday: Charleston, Savannah, Saint Augustine.

"Most everywhere. India, Japan, Russia, Persia, Africa. Venators often act as diplomats, carrying messages between septs."

"You must know a lot about people if you've been to all those places."

"Cultures have their own flavors, but human nature stays the same." Phillip reached back, rustled in his saddlebag, and pulled out two sage leaves. "Crush these and rub them in your hair."

I ran the crumbled leaf across my neck and imagined dancing under sky lanterns. "You think when I get to Amaranth, Rowan and I will travel to far-off countries?"

"Perhaps." Phillip glanced down. There was a kind of sorrow about him. "We should move our bedrolls out there." He nodded to the meadow that flickered with lightning bugs. "I'm afraid ticks will fall on us under these trees."

We spread our blankets side by side and lay down under the stars. Phillip pointed out the constellations, and I half-listened to what he said while I let myself imagine that I could float up to the heavens. His voice drifted over my own thoughts.

"It doesn't make sense," I muttered.

"What?"

"If I can heal, then why did my real mother die?" I leaned up on my elbow and patted down the wildflowers that separated us so I could see the shadows of his face. "I should've been able to save her."

Phillip shifted to look at me and was quiet for a long moment. He spoke at last. "I don't know. Perhaps your abilities weren't fully developed when you were born." He lay back down. "Do you recall the first time you healed someone?"

"You mean besides animals?" Stuttering Joe sprang up in my mind. He lived in the settlement on Cusabo and came out to our farm from time to time, set on courting Mama Jane.

I'd been sitting on a hickory stump watching Ol' Joe show Abel and Noah how to split wood. The boys must have been six years old, so I was probably eight. Noah had asked Joe about the boils that covered his arms. Stuttering Joe told us that he had gotten warts from handling too many toads. Abel asked if he could touch a wart, just to see what it felt like. Joe propped his ax against a tree and held his muscled arm low. Noah's hand hovered over a weeping boil for a moment, but he couldn't bring himself to swipe his fingers over Joe's skin. The blisters seemed angry, and something inside of me wanted to make them go away. I laid my palm just below the crook of Joe's elbow and felt a jolt to my chest, like somebody had shoved me backward. Joe snatched his arm back and held it close to his stomach like he had been burned. Then he held out his arm to me and said in a clear voice, "Miss Anne, do that again."

I never heard Joe stutter after that, and his warts never came back either.

Phillip listened, then we lay quiet for some time, sifting through our own thoughts.

He turned to me, and in a soft voice said, "It's not your fault your birth mother died."

His words made my eyes sting.

"What makes you think I feel guilty?" I asked.

"We all do."

I don't know what affected me more: the fact that he seemed to know just what I was thinking, or that he shared my feelings. I took a deep breath and gathered my courage before I asked, "Do you know who my father was?"

Phillip rubbed his forehead. "You're full of curiosity tonight."

"D'you know the answer?"

"I know what I was told when I asked the same question."

When he didn't continue, I prodded, "Well?"

"First, I want to tell you something that I've learned."

"Go ahead."

"All over the world, every group of people have their own traditions, their own beliefs," Phillip said. "And on top of that every culture has their own creation story."

"Like how God created Adam and Eve?"

"Exactly." He propped himself up on his elbow and faced me. "In the Bible, do you recall that an angel appeared to Mary, a virgin, and told her she was to have a child? God's child?"

"I do." Mama Jane told us Bible stories every night.

"You are also a child of the gods," Phillip said. "The god Phanes is your father, and the goddess Gaia is your mother. Together, they chose an Earthly mother, a virgin, to carry you."

"Phanes and Gaia." In my mind's eye, a girl knelt before two figures carved out of stone. "They aren't in the Bible."

"There are a great many things that aren't mentioned in the Bible."

"Like what?"

"Cats, for one, and volcanos."

These new particulars sunk in, and I felt disappointed. I thought to say that Mama Jane had never spoke about Phanes and Gaia, but then again, she hadn't told me about a lot of things.

"Mortals have short memories; they've forgotten the ancient ways. Now days most people worship one god—I suppose it's easier that way—but long ago, people and immortals worshiped many."

A thought crossed my mind. "Are Phanes and Gaia your parents too?"

"My soul comes from them, but my body and blood come from the woman that birthed me."

"So we aren't brother and sister," I said.

"Spiritually, yes. By blood, no."

It was the same with Mama Jane and me. She always said the Lord brought me to her. "Have you ever seen Phanes or Gaia?" I asked.

"I see them all around me, in the stars, the wind, the sun."

"Mama Jane says that God gives breath to all things."

Phillip yawned. "I like to think that we all have the same gods watching over us; we just call them by different names."

23

A sob broke the darkness. An animal was hurt—or at least that's what it sounded like. I sat up and rubbed the sleep out of my eyes. Phillip lay just out of arm's reach, breathing slow and deep. I must've been dreaming; surely a cry would've woken him. A solitary frog croaked, then another answered, and more joined in. Crickets began to chirrup, and I knew that it would be light soon because the forest was waking up.

A whimper echoed through the trees.

I sat up and cupped my hand on the roundness of Phillip's shoulder. He sighed and laced his fingers into mine. Our hands fit together perfectly.

A wail pierced the predawn.

Phillip sat up like a shot and crouched next to me before I could make sense of what was happening. A swish of steel slid out of his scabbard. I pushed myself to my knees and peered into the night.

Phillip stood and moved quietly toward the woods. I followed his shadow with my heart pounding. Something shifted behind me and nudged my shoulder. I turned on my heel, ready to scream. To my relief, Safeen pushed his wet nose against my cheek.

"Stay here." Heart pounding, I reached out and brushed my hand along his jaw, then followed Phillip. He ducked behind a bush, and I slid in beside him. Phillip pointed down to the Indian trail, where the first rays of sun filtered through the leaves, giving the path a hazy purplish color.

A child cowered in the dirt. They rocked back and forth in a stiff, scared way that made an ache rise up in me.

"That child hurts," I murmured, then moved to stand up.

"Wait." Phillip pulled me back, and I toppled onto him. He wrapped his arm around my waist. Our noses were almost touching.

"Who's there?" the child asked, in a soft, high-pitched voice— probably a girl's voice.

Silence.

"I need to help," I mouthed.

"Runaway slave." Phillip's breath was hot on my face. "She'll be hunted."

"I've got to go to her." Suffering gnawed at my spirit.

Phillip gave a nod and released me. I scurried down the embankment and landed a horse-length away from the girl. I caught a whiff of wet rust, and my feet stung like they had been dragged through a briar patch.

"Hey." I spoke softly. "You got hurt feet."

The girl balled herself up tight and hid her face. She was twig thin, just like Noah and Abel were when they first came to live on Cusabo.

"I'm far from home too." I inched closer. "When I was little, and I was hurt, my mama would make a comfrey poultice." I grazed my fingertips along the bottom of her foot and felt the slickness of blood. Deep gashes ran through the thick skin. I closed my hand around her ankle. The palm of my other hand pressed against the sole of her foot. She stilled, and whooshing filled my ears.

Phillip slid down the slope and landed on the path. The girl hid behind my back.

"It's alright," I said. "He's with me." Faint beams of sunlight seeped through the trees. Birds whistled calls to each other.

"We need to get back," Phillip said, glancing up and down the path.

"C'mon," I coaxed. "You hungry?"

The girl's eyes darted from me to Phillip.

"What's your name?" I wiped my palms on my britches, then held out my hand.

Her brown hand clasped mine. "Elodie."

24

Phillip got the fire going and went to check his snares without saying a word.

The dried moss and bark hissed as smoke wafted through the air. I busied myself rolling up the blankets while Elodie washed in the creek. Her skirt was tattered, and her shirt just about swallowed her whole. Ruth would've called her "thin as hen's skin" and made she-crab soup to put some meat on her bones.

Elodie cut her eyes my way when she thought I wasn't looking. I suppose she was deciding if I could be trusted.

Phillip returned with two jackrabbits.

"You angry?" I asked him in a low voice while he skinned breakfast. He glanced over my shoulder at the girl, and his eyes softened.

"Then what is it?" I pressed.

"I'm trying to figure out what to do with her." Phillip wiped his knife across his pants leg. "Slave hunters will be tracking her, and if we help her, they'll be searching for us too."

Elodie sat on the side of the creek bank, admiring the horses.

"Guess I wasn't thinking about consequence," I said.

"Don't apologize for kindness," Phillip said as he turned the meat over the cooking spit.

I rummaged through my saddlebag and found a lump of

oat cake that Brother Barnabas had packed, then stepped to the stream.

"You like oats?" I asked Elodie.

Elodie rolled a pebble between her thumb and forefinger and didn't say a thing. I broke off a tiny clump of oat and slipped it into my mouth. She watched me chew, and I held out the cake to her. She took it, gave it a sniff, and stuffed it into her mouth whole. I sat in the grass across from her and eyed her scarred feet. I'd heard tell of slave owners threshing the feet of slaves who tried to run but had never seen the like.

"How many times did you try to escape before this?" I asked.

Elodie shrugged. All her attention was on chewing. She cupped her hand under her chin to catch the crumbs, and when she was done, she licked the last morsels from her palm.

"Where you headed?" I asked.

She lowered her head to the stream and drank.

"We're not gonna turn you in, but it's not safe to leave you here either." I pushed my hair behind my ears.

Elodie rubbed the skin on the ball of her foot. Although I had healed her fresh wounds, deeper scars remained.

"We're riding north," I said.

She twisted a loose thread that dangled from the bottom of her skirt. "What're you called?" Her voice was small.

"Anne-drew." I stumbled through my name, remembering that I was supposed to be a boy.

"Why you wearing britches, Anne Drew?"

Of course she knew I wasn't a boy. "It's hard to ride in skirts," I answered.

"Them's fine horses."

"You ride?"

Elodie dipped her ear to her shoulder and stared out at the meadow. We sat in silence for a bit, listening to the slosh of water over the rocks.

"Still hungry?" I asked, but she didn't answer. "We've made breakfast. Let's fill our bellies, then you can decide what you want to do."

Phillip and I picked at our food, allowing Elodie to get her fill of roasted hare. She sat away from the fire, away from us.

When we were done, Phillip picked up his saddle and gave a tch for the horses.

"We can't just leave Elodie here," I whispered as I lugged my saddle behind him. "Slave catchers use bloodhounds. They'll get a sniff of her, and she'll be done for."

"She'll slow us down," Phillip replied over his shoulder without glancing back. "We've already wasted the better part of the morning."

"I don't care." I dropped my saddle in the grass.

Phillip glanced down at my saddle, then up at my eyes as if he were trying to determine how serious I was about helping her. "She reminds you of your family."

"A bit." I held strong. There was no way I was leaving a child to fend for herself.

Phillip's eye twitched as he gave the girl a long stare over my shoulder. "I was in her place once."

"Rowan saved you at the slave market," I murmured, remembering what he'd told me.

He grimaced, then shook away the memory.

"This here is your chance to do the saving." I leaned closer.

"We can't force her to come with us." Phillip slung his saddle over Salaa. "She'll fare better with the slave catchers than she will with Rex."

"Rex won't catch us," I said.

"D'you know something I don't?"

I almost blurted out how safe I felt when I was with him, but I wasn't sure of how to say it without blubbering, so I just said, "No."

"We could be placing Elodie in worse danger than she already is."

"Rex will be hunting two people, not three," I said, then added, "Maybe Elodie's scent will mask ours."

Phillip gave a half smile up as he fit the bit into Safeen's mouth, then handed me the reins. I watched him walk back to Elodie.

"We're headed north," Phillip said. "I can't promise you'll be safe, but I think you'll be better off with us than on your own."

The girl scrunched her face up, like she was trying to make a decision.

"We won't hurt you or turn you in." Phillip sounded earnest.

"You swear?" Elodie asked in a whisper.

"On my honor." Phillip spit in his hand and held it out for Elodie to shake. Elodie gawked at Phillip for a minute, and then spit in her palm and took Phillip's hand.

"How old are you?" Phillip asked.

"Not sure."

"You know where you're going?"

"Bound for Dunn," Elodie said.

"North Carolina?" Phillip asked.

Elodie nodded. "There's a tobacco farm there. Hear tell there's a man who helps folks north."

"A Quaker?"

"A farmer."

"You know his name?"

"Brewster Tate."

Phillip nodded.

"You heard of him?" A glimmer of hope crossed Elodie's face.

"No," Phillip said. "We'll be passing just east of Dunn. It won't be too far out of our way to see you to this Brewster Tate."

25

The trail ended under a cloudless blue sky. Scorched farmland strewn with charred plant stalks stretched out as far as I could see.

"Is this how it's supposed to be?" I asked.

"No ma'am." Elodie shifted in the saddle in front of me. "The army has been through."

"What the soldiers don't take, they burn," Phillip said, standing in his stirrups to survey the land. "We'd better stay close to the tree line."

We skirted the woods, cutting across open fields only when necessary. Every so often, we'd happen upon the shell of a burned-out farmhouse or cow carcass that had been picked clean by vultures and the like.

At dusk, we came across railroad tracks and followed them northwest. The moon was directly overhead when the tracks led us into a town. Salaa gave a jittery snort, and Safeen dug his heels in the dirt.

"What is it?" I asked. The railroad irons were twisted and bent back on themselves, resembling iron bows.

"Sherman's neckties," Phillip said. "Union soldiers have torn up the rails to keep supplies from getting through."

The horses stepped lightly around the crooked iron ties to the depot. Phillip dismounted and struck a match to read the depot sign: "Tabor Junction, North Carolina."

"We're out of South Carolina," I said.

"Slave catchers can cross state lines," Phillip replied.

So can Rex, I thought.

"Are you good for a few more hours?" Phillip asked.

"Think so." Elodie leaned back against my stomach, her head just below my chest.

"It's best to get as far as we can tonight and sleep during the day."

As we rode on, the stars spread themselves over the sky like a patchwork quilt, certain ones blinking brighter than others. It was possible that Ruth was looking up at the same sky, and maybe even Rowan was too. If we were all seeing the same stars at the same time, then we were all connected. Maybe right now, Ruth and Rowan were thinking about me, just like I was thinking about them.

The horses were as sure-footed at night as they had been during the day. I tried my best to stay awake, but my head felt like it was full of steel wool, and I nodded off in my saddle.

Sometime later, a rooster crowed. My head bobbed forward, and my eyes sprang open. Pinkish streaks lit the gray sky. Early cotton plants sprouted in the surrounding fields.

Up ahead, Phillip and his mount stood on the side of the road. "There's a glade just beyond this thicket." He motioned behind him. "It'll be a good place to hide."

We led the horses off the road and through the trees. Elodie woke up and insisted on keeping watch while Phillip and I slept. Both of us were too tired to argue. We spread our bedrolls on the damp grass and lay down. Phillip rested his sword between us, and I did the same.

"We covered a lot of ground," Phillip said.

"How far do you think we are from Dunn?" I asked.

"A night's ride, maybe two." He closed his eyes, and his face relaxed. His eyelashes were dark and long, and his lips parted just a touch as he fell asleep.

○))) ❭ ❭ ● ❰ ❰ (((○

Tobacco fields replaced cotton as we journeyed north that evening. The green leaves and clay soil gave an earthy sweetness to the night air. Elodie was good company. I suppose I'd taken a shine to her because she reminded me of Ruth and my brothers, but there was something deeper. She was searching for more than she had been given, and I understood what that was like.

"You spin a good story," Elodie said.

I had just finished explaining how Noah and Abel had smoked out a hive of honeybees and taken the comb.

"My friend, Josiah, tended the hives on the plantation," Elodie said. "He was the one who told me about the farmer in Dunn. Josiah helped me run."

"How'd he do that?" I asked.

Phillip leaned back on Salaa, and the horse slowed.

"Well, first time I took off, the overseer used dogs to find me. That's when he threshed my feet and told me he'd do worse if I tried making off again." Elodie gave a shiver. "Josiah caked honey on my feet to help them heal."

"That was kind," I said.

"Once my feet were put right, I told Josiah I was gonna light out again." Elodie's voice grew steely.

"What'd he say to that?" I asked.

"Told me how to be crafty." She spoke low. "Said if I was gonna run again I needed a plan, then once I'd hatched it, I had to wait for a sign."

"What kind of sign?" Mine and Phillip's voices rose together.

"A ruckus," Elodie said. "Josiah said the runners who made it past the swamp and outta the woods all ran when the overseer had his hands overfull."

"What happened?" Phillip asked. Our horses were so close that his knee brushed mine.

"A stranger rode up hunting his sister and the man she'd run off with from Charleston," Elodie said. "He offered a fist of gold coins to whoever found his sister."

My mouth popped open, and I felt as if I'd been punched in the guts.

"What did the man look like?" Phillip asked. "Did you catch his name?"

Elodie shook her head. "He was beefy-like and mean-eyed." Elodie lifted her left hand and wiggled her fingers. "And he only wore one black glove."

Phillip twisted in his saddle and searched the darkness. My head was sloshy; I thought I might throw up.

Elodie continued on with how she had watched the overseer round up a gaggle of men and ride off with the stranger, but I could barely pay attention. My heart was thumping so hard I thought I might splinter a rib. Without thinking, I clenched my legs against Safeen, and we began to gallop. Phillip kept pace with me.

The moon was waning when we rode into the village of Dunn. Phillip checked the notice board posted outside the railroad depot and telegraph office. Brewster Tate's name was typed out under the telegraphs received column.

"Looks like we found our tobacco farmer," Phillip said.

"Now what?" I asked. It wasn't like we could just ride up and ask him if he was helping runaway slaves north.

"We find a place to hide Elodie. You and I can find Brewster's farm in the morning."

26

Brewster Tate's flat-roofed, clapboard farmhouse was set back from the dirt road. Long rows of mustard greens stretched out from the front yard to the ditch that bordered the farm. Behind the house, the drying barn stood at least three stories tall. Tobacco fanned out to the back and sides of the property. Several field hands were slowly making their way down the rows shaking each leafy plant. The entire farm stood isolated at the end of the road encased by pine forest on all sides.

We tied Safeen and Salaa to the hitching post at the stable and dodged chickens as we cut a path to the rickety front porch. The door swung open, and puffs of dust whirled out of the house. A wiry woman stepped through the doorway, caught sight of us, and lifted her twig broom like she was aiming a rifle.

Phillip removed his hat, and I quickly did the same. "Pardon us, ma'am, we didn't mean to startle you." Phillip dipped his head.

She lowered her broom and ran her eyes down Phillip's torso and rested on his sword, then did the same to me.

"We ain't got no work needs doing," she said. Inside the house, a baby cried.

"We're here for Mister Brewster Tate, ma'am." Phillip's accent had gone flat into a twang.

"He don't take callers," the woman said.

A silent stand-off began. Phillip waited it out by squinting down at the wooden slats of the porch and shifting his weight from one foot to the other. The woman swept some feathers off the porch and acted like we weren't there. She had on a pair of leather slippers, the same kind Mama Jane had sewn for me in the winter.

"Where you boys headed?" the woman asked finally.

"Virginia." The wail of a child drowned out Phillip's voice.

The woman sighed and turned to go inside. "He's out in the barn," she called over her shoulder.

Hogshead barrels were stacked four high against the back and side walls. The dizzying aroma of dried tobacco hung in the air. An old black man with curly white hair sat hunched over a sharpening wheel, honing a sickle blade. Several other slaves were high in the side rafters, arranging drying sticks that crisscrossed up to the ceiling, but once they spied us, all work stopped. In the corner, a block of a man with a ruddy neck and brassy hair was bent over a barrel with a mallet in his hand. He lifted his freckled face at our footsteps and regarded us for half a shake, then spit a stream of brown juice on the floor.

"What y'all want?" His voice echoed like a plucked banjo string. He tugged a kerchief out of his pants pocket and dabbed at his forehead.

"You Mister Brewster Tate?" Phillip asked.

"Who's asking?" The man cocked his head to the side.

"I am, sir." Phillip twisted his hat in his hand. "We need assistance with some cargo."

"Assistance?" Brewster narrowed his eyes and shifted the plug of tobacco in his lower lip.

"We have a friend who's been following the North Star, a child. She believes you can help her."

Brewster gave us a steely glare, then stepped to where the old man sat, now sharpening a hoe. He jerked up a pitchfork from the throng of tools that lay beside the honing wheel, marched over to

Phillip, and shoved the pointed tines right under Phillip's chin.

"Git off my land!" His face had turned the color of a beetroot. "I don't know what lies you been told, but you best git while the gittin's good."

"We can pay you." My voice was shaky. Phillip held his arm out and blocked me from stepping forward.

"How you gonna pay me, boy?" Brewster's voice rose up. "You don't look like you got a pot to piss in yo'self!" The men in the rafters snickered.

"Come on, brother," Phillip said to me, then dipped his head to Brewster. "Sorry to have bothered you, Mister Tate. We've been misled."

Brewster Tate stood with his chest poked out like a prize game-cock. Phillip nodded to the man at the honing wheel.

"Guess Elodie was wrong," I mumbled as we untied our horses from the hitching post.

"Ahem." The old black man stood in the barn doorway holding a hoe.

Phillip raised his eyebrow and waited.

The old man took a step closer. "If your friend's aim is true, she needs to search for the light." He pointed to the roof of the barn, then turned and went back inside.

"D'you think we can trust them?" I asked as we walked Safeen and Salaa to the road.

"Did you see how comfortable those men were with Brewster Tate?" We had reached the dirt road. Phillip swung his leg over Salaa and studied the rows of tobacco that sloped upward to a copse of trees to the back of the farm. "This is the place."

27

We had almost made it back to the outcropping of rocks where we had left Elodie when I caught a whiff of wet dog. Phillip must have smelled it too; he cocked his ear for a moment, then slid off Salaa and stepped to a pine tree. He ran his hand up the bark and tugged away a few strands of gray hair, then held them to his face and inhaled. His mouth formed a hard line as he inspected the ground.

The jangle of bells tolled through the woods. Phillip motioned for me to get off Safeen. We walked the horses downhill through the trees in the direction of the bells, stopping to listen every little while.

A dog growled, and a cry warbled through the trees.

"Elodie!" I took off running.

"Anne!" Phillip called after me.

Shadows darted between trees, and the bells chimed louder. The rocky ground was steep, and my weight pushed me forward as I bounded down the hill, faster than I'd ever run in my life.

"Somebody's coming," a strange voice hissed.

I skidded on a patch of wet leaves, fell on my shoulder, and tumbled head over heels down the hill. When I managed to sit up, the barrels of two rifles were leveled at my nose.

Phillip skidded down the incline and landed beside me. The

horses had found a flatter path and meandered into the glade to my left.

Two bearded men in slouch hats stood side by side. A scrawny bluetick hound nosed at something behind them. I leaned to the right, and my heart sank. Elodie was crouched in the weeds, her shoulders hunched forward. A metal collar circled her neck. Three long rods extended from the neckband, and at the end of each rod hung a bell that clanged with every movement. Elodie kept her eyes cast down. Her shame lit a fury in me, and I sprang to my feet.

"Halt there!" the thicker man hollered. He prodded the brim of his hat back, and it toppled to the ground, revealing stringy black hair with a broad streak of gray, like a skunk. "This here's our catch. We found her first, and we ain't splitting no reward."

His partner adjusted his gun against his shoulder, his finger twitching at the trigger.

I opened my mouth to speak, but Phillip beat me to it. "You've found my slave."

"Tug, show 'em that notice," the skunk-haired man said.

Tug lowered his gun and twisted his hand into his grimy jacket pocket, fished out a crumpled piece of paper, and shook it open. "Got a notice that calls for a hundred-dollar reward for a ten-year-old girl that took off from Florence County, South Carolina." The notice floated to the ground as he repositioned the gun. "Says she goes by the name Elodie."

Tears welled up in Elodie's eyes.

"You've made a grave mistake." Phillip squared his shoulders and took a step forward.

"Get back!" Tug rasped. "I ain't yearning to kill you, but I will."

"We got the right girl." The skunk-haired man grinned.

"Show 'em, Bo," Tug said.

With one hand, Bo reached back, grabbed Elodie by one of

the rods, and jerked her forward. The clanging of the bells scraped at my nerves. He yanked the back of Elodie's shirt up to show a raised V etched into the skin over her right shoulder blade.

"That mark means nothing to me." Phillip's voice was icy and his jaw was set. "This slave is mine."

Bo nudged Elodie forward and pressed the muzzle of his rifle to her neck. "What's the name of the farm she ran off from?"

No one said a word for several breaths. The bluetick hound wandered over to me and snuffled my leg.

"If this slave is truly yours, then you should be able to answer the name of the farm from whence she escaped." Bo used the heel of his boot to grind the wrinkled notice into the dirt.

Elodie had never shared that information with us, and we had never asked. She blinked, and a single teardrop spilled from her eye. I was struck by how shiny the rivulet was against her skin as it streamed down her cheek. A moment of beauty in the midst of horror.

"Victory," Phillip said, staring Bo straight in the eyes.

"Wrong!" Tug announced as if he was the caller at an auction.

"Perhaps we can come to an arrangement." Phillip jangled the coins in his pocket, then drew out a solitary gold piece and turned it over in his fingers.

Tug's eyes locked on the gold, and he licked his lips. "How many of those you got?"

"How many will it take to release the girl?" Phillip flipped the coin with his thumb high in the air. Tug and Bo leaned in as the gold piece spun—head-tails, head-tails, head-tails—then arced and fell back into Phillip's open palm.

"What you think, Bo?" Tug scratched at his neck.

Bo leered at Salaa and Safeen. "I think them's mighty fine horses."

I took a step backward to Safeen and stroked his mane.

"Ten pieces of gold, right now, for the girl," Phillip said.

"That saves you the trouble of carting her back south."

"We want them horses too," Bo countered.

"Our horses aren't for sale," Phillip said.

"We ain't looking to buy 'em," Tug snickered, showing a mouth jammed with crooked teeth. "We got something you want, and you got something we want. That's called bartering."

"Tell you what," Phillip said mimicking Tug's drawl. "I've got fifteen gold pieces. You give us the girl and you can have it all."

"We'll take it all," Tug said, knowing he had the upper hand. "Plus, them horses."

Bo jabbed Elodie with the muzzle of the rifle and the bells on her collar jingled as she shuddered. He pulled down the loose collar of her shirt and admired her collar bone.

"Free Elodie, and the horses are yours," Phillip said. I couldn't believe what I was hearing. Surely Phillip had the wits to figure a way out of this without handing over Safeen and Salaa to these scallywags.

"This is how it's gonna work," Tug said, proffering a key from his pocket. "Yer gonna put your sword down on the ground, nice and easy. Then yer gonna toss me those gold coins, one at a time. I'll toss you this here key in return that's gonna unlock her bell-collar."

Phillip nodded and slowly placed his sword at his feet.

"Stay behind me," Tug said to Bo. "If they make one wrong move, put a shot o'lead in her." Bo nudged Elodie behind him.

"Nice and gentle now." Tug motioned for Phillip to lob a coin.

Phillip did as he was told. Once Tug had the coins, he tossed the key to Phillip.

"Have that whippersnapper there," said Tug, pointing at me, "tie those horses to yonder tree." He dipped his head toward a loblolly pine to the right of the clearing.

"Andrew, give them your horse." Phillip's eyes never left the men.

I wanted to scream "No!" but instead I took Safeen by the reins, led him to the loblolly pine, and tied his reins to the trunk. I placed my hands on either side of his face and rested my forehead against his. "I'm gonna miss you." I kissed his nose and walked back to Phillip.

Phillip whistled for Salaa, who nosed his shoulder. He ran his hand along the horse's neck: its ears flattened back as Phillip muttered, "Lugus."

"Here." Phillip passed Salaa's reins to me, and I walked him over to the same tree where Safeen waited.

Tug raised his shotgun at Phillip, who seemed unnaturally calm. On the other hand, I was about to chew the inside of my cheek to pieces. I did the only thing I could think to do in such a situation: I prayed. Dear God, please don't let this nervous man shoot us. Tug's eyes darted from Phillip to me to Bo, who was busy tying Elodie to a hickory tree on the left side of the clearing. Elodie bent her head forward as if in prayer as Bo wound a rope around her and the tree several times, tying a knot every so often so she couldn't get loose easily.

"Walk them horses up the hill," Tug said to Bo. "I'll be up directly." Bo untied the reins and made off into the trees.

The bluetick hound followed Tug as he slowly backed away, keeping his rifle trained on Phillip and me. Once he was a good distance away, he turned and took off running in the direction of Bo and our horses.

Soon as Tug had turned his back, I ran to Elodie and loosened the knots and rope that bound her.

"We're gonna get you loose," Phillip said as he unlocked the collar. Elodie staggered to stand, and I wrapped my arms around her shoulders.

"What if they come back?" Elodie asked, trembling and her

eyes wide with fear. She had held herself together as best she could, but now that the slave catchers were out of sight she crumbled like week-old cornbread.

"I'm proud of you," I said as she bawled. Tears and snot dripped from her chin. "You were brave."

"Let's get out of here," Phillip said as he slipped his sword back in his scabbard.

28

We hid deep in the woods, in the opposite direction from the way the slave catchers had gone, and waited for the day to pass so we could make our way back to Brewster Tate's farm in darkness. Elodie refused to leave my side. After we had untied her from the tree, she had broken down into hysterics, which had worn her out, but she was afraid to sleep in case Tug and Bo returned. I settled back against a hollow log with my knees pulled up to my chin and wrapped my arms around my shins.

How long had it been since I left home? One week? Maybe two? The days all mashed together, and nothing made sense anymore. I couldn't believe Phillip let those scallywags have Safeen and Salaa. In my heart, I knew that the horses would make their way back to the Hermitage. I could feel the truth in my bones. Still, it didn't much ease my mind.

I sensed Phillip approach before I heard him. The touch of his hand on the top of my head soothed me.

"It's time," he said.

Night had come quickly, and the charged air smelled like rain.

Phillip motioned for Elodie and me to follow him. The woods ended in a wide pasture, which we crossed before climbing a stile over a fence. The drizzling rain chilled my nose. We trudged through rocky farmland and tobacco fields. At last, we crossed a stream and scuttled up a muddy bank. Under the cover of trees we formed a tight circle, catching our breath as the heavens opened up. Lightning streaked across the sky, followed by the roll of thunder.

"We're almost there," Phillip said. "It's just on the other side of this grove."

We picked through the tangle of bushes and privet until finally we gazed down at Brewster Tate's farm.

Rows of tobacco spread out, and in the distance, dim light flickered through the slat walls of the drying barn. The rain had stopped, and mist hovered over the ground.

"What now?" I whispered.

"We wait," Phillip said.

One by one, we crept into a ditch between the leafy plants until we were shouting distance to the drying barn. We hunkered down in the mud, deep in the furrow of a hill. Tobacco leaves, heavy with dirt, hung over the tops of our heads.

"What are we waiting for?" I murmured. The moon's light flickered between passing clouds.

"A sign."

I barely heard him. Stretching my legs to the mound of wet clay in front of me, I wondered what sort of signal Brewster Tate would send, and hoped Phillip was right in trusting him. The wet tobacco gave off a musty smell, like spoilt honey, that soured my stomach. I took my hat off and rubbed my temples. My head felt like it might split into pieces. Elodie leaned into me, and I wrapped my arm around her shoulder. The lantern light from the barn went out, and I wondered if that was our signal, but Phillip didn't move.

The night took its time passing. I tried counting blessings, but couldn't keep my mind aimed in one direction, so I watched the moon slowly track across the sky and tried not to think of how empty my stomach was, or how the water dripped from the ends of my hair and rolled down the back of my neck. I imagined Safeen bucking Tug into a bramble of thorns and galloping back to the Hermitage with Salaa. Perhaps they were retracing their steps through the swamp at this very moment.

The pounding of hooves against the dirt road echoed in the darkness. I opened my eyes just in time to sense Phillip stiffen. He brought his finger to his lips and stretched his back to peer through the layers of leaves toward the road. Pulling my arm free of Elodie, I crouched behind Phillip and placed my hands on his back to steady myself. It was too dark to see anything that wasn't right on top of you.

Someone was approaching the barn. The tiny hairs on my neck stood up, and my stork bite prickled. A horse snorted, and boots slapped the dirt. The echo of splintering wood beat through the night. The barn door opened, and Rex's face lit up with lantern light. He'd been sweating, and his thick black hair was matted to his head.

A stab of panic shot through me. Rex towered over the old man, who had been honing tools this morning. His mouth was moving, but I could only hear bits of what he said. Rex barked my name, then Phillip's. The old man shook his head. Several more men came out of the barn holding pitchforks and shovels. A figure ran to the barn from the house in a union suit that glowed red in the light. Brewster Tate was half as big as Rex in stature, but made up for it in a thundering voice.

"They was here this morning, but we sent them away!" Brewster bellowed. "We don't take kindly to strangers!"

Rex shoved him to the ground, and Brewster scrambled back to his feet.

"Git off my farm!" Brewster yelled.

"Where did they go?" Even though we were half a field away, Rex's voice tore through me.

"I don't know!" Brewster was hopping up and down, sticking

his fists out ready to fight. His men formed a semicircle behind him.

Rex stood very still, then pushed past the men and into the barn. I could hear banging, and Brewster hollered. It seemed to take forever until Rex came back outside. Brewster and his men huddled together and glared as Rex rode off.

Rex's horse slowly clopped to the road, then stopped. He could feel that I was close; I could feel his pneuma pulsing through me like a rip current. Rex's shadow had a greenish glow to it, like shimmering algae. He slid out of his saddle and drew his sword, tramped along the road, then slid into the ditch. The thwacking of a sword hacking at tobacco plants beat up the hill.

"Phillip!" Rex howled at the night. "I'm coming for you!" He sounded mad as a hornet who'd lost its stinger.

I squeezed my eyes shut and pressed my forehead against Phillip's spine. Finally, Rex scrambled back to the road, and his stirrups jangled as he rode away.

Phillip slumped down in the ditch and exhaled. I clasped his wrist; his heartbeat pounded beneath my fingertips.

"Why did he leave?" I mumbled into Phillip's ear.

Phillip shrugged his shoulders and motioned to the ground next to him, and I sat back. All of my edges were frayed, like a bolt of lightning had gone right through me. Phillip slipped his hand in mine, and for the first time, I realized that I was shaking.

"It's okay." His breath ruffled my hair as he pulled me to him. I tried not to think of Rex tracking us to where we had come up against the slave catchers, then stalking us to where we sat now.

The night had become silent and black as pitch. Soon it would be dawn. A flicker caught my eye. The flame of a solitary candle winked from a tiny opening near the eave of the drying barn. I squeezed Phillip's hand and nodded to the light. The flame winked and then disappeared.

"The sign," Phillip said.

I shook Elodie awake. We crouched low and crept to the barn door, which was ajar.

"This way."

The old man led us to a ladder and held it steady as each of us climbed. Brewster was waiting for us in the barn's loft.

"Gimme your weapons." Brewster's eyes were slits. "You can hand 'em over or git out."

Phillip unbuckled the belt of his scabbard, and I did the same.

"Anybody else gonna show up rooting around for you?" Brewster asked. "Because if they do, I'll hand you over faster than stink on a skunk."

"No, sir," Phillip said.

"Come with me, then," Brewster said.

We skirted around the ledge to the next ladder and climbed the rafters to the third level. This overhang was wider than the first, and dried twigs and shredded leaves covered the floor.

"Take 'em up, Nat," Brewster said.

A massive man with steel gray eyes led us to a hatch that hung down from the ceiling. The man boosted Elodie through the ceiling, then me. Phillip's head and arms popped through the hole, then he boosted himself up and in. The hatch closed, and we were swallowed by darkness.

29

The splatter of raindrops on the tin roof roused me just enough to remember I was in the drying barn. Bone-tired weariness overtook me, and I let myself be lulled back to my dream where the sun warmed my face. My head rested in the man's lap, and he ran his fingertips through my curls. The sun was behind him, casting his face in shadow, but his hair was a mass of dark waves. Delicately, he traced the line of my jaw down to my collarbone, and his fingers lingered on the ruby at the base of my throat. "Meus dilligo." My love. I floated, light as a puff of air. The surrounding olive trees shook, and the ripe fruit fell around us.

Water dripped on my cheek, and the roof shook from the thunderclap. I buried my face in the crook of my arm and replayed the dream in my mind. Who was this man, and why did he fill my dreams? My throat tingled where he had touched me. I laid my hand at the base of my neck, holding on to his warmth.

"You awake?" Phillip asked.

"Morning." Shafts of light sifted in through the knotholes in the wood wall.

"Afternoon." He pushed a pail toward me with his boot. "Brewster sent up some food."

My stomach gurgled. I sat cross-legged and pulled a mason jar half full of milk and a brick of crumbly cornbread from the pail. I ate, obliged for each stale morsel. Phillip handed me a piece of cloth. I thought he meant for me to wipe my face with it, but when I took it I could feel that it held something: a slice of cured ham. Memories of the smokehouse on Cusabo Island gushed inside me as I held the meat to my nose.

"What's wrong?" Phillip's voice was full of concern.

I shook my head to weaken the memory of home. "Where's Elodie?"

"Brewster took her to the house. His wife takes down the stories of the people who pass through. She was raised by Quakers." Gruff voices floated up from the barn floor. "Brewster's men aren't pleased with us for leading Rex here."

"That wasn't our fault," I said.

"Doesn't matter. We've imperiled their operation."

I fought the urge to groan. Can't anything be easy? Then a thought struck me. "Rex." His name scratched against the back of my throat. "If he was able to track us here, then why didn't he know we were hiding in the tobacco field?"

"I've been pondering that very question." Phillip ran his hand through his hair. "Rex followed our trail the way we approached yesterday morning on horseback. He knew we had been here—he searched the barn. When he left, he seemed uncertain, like our trail had vanished." Phillip picked up a dried tobacco leaf, turned it over in his hand and held it to his nose. "Perhaps the tobacco masks our scent."

"Last night, in the field, I was dizzy and sick to my stomach." I leaned forward. "Maybe Rex felt the same."

"It's possible." Phillip traced the scar on his eyebrow with his thumb.

"You do that when you're thinking." I pointed to his hand.

"What?"

"Rub the cut in your eyebrow," I said.

"Oh." Phillip dropped his hand. "I guess I do." One side of his mouth curled up.

Raindrops pattered against the roof, and I tugged my jacket tight around me.

"Does Amaranth have fireplaces?" I asked.

"Many," Phillip said, and his jaw relaxed as he stared at me, like he was picturing me there. "Some of the larger rooms have two fireplaces."

"Two?" I'd never heard of such a thing.

"There are curved ceilings that arc into domes; some have an opening at the top to let in sunlight." Phillip raised his arm over his head and spread his fingers out. "When it's cold, you can stand under the oculus and let the sun warm you."

"Oculus?"

"The opening at the top of the dome. In the summer, when I was a boy, I used to wait for it to rain; then I would run under the oculus as the drizzle came down. It cooled the whole room."

"Does it rain often?" I thought of the thundershowers that blew in off the sea and flooded our garden on Cusabo.

"Mainly in the fall, but Amaranth is an island, so the weather is mild."

"An island?"

"What had you imagined?"

I shrugged. "A castle in the forest."

"With a fire-breathing dragon and maybe a herd of unicorn?" Phillip chuckled. "Amaranth is a tidal island, but it does have a fortress."

"What's a tidal island?"

"When the tide is high, Amaranth can only be reached by boat, but when the water recedes, a land bridge emerges." He leaned forward and gestured with his hands. "It's like a wedding cake. The base is thick, and it gets smaller with each rise so at the top there is only a point. The village sits along the bottom, and a narrow road winds up and criss-crosses to the top of the cliffs, and that is where the fortress sits."

"So there is a castle," I said.

"Of course." Phillip scooted closer. "It's our home."

"And the village?" I glanced down. The toe of his boot pressed against mine.

"Farmers, fishermen, and shopkeepers live there. They're descendants of the workers who built the fortifications centuries ago. Some of the villagers work in the castle as cooks or maids."

I shivered, and Phillip shifted closer.

"You're really cold." He shook off his coat and draped it over my legs.

"Aren't you?" I asked.

"Not really."

"Ruth says I give off heat." I wrapped my legs in his jacket. "But if I'm not in the sun, I get weak."

"Rowan says the sun strengthens her," Phillip said. "In the afternoon, she sits on her balcony to write letters and read." He leaned his lead back against the wall. "Her rooms are in a corner tower, and she has tall windows to capture as much sun as possible."

"Tell me more," I said.

"She rises early, every day, to pray for your return." Phillip's voice was soft. "Then she trains the venators."

"She's a teacher." My heart swelled as I recalled her patience with others.

"It was Rowan who decided that venators should be taught to go out and find other immortals."

An image of a girl with a mass of black curls floated in the back of my mind.

"She foresaw your coming," Phillip said. "She had a vision that you would be reborn in the new world and found during a time of war."

The barn door grated open, and boots stomped across the floor-boards. Phillip lay on his stomach and squinted through a crack in the wood slats.

"What's happening?" a thick voice asked from below.

"We got us a shipment coming in," Brewster cawed. "Git Elodie back to the loft and lay some quilts down. We take delivery at nightfall."

"How many?" someone asked.

"Don't rightly know," Brewster said.

The hatch squeaked open, and Nat handed up several folded quilts, then boosted Elodie up to us. She had the scent of lye soap, and her face and neck had been scrubbed clean.

"I told 'em how you helped." Elodie's words tumbled out of her mouth. "Told 'em how you saved me from those slave catchers and gave up your horses."

"Thank you," Phillip said.

"You get the ham?" Elodie crawled toward me.

"It was tasty," I said.

In low tones, Elodie told us how Brewster's wife had written down her name and everything she could remember about herself in the back of her Bible.

"Missus Brewster says there's a Quaker settlement in Delaware where I'd be welcome. She said the wagon that's due in tonight is headed there." Elodie chattered on about her plans.

Later, we heard wagon wheels sloshing through the muck and the barn doors creak open. I pressed my eye to a gap in the floorboards. Brewster and his men helped guide two lathered horses into the barn, followed by a wagon overflowing with loose hay. The driver stepped down and walked to the back of the wagon.

"We made it," the driver said. The hay in the wagon shimmied as arms and heads poked through the straw. Men and women stood, shaking themselves off and stretching their limbs. Brewster and the driver helped everyone down.

"We got blankets for you upstairs and grub on the way," Brewster said. "Nat, get these folks to the loft."

One by one, the runaways followed Nat. The hatch swung open, and Phillip, Elodie, and I scurried to the far wall.

"You and your brother gonna have to get down," Nat said to Phillip.

"Can Elodie stay with the others?" Phillip asked.

"Yep," Nat said.

Phillip and I lowered ourselves through the hole and onto the ledge. Nat and Phillip helped boost the runaways up to the loft.

Below, Brewster and the driver talked as they unhitched the horses.

"They showed up yesterday," Brewster said.

"Ain't got room for no more," the driver grunted.

"Well, it'd only be three, two and a half really. The girl's no bigger than squat."

"We'll see," the driver said, and led the horses outside.

30

Long sticks crisscrossed over the open interior of the barn, which Phillip explained would be used to hang the tobacco out to dry when it was harvested. There was a squeak on the ladder. I peeked over the edge and saw a wiry mess of hair.

Brewster's head popped over the edge of the loft. "Elodie says you're headed north."

"Yes sir, we are," Phillip said.

"Says you traded yer horses for her." He eyed us.

Phillip nodded, then fished two gold coins out of his pocket and offered them to Brewster.

"You don't need to pay me," Brewster said. "But the driver will need to be provided for."

"We need to get to Norfolk," Phillip said.

"Driver can get you close." Brewster shifted the plug of tobacco in his lower lip. "It'll be mighty tight in that wagon."

"We'll manage," Phillip said.

"All right then," Brewster said. "Y'all gonna be leaving once the driver and horses get some rest." He climbed down, and his men sprang into action, changing wagon wheels and replacing axle clips. Nat brought a basket of food to the hidden attic.

"There's a train that runs to Norfolk. Once they let us off, we can follow the tracks or jump a train if one comes by. It shouldn't take long to get there." Phillip flicked his fingers as he silently counted. "We've been gone nine days. If all goes well, Ram-An and the others should be at the port when we get there."

"Won't Rex expect us to go to Norfolk?" I asked.

"Hopefully the rain and tobacco will throw Rex off our scent." Phillip crushed a handful of leaves and stems and stuffed them in his jacket pockets. "Rex knows we have venators in Wilmington, so he'll expect us to go there."

"Unless he thinks like you," I said. "If he's smart, he'll try to predict what you'll do instead of doing what you think he'll do." I shoved several fistfuls of tobacco into my pockets; my aim was to smell like a pipe.

"True." Phillip leaned closer to me. "We need be ready for anything." He glanced down at the men hammering at the underside of the wagon, then turned to me. "Did you ever wrestle with your brothers?"

"A little."

He tilted his chin up. "What would you do if Rex came at you?"

"Run," I said.

"What if he catches you?" Phillip's hand darted out and thumped my hip. "He takes your sword. You have nothing to protect yourself."

"He'd never catch me. I'm fast as a jack rabbit." I could easily outrun Noah or Abel.

"What if Rex is on a horse, and he runs you down?" Phillip said. "You have no choice but to fight him with your wits and your fists." Phillip crouched into a fighting position. "What would you do then?"

I hunkered down and readied myself for whatever he was aiming to do. I'd seen Abel and Noah go at each other like this a hundred times, but Mama Jane never allowed them to tussle rough with Ruth and me. Phillip lunged forward, and I jumped back. My head brushed against the ceiling, and the heel of my boot hit the wall.

"What now?" Phillip's eyes grew wide. "I got you in a corner, and there's nothing you can do." He took hold of my arm and squeezed.

Using my free hand, I balled up my fist and beat against his chest.

"You'll have to do better than that," Phillip said. "I'm bigger and stronger." He punched my shoulder with his fist, just hard enough to prove his point.

Using all my strength, I shoved him. He easily held me back, then spun me around and twisted my arm high behind my back. "I can't kill you." His breath was hot on my ear. "But I could break your arm or force you into my carriage for nefarious purposes."

I tried squirming free, but it was useless. My nose was pressed against wood slats where the ceiling met the wall. I bent my neck to bite his shoulder, but he strengthened his hold by pressing his chest against the back of my head. His heart was racing.

"You'll never escape," Phillip whispered in my ear. I shimmied my shoulders and kicked back with my legs, but he squeezed my arms till I quieted down. "Reason what your next move should be," he said through gritted teeth.

My eyes began to sting, and I clenched them shut. Don't get riled, I told myself. "You're hurting me." I whimpered. Though this was true, I wasn't eager to admit it, but it was the only thing I could think of to say. He loosened his grip, and I slipped away, twisted my body, and kicked him. The heel of my boot cracked against his knee.

"Ow!" Phillip sprang back, his mouth and eyes wide with shock.

I ran forward with my head low. Phillip caught me; his arms were longer and stronger than mine, so he easily wrangled me into a bear hug. We were a hair's width from the ledge of the loft. I doubted the drying sticks would break my fall if we took a tumble.

"You're good." Phillip's breath came hard. "Truce." He held up his hand, then bent to rub his knee.

Blood rushed through me, and I shuffled back.

"I thought I'd really hurt you." He started to laugh.

"You did." I rubbed my arm where he had grasped me.

"When you're up against a man, it's best to let him think you're frail, then aim for his weak spot." Phillip jabbed his fingers at my face. "His eyes, ears, and nose." He held the base of his palm up to my nose. "You won't kill an immortal this way, but you'll slow him or her down." He ran his thumb along the front of my neck and gently pressed against my windpipe. "Do you feel that?"

"Yes!" I shoved him away. "I hate that."

"Everyone does. If you get the chance to punch your attacker in the neck, punch hard. You can crush their windpipe and that will put them down." Phillip extended his neck. "Do you see where my Adam's apple is?" He took my hand and placed it on his neck.

"Yes," I said. "It feels like a flexible bone."

"It's actually cartilage, which is more pliable than bone. Now place your thumb right below my Adam's apple."

He swallowed, and the cartilage bobbed up and down under my thumb.

"If you jabbed your fingernail right into that soft spot, you could tear my windpipe."

A shiver ran through me. "I can't abide anyone touching my neck."

"Looks like I found your weakness," Phillip said. "Everybody has one."

"What's yours?" I swallowed.

Phillip opened his mouth to speak, then closed it. Color rose in his cheeks as he examined the floor.

"Do immortals fight much?" I asked.

"Most of us live in peace, but Valen's people use force to get what they want."

"Why don't the peaceful septs band together and overtake Valen's tribe?" It seemed like a simple solution.

"Valen's sept is powerful." The lightness in Phillip's voice faded. "He has formed alliances with kings, high priests, and politicians. An all-out war would benefit no one."

"Why would anyone want to band with Valen?"

"Money." Phillip rubbed his thumb against his forefingers. "The sept of Valen is the wealthiest bank in the world. When countries want to go to war with other countries, they borrow from Valen. Many of the world's nations owe him a great deal of gold, which gives him influence over them."

"What does that mean?" I asked.

"That Valen's gold can buy almost anything he desires, and that he has many governments in his pocket." Phillip said.

"I don't care about gold," I said.

"Others do."

"Like Rex?" I asked.

"Yes, and venators for hire." Phillip extended his palm, and I inched my hand into his. "Be careful who you trust. Not everyone will take your best interests to their heart."

"I don't need to fret about that." I tugged at his hand. "You're gonna teach me to fend for myself. I'll be able to fight all the bad folks off."

Phillip grasped my wrist and kicked the back of my leg, and I crumbled to the floor.

"You have a hundred years of skills to master." He grinned down at me.

31

A lone moth flitted from rafter to rafter, beating its wings against the low ceiling. A vision of a tower rising out of the sea spread across my mind. My heart ached to be there, to be with my sister. I held up my finger and examined my ruby ring. I had no doubt that Rowan had sent it to draw me to Amaranth.

A screech echoed in the barn, and I sat up. Phillip lay on the floor, eyes closed and still, but I knew he wasn't sleeping. I crawled over to the ledge and peered down to the dimly lit floor. The horses gave soft neighs and stomped as they were hitched to the wagon. I shook away the memory of Safeen and Salaa. It wouldn't do me any good to pine for them now.

"Load 'em up," Brewster called. Phillip and I backed against the wall to make room for Nat to swing his leg off the ladder and walk around to the hidden attic. Nat joggled the board loose and undid the latch, and he and Phillip helped seven people out of the hiding place. Elodie emerged last. I removed my kepi and placed it on her head, then followed her down the rungs of the ladder.

Brewster handed over my and Phillip's swords without a word.

The wagon boards creaked under the load as we crawled in. I was wedged between Elodie and Phillip, my leather scabbard pressed against my thigh. Brewster's men covered us with fresh hay until I was buried under thin stalks of straw. Elodie sneezed from the hay dust, and I hung my face down so not to get any in my eyes. The irritating straw made it nearly impossible to breathe. I craned my neck back and blew out until I made a little hay window through which to see and breathe.

The wagon lurched forward, and we bumped onto the road. Stars glinted against the inky night. The tips of my boots were wedged between the feet of a hollow-eyed man who sat across from me. I held my left leg straight so my sword wouldn't dig into my thigh.

"Tch, tch!" the driver called from his high seat. No one in the wagon spoke. The hay shifted and settled down around my chin.

Our bodies jostled against each other with each shake of the wheels. The air was warm, and hay stuck to my damp skin, making the ride miserable. Shreds of tobacco clung to my hair. The toasted pipe smell reminded me of the men that smoked pipes on Cusabo.

I gritted my teeth as the wagon wobbled along, chafing at the notion that I could walk quicker than we were moving. Phillip's knee pressed against mine, a reminder to stay calm. He hooked his arm through the crook of my elbow, and I rested my temple against his shoulder.

Just a while longer, I told myself when I began to get restless. At least you're not in a casket, and there are no rats in this wagon. I bided my time thinking about what Phillip had shown me in the loft. The idea of brawling with someone made me uneasy. Mama Jane always insisted that fighting wasn't ladylike, that she wanted Ruth and I to be respectable. The idea of respectability rolled around in my mind. What good was being dignified if you lost your head? The way I figured, it was better to seem respectable, but know how to fend for yourself too.

My hips were numb and it was still dark when the wagon finally turned off the road and onto grass. I stretched my neck and blew the hay dust out of my face. As the driver slowed, I could see a white steeple aglow in the moonlight.

"Whoa," the driver called low when we reached the back of the church. He climbed down and knocked on the door with three hard then two soft thumps, waited a spell, then repeated his rap.

"Who's there?" a deep voice asked.

"Friends," the driver called. A latch clacked, and a large barrel of a man stepped out.

"How many?" the man asked.

"Nine," the driver said.

"Take 'em down."

The back hatch of the wagon creaked open, and crush of bodies eased. The folks closest to the back hatch rolled out with a mass sigh of relief. We could all move freely again. Elodie slid out and helped a woman in a yellow kerchief steady herself. My legs shook as I hit the dirt, and I brushed off the hay that was stuck to my skin. All around me, people were stretching their legs and shaking off the dust.

"This way," The barrel-chested man said. I followed the others through an open door that slanted oddly into the foundation of the church. Stone steps led to a dug-out earthen cellar that smelled of wet clay. The door latched behind us.

Phillip's hand pressed firmly against the small of my back and guided me to a corner. Grains from the dirt wall crumbled under my fingers. An arm rubbed against mine.

Phillip breathed into my hair. "Are you okay?"

"I think so." I raised my face to his. "You know where we are?"

"No." He rested his forehead against mine. The muted prayers and whispers that filled the dank air seemed miles away. Inhaling Phillip's breath made me tipsy, like I'd taken an overlong swig of muscadine wine.

The door creaked open, and a shaft of lantern light cast the root cellar in a haunted glow. Elodie was wedged between the stairs and the woman with the yellow kerchief. A basket of cornbread was handed down, along with several jugs of water. The woman made sure Elodie got water and a large chunk of bread before she passed the basket along. The door shut, and darkness swallowed us whole. Across the room Elodie whimpered, then calmed at the murmurs of the woman.

"D'you want to sit down?" Phillip asked.

"Yes." I started to scoot down the wall.

"Wait." He worked off his jacket and spread it on the floor. "Sit here."

"Thank you." I stretched my legs out.

"You're chilled." Phillip cupped my hands in his and breathed on them.

"Am I?" His touch was like nothing I'd ever felt. I flattened my palms, and he laced his fingers into mine.

Water sloshed in a jug, and someone smacked as they chewed.

"Sitting next to you all night helped me to realize what my weakness is." Phillip's mouth brushed against my ear.

"What?" My lips curved up as I remembered our play fighting in Brewster's loft.

"It's you."

The backs of his fingers traced along my jaw and rested on my cheek. I had no words, just a tingling warmth on my skin. A fire welled up inside me. The toe of my boot tapped his, and I leaned my face into his touch.

Someone passed the basket of cornbread to us.

"Are you hungry?" Phillip asked. I shook my head. "Me neither." There was a smile in his voice. He passed the basket along, then wrapped his arm around my shoulder and pulled me close. I rested my head against his chest. His heart was pounding.

Someone started humming in the darkness. I was thankful for the noise because I was sure that everyone could hear my heart going a mile a minute.

32

Dusk melted into night as our band of travelers climbed back into the wagon. Phillip took my sword in its scabbard and laid it flat between us so it wouldn't dig into my side as it had done the previous night. Shyness had taken hold of me; I imagined that everyone knew that Phillip and I had slept with our bodies pressed against each other in a tangle of arms and legs.

The driver shook the reins, and we began to lumber north. Clouds blanketed the stars and the moon as the hay shifted and settled around my shoulders.

Underneath the dried grass, the back of Phillip's knuckles grazed mine. He twisted my ruby ring with his fingers, tugging at the gold band and twirling it against my skin. We rode like this for some time, Phillip outlining my fingers with his, making my stomach buzz like I had swallowed a hive of honeybees.

A puff of wind stirred the straw. Phillip stiffened and gripped my hand.

Metal jangled in the night air. "Ho!" a man's voice cried from the darkness. The wagon shimmied to a halt.

Phillip unlatched his sword handle from its scabbard. I felt between us for my sword and wrapped my fingers around the grip.

"Who goes there?" The driver peered into the darkness. Elodie skulked down under the hay beside me.

"Check the wagon," a familiar voice twanged. Several horses stomped and neighed.

A sour taste curdled against the back of my tongue as I searched my memory, trying to place the drawl. There was a strike of a match, and light seeped through the slats of the wagon wall. Phillip pressed against my shoulder, and I slid down as far as I could next to Elodie, who was trembling.

"Hobble them horses!"

Just then, it dawned on me where I'd heard that drawl: Tug, the slave catcher. I strained my ears for any sound from Safeen and Salaa.

"You're wasting your time," the driver said. "I'm toting this hay—" The sound of a gun being cocked stopped him short.

"Do it!" Tug commanded.

The wagon shook as the driver jumped down and walked around to the back of the buckboard. The driver fumbled with the latch and cleared his throat, as if to warn everyone in the wagon that danger was at hand.

The back board swung down, and passengers rolled out and onto the ground. The brightness of the lantern was blinding. I raised my hand to shield my eyes. Phillip scooched forward and got to his knees, holding his sword in front of him ready to fight. Tug and Bo, the slave catchers, stood on either side of the driver. A leather-clad hand came out of the shadows and shoved the driver out of the way.

Rex towered over the other men by a head and neck. I was taken aback for a moment, having forgotten how powerfully built Rex was. He ran his eyes over the back of the wagon expectantly, like a child searching for seashells on the beach.

Phillip had brought one knee up and had almost pushed himself to standing when Tug leveled a rifle at him.

"No!" I managed to holler.

"That's him." Rex pointed to Phillip.

"Anne!" Phillip shouted as the rifle exploded.

Sparks and white-hot smoke burst from the barrel. The blast was so loud that my ears rang. The other travelers looked to be screaming, but all I could hear was a high-pitched peal.

Blood splattered across my face, and I recoiled as if I'd been slapped. Phillip toppled backward and landed on the passengers across from me, who broke out into a ruckus of arms, screams, and legs. Sprigs of hay flew everywhere, kicking up a ghostly dust cloud. I blinked, dazed, as my brain tried to decipher what was happening.

"Phillip!" I pawed at the leg of his britches, but a hollow-eyed man shoved me back. He lifted his foot to my shoulder and used me as a toehold to bound over the wagon's wall. The weight on my shoulder pinned me against the wall. I would have been mad about being used as a step if I had my wits about me, but I did not, and there was no time. The lady in the yellow kerchief boosted Elodie over the side, but the wooden slats splintered and gave way, and the two of them tumbled to the ground. Elodie's eyes were wide with fear as she grabbed my arm.

"Run!" I shooed Elodie away, and she and the woman took off in the darkness.

"The slaves!" I could tell Bo was shouting, but he sounded like he was under water. "They're getting away!"

The horses reared and bucked, causing the wagon to wobble and bounce, making it impossible to stand. Phillip was on his back, using both his hands to try and lift his sword. A trickle of blood ran from the corner of his mouth, which I knew wasn't good. The shot had ripped his stomach wide open, and blood was gurgling from his injury. My mind focused on the problem. Pressure, I thought. I needed to press down on the wound to stop the bleeding. He and I were the only two folks left in the wagon. I stretched my arm out as I crawled to him. Nothing mattered but Phillip. All I wanted was to lay myself on his chest and share my cure with him.

The light dimmed then brightened as I took hold of his boot. I reached out my hand to touch his belly—but somebody tugged on my hair. The bones in my neck ground against each other as my head jerked back. I held on to Phillip's boot as I was towed across the planks. For a few seconds, I dragged Phillip's body with me, until his boot slipped off his foot and into my hands.

Another gunshot exploded as Rex lifted me from the cart.

Metal buttons dug into the side of my cheek. Rex knocked the boot out of my hands and spun me around so I saw Phillip half-hanging off the tail of the wagon.

"The horses broke free of their hobbles," Rex said. The wagon barreled away with Phillip in it.

"No!" I reached out, as if by some miracle I could stop the wagon and take hold of Phillip.

Rex lessened his hold and buried his face in the crook of my neck. "That went better than expected."

I spit dust out of my mouth and shrieked as I kicked Rex's legs, trying to get free of his grasp. My mind only knew one truth: I had to get to Phillip. I must heal Phillip.

"You're a slippery one," Rex said as he wrapped his arm around my middle. I kicked at his shins, and he clasped his good hand around my neck and pressed his thumb against my windpipe till I sputtered to breathe. The outer edge of my vision went dark, as if I were staring down a tunnel, and the world started to slip away. As soon as I went limp, he released his hold, and I fell to his feet, gasping and gagging.

The horses' hooves grew distant, and the runaway slaves' shouts of "Over here!" and "This way!" echoed in the darkness.

"Slaves are getting away!" Bo yelled.

"Let them go," Rex said.

A rifle blasted, and I jerked. A cloud of gunpowder rose above our heads.

In one swift movement, Rex shifted his weight, drew his sword, and ran Bo through with his blade. The slave catcher slumped a rifle's length away. The coppery-sweet smell of blood mixed with the hot sulfa of gun smoke. Tug lowered his lantern and shrank back from us.

"Where are Safeen and Salaa?" I croaked at Tug. "Our horses." My voice was raspy. I'm not even sure he understood me.

Tug's slouch hat tipped to the side as he shook his head. Rex lunged forward and thrust his sword into Tug's belly. Tug's eyes and mouth gaped wide as he fell back. I opened my mouth to scream, but nothing came out. I'd never seen anyone killed before, and watching two men be cut down right in front of me made my body shake like I was having a fit.

"Don't fret, my lamb." Rex spoke all gentle as he slipped his hand under my arm and lifted me to standing. "Phillip will live to fight another day." He wiped the blood from his blade on my britches leg, then slipped it back in his scabbard.

Rex was right. That gunshot would have killed any mortal man, but Phillip would live. I nodded, soothing myself that he spoke the truth.

Rex pinned my arms behind my back and twisted some rope tightly around my wrists.

"Why didn't you take Phillip's head?" I managed to ask.

"Didn't see any need to." Rex took me to his horse. "I got what I came for."

"Take me to him," I pleaded. "Let me heal him, and I'll go anywhere you want without a fight."

Rex gave a chuckle as he heaved me over the saddle on my stomach, my legs and arms dangling on either side of the animal. "You go ahead and put up a struggle if you mean to," he said. "I'll just choke you till you pass out."

He would too. I tried to calm myself by taking several deep breaths and staying still. I needed to think, to plan how to get myself free. Rex had me overpowered. It was useless to fight back right now. I needed to just go along and save my strength for later. Bitterness rose in the back of my throat.

He climbed on behind me and gave the horse a kick. The stench of manure wafted from his boots and legs. Draped as I was over the saddle, my ribs and hip pressed against Rex's thighs. Being so close to him made my skin prickle like I was crawling with fleas.

With every trot, I thudded against the saddle like a doll made of cast-off rags. Rex gripped the back of my belt to steady me, and the horse broke into a gallop. I was too dazed to cry. Too much had happened in a matter of minutes for me to be sure if all this was real. All I could think about was the gaping wound in Phillip's belly.

A steam whistle pierced the night, followed by the rumble of a train. We clambered over a hill, and Rex dug his heels into the horse as we bounded down the slope. The horse galloped to the tracks and cut close to the train.

A silhouetted line of boxcars came into view. Rex ran the horse parallel to the train, picked me up like I was a bale of cotton, and heaved me into an open boxcar. I flew into the blackness, then landed hard on my stomach. There was no chance of hollering; the wind had been knocked clear out of me. I skidded across the floor and banged into a wall. White heat exploded on my scalp as my ears filled with the crack of my head against wood.

33

A high-pitched whistle jolted me awake. I was rocking to and fro, face down on a wooden floor. In that muddled, half-asleep, half-awake moment, I imagined myself back in the casket on my way to the Hermitage. Then it occurred to me that I couldn't feel my arms; they had gone numb from being tied behind my back. Hot breath puffed against the back of my head, and something nuzzled against my side. I rolled away and blinked, trying to understand what I was seeing: Rex fast asleep. His lips were parted, and it struck me that he looked almost angelic, like a child. I kicked my boots against the floorboards and scooted myself away from him.

Calm down, I told myself between the throbs of my skull. I quickly surveyed the room, searching for any means of escape. The rail car's door stood ajar. Specks of dust danced in the first rays of sunlight.

Rex blinked, sat up, and rubbed the sleep out of his eyes.

I rolled to my stomach and managed to rock myself up to my knees, then wobbled to one side and pushed myself to standing. Rex's mouth curled up as he watched me struggle.

I smiled back at him, just to let him think we were of the same mind, then I took off running for the train door. Rex moved quickly for someone who had just woken up, sliding forward and jutting his foot out to trip me. I fell flat on my belly. A puff of grit rose around me, and I let out a sneeze.

"Gezuntheit." Rex stood and fished out a length of rope from his coat pocket. He tied the doors of the freight car shut as best he could and turned to face me. Rex was a bull of a man with a thick neck and broad shoulders. He moved deliberately, confident of his strength. For a moment, I considered playing frail, then running when I got the chance, but his lips pulled back into a smile as if he was reading my thoughts. Right then and there, I made up my mind not to show a grain of weakness. Just to show myself that I meant business, I twisted my face into a scowl, then scooted backward until my back was against the wall of the rail car.

"No reason to fret." Rex's voice was all honeyed. The sword that hung at his hip was huge, the weight of it causing his belt to sag. Crafted into the metal of the pommel was an eagle, its beak gaping wide in a screech. On seeing his sword, I instinctively reached for mine, then squeezed my eyes shut when I remembered the last time I'd had my sword was the previous night in the wagon.

Rex drew a thin dagger as he took a few steps closer to me, and my whole body went stiff. "Lean forward," he said. When I didn't budge, he lifted me off the floor, then set me back down with my back facing him. He sawed at the rope until it frayed loose, and my hands were free.

I rubbed my blistered skin.

"I'm not so bad," Rex said. His bottom teeth were crooked, and his eyes were a touch too close together, yet by some miracle, when he grinned his eyes lit up, and his face became almost attractive. A gold rope with several charms, one a gold coin, hung around his neck.

Slowly, the memory of the past night's events began to take form, and I chewed on my lip to keep from fretting about Phillip's bloody shirt. He hadn't even been given the chance to fight before he'd been shot like a rabid dog. My hands squeezed into fists at the thought. Thank goodness he'd only been shot, but bullet wounds tended to fester unless the ball was removed and the flesh cleaned. Tears clung to my eyelashes. Phillip was God-knows-where and bad-off, all because of me. Everyone had been cast out into the night just because they'd been in the same wagon as me. Maybe I was cursed.

Rex cocked his head to the side, reached into his jacket pocket, and pulled out something small and round. "I plucked this a few days ago." He held it to his nose and inhaled. "I've been saving it for a special moment." He sank his teeth into the fruit, and the sweet balm of apricot wafted past me. My mouth went dry, and I forbade my stomach to growl.

Rex ate slowly, savoring every bite to the last. "Isn't it magnificent when something so simple and pure ripens to perfection?" Rex wiped his mouth with the back of his sleeve and tossed the fruit's pit over his shoulder. He'd not taken his eyes off of me for a second, and I returned his leer with my evilest eye.

"I've been told of your beauty, but to be quite honest, mere words could never have prepared me for the depth of you." Rex inched closer. "You are a siren that I am compelled to follow." He fell to his knees in front of me and unlaced his glove.

Nausea replaced my hunger.

"It must have been torturous for Phillip to be so close to you, but not to have you." Finger by finger, Rex tugged at the leather, until at last, he presented his stump to me. The skin on what was left of his hand looked like it had been melted, folded over on itself, and hardened. Only his pointer finger and thumb were undamaged; the other fingers were just nubs.

"Heal me." Rex held what was left of his hand out to me.

I drew back. The thought of touching him made me ill.

"Do it." He grabbed my hand and laid it on his. His skin was thick and calloused in some patches, but thin and impossibly smooth in others. My fingers curled over his scars. There was no feeling, just emptiness. I closed my eyes as he wiggled his nubs against my palm.

"The wound is too old; there's no spirit left in it," I said. "I can't put back what's already been taken."

"Charlatan!" Rex jerked himself free and curled his injury under his neck, like a wolf licking a wounded paw. He flapped the glove in the air a few times to expose the finger holes, and little pieces of steel wool spilled out. He worked the leather back over his hand.

"What happened to you?" I asked.

"Not your concern." Rex walked to the crack in the rail car door. The wind blew his black hair back while he fiddled with the laces of his glove until he had them tied at the wrist. He molded the leather where the tips of his middle, ring, and little fingers should have been. I supposed the shards of steel wool filled out the hollows in those fingers.

Rex saw me watching him and straightened himself. "Wishing you'd never left home?"

I wondered what he knew about me and where I had come from.

"You're quite intoxicating, Anne." My name dripped from his mouth. "I feel heady, just being close to you, as if I have been victorious in battle and am now ready to reap my rewards." He crouched beside me.

I brought my heels close to my body, making myself as small as I could.

"Not to worry, my lamb." Rex tapped his fingers on my knee, then ran his good hand down to my ankle. "I won't take you, although by all rights you are mine." He hooked his finger inside the rim of my boot. "No, you must remain pure for Valen."

"No." My voice cracked. I cursed myself for speaking, but I couldn't help it: Valen's name filled me with a hellcat fury.

"Ah," Rex said. "So you remember him."

I closed my eyes tight and tucked my chin to my chest.

"Phillip has no doubt poisoned you against Valen."

My eyes shot open at the way he spit out Phillip's name. "Phillip's a gentleman!" It was all I could think of to say.

Rex lifted the back of his gloved hand to his mouth as if my words had stung him. The corners of his lips curved up, then he gave a laugh. "You love him," he said. "Your eyes light up when you say his name."

I kicked out, but Rex grabbed my leg and squeezed my shin hard.

"Don't fight me," he said. "I could break you like a dry twig, and trust me, you'd be much easier to handle broken." He released me, and I drew my legs together and brought them close to my side.

"Now," Rex said, sticking with his thought, "I suppose that you believe Phillip loves you too." He pursed his lips. "Did he tell you that he loved you? Is that why you followed him?"

I considered Rex's weak spots. Could I move fast enough to jab him in the eye?

"He was taking me to my sister." My voice was as tight as I could make it.

"Was he now?" Rex cooed. "I suppose the noble Phillip never once mentioned the glory and riches he would receive once he returned you to your lord and master, Bello."

"What?" I heard my voice before I realized that I had spoken. My mouth and mind unyoked. The name Bello made my lips ache. A sweetness ribboned through me.

"I see that he did not," Rex said.

Bello. The image of a man filled my memory. I saw his face clearly: eyes that took in the smallest details, the sharp line of his jaw, the bridge of his nose slightly crooked from where it had been broken with the pommel of a sword. I had healed him, but not completely. I remembered telling him that I preferred him slightly blemished, not so perfect. He had been mine, and I had loved him completely.

"Did you honestly think that Phillip was escorting you to Amaranth out of the goodness of his heart?" Rex's voice rose high. "To your sister?"

The steam whistle blew. "Who is Bello?" I asked.

Rex held my stare for a moment. "The ruler of the Amaranthine sept." He spoke with a tinge of respect.

"He was my husband." I touched my ring.

"You were bound to him," Rex said. "It's curious that Phillip or Ram-An did not speak of him. What did they tell you of Valen?"

"Only that he is vile and craves power above all else," I snapped.

"I suppose the valiant Bello only wants you to love and cherish." Rex's eyes flashed. "The truth, my dear Anne, is that you are a talisman. Whoever possesses you has health and wealth." He settled himself next to me and pressed his shoulder against mine. "Don't be a little fool. Bello wants you for the same reasons Valen does."

I only wished to be alone to sort out all that I was feeling.

"It does me good to be close to you. You are a tonic to these weary bones." Rex rubbed his cheek against my head, then took my hand and examined my ruby ring. "Dolomite gold from the Amaranthine mines," he said.

I tried to wrestle free, but his grip on my wrist was tight. He tugged the ring off my finger and turned it over in his palm.

"Healing ruby." Rex's words came out as a whisper. He bit the gold to test its strength, then polished the metal against his shirt.

"It's mine." I held my palm out.

He reached behind his neck and unclasped the gold rope, then added my ring to his collection of charms: a black pearl, a gold coin etched with my profile, and a jeweled silver cross.

"You can't have it." I snatched at the necklace, but he raised his elbow and blocked my reach.

"It will pay for your passage." Rex rethreaded the necklace.

"It was a gift from my sister," I said through clenched teeth.

"I'll keep it safe for you." He slipped the necklace under his shirt, then ran his fingers through the tips of my hair. "It's a shame they cut your tresses."

I kept quiet.

"Would you like to know how Valen spoke of you?"

"No."

"Hair, black as a raven's wing, that cascades in loose curls down her back." Rex pressed the flesh of his thumb against my stork bite. "Eyes blue and clear as the Aegean Sea." His finger traced the outline of my ear and down to my jaw. "Lips full and red as a budding rose."

"Enough." I twisted away from him.

"You will find that Valen—and I—can be quite generous. When we get to New York City, you will be fashionably dressed and shod. I will give you all that a lady of your status requires."

He had raised his eyebrows and uttered the words "New York City" as if it was a special treat. I hummed a ditty that Mama Jane used to sing when we were sowing seeds in the garden, shutting my ears to Rex's nonsense.

34

The train's boxcar measured seventeen of my boots long by eleven wide, and as far as I could see, there was no escape. When I paced the walls, Rex stuck to me like a second shadow, always a hand's grasp away. When I managed to fall asleep, I awoke with his fingers braided into my hair. I slapped him away, but he offered no apology; he just grinned like a hungry child caught with his spoon in the jam jar.

The train slowed to a crawl as we approached yet another station. Rex untied the rope that held the door shut, then coiled it around his wrist as he studied me.

"I won't run," I lied.

"Hold your arms up." Rex wrapped the rope around my waist, tied a knot, and coiled the remaining length around his gloved hand. He walked me to the open door like I was a dog on a tether. The wind rustled my jacket as the train rocked over a wooden trestle and into swampland. In the distance, brick chimneys rose above the treetops and black smoke curled into the clouds.

"Are we going to get off at the station or jump?" As soon as the word "jump" escaped my lips, I noticed Rex's hand on the small of my back. Without a word of warning, he shoved me from the train.

Arms flailing and screaming in terror, I flew through the air and splatted face down in a bog. Rex splashed somewhere close by. The pit reeked like dead skunk, and it didn't taste any better. I gagged, spit, and blew out of my nose. Rex fumbled with the rope at my waist, then towed me out of the muddy water, up an embankment, through some willows, and onto dry land.

"Wait." Using the inside of my shirt, I dabbed at my watering eyes as I caught my breath. "What is wrong with you?" I shoved his chest, but he didn't budge.

Rex regarded me with a mixture of curiosity and mirth. "Welcome to New York," he said. "Hold out your hands."

I spit in his face.

"Feisty." Rex arched one eyebrow as spittle dribbled down his chin. "I like that." He wound a length of rope tightly around my wrists and yanked it so hard that my hands grazed just below his belt. He gave a low, guttural sigh and raised an eyebrow. My face wrinkled in disgust. I wanted no part of him or his vulgar games, so I dropped my eyes and kept them glued to the ground.

Rex's long, muscular legs took much longer strides than mine. I had to take two steps for every one of his just to keep pace. I feared that, had I not been able to keep up, he would have dragged me behind him like an anchor. We scrambled up a hill to a pasture where a herd of sheep grazed and a ribbon of smoke rose out of a narrow shed. Before us, garden plots stretched out to the tree line. Women and children worked between the rows of vegetables. I stared and nodded to them as we passed, wanting them to see me, to remember whatever they could about me. Their shoulders tensed as they cast their eyes down and turned away.

The hay-strewn dirt streets of New York City were bustling with activity. A group of men unloaded crates from a wagon, and a mob of children chased each other. Signs hung over shops advertising wares, and long boards had been laid over the ground in front of the storefronts to keep the mud out of doors. The wooden planks bounced and creaked under our weight.

Rex guided me across the street and between two buildings.

A woman carrying a chicken backed away and pinched her nose as we passed. The alley opened into a long yard that ran as far as I could see. Speckled guinea hens squawked and cleared our path. Scrawny dogs with whip tails trailed us past privies, chicken coops, and cook fires. Rex stopped short as a bucket full of dirty water sloshed out from a door and splashed on his boots. A plump woman with a ruddy face caught sight of us and shrank back into the shadows.

We stopped in front of a faded red door with chipped paint. Rex knocked once, and the door cracked just enough for a man to poke his head out. He was lean, no taller than me, with narrow eyes and skin the color of mustard root. I took a quick step back, and Rex yanked at the rope, stopping me from going any further. The man swung his head from side to side. Satisfied that we were alone, he waved us in, then bolted the door behind us.

Rex and I stood in a corridor at the foot of a staircase. Rex shrugged off his wet overcoat, and it fell to the floor in a heap. My stomach let out a growl at the aroma of roasted meat. Rex untied the rope at my waist and let the length of it puddle on the floor. I held my bound hands out, and he loosened the knot.

"Panita," he called.

A petite woman glided down the stairs. Her black hair, fine as silk, was piled on her head and held in place with silver combs. She wore a shimmery red dress embroidered with dragons. She ran her eyes over me and wrinkled her nose.

"No good," Panita said to Rex.

Rex shoved me toward her. "Bathe and dress this girl in clean clothes—something pretty, with lace—then bring her to me." Rex lumbered up the stairs, his boots leaving a trail of mud.

Panita called out something in a foreign tongue, and two young girls appeared from another room. She pointed to me, then shooed them outside. She gave a sigh, then motioned for me to follow her upstairs.

The second-floor landing was open to the parlor below. Mirrors and paintings of naked women hung on crimson walls. Cigar smoke wafted through the air, and the faint trill of laughter echoed from closed doors.

Panita stepped to the banister and tapped her painted finger-nails against the wood as she glanced down on the room below. Several women, all wearing sheer shift dresses, leaned over the men, rubbing their necks as they sat around a table playing cards. One of the men reached down and pinched a girl's bottom, and she giggled.

I must be on guard, I thought as I backed away from the balcony. Why had Rex brought me to this place? He was dead wrong if he thought I was going to wear next to nothing and sit on his lap.

"Come," Panita said. She led me along a hallway and up another flight of stairs, these more narrow than before. She fished a skeleton key out of her pocket and unlocked a heavy door. The room we entered was bare, save for a bed and a wooden hip bath. Sunlight streamed through lace curtains, casting snowflake patterns on the floor. The two young girls appeared behind me, each lugging two pails of water. Panita said something to them, and they dumped the water in the basin and scurried from the room.

"You wash." Panita motioned to the bath, then crossed her arms and stared at me, waiting.

The idea of undressing in front of a total stranger in broad daylight seemed shameful and improper. I tugged at my shirt collar and grabbled with the top button, managing only to undo it partway. Then I went down on one knee to untie the laces on my boots, but the knots were caked with mud and near impossible to undo, so I gave up. Straightening up, I glanced around the room, wishing for a screen or door to hide behind.

"Now!" Panita screeched.

"The door." I pointed to the open door, and Panita rolled her eyes, then closed it. Slowly, I peeled off my jacket and let it fall to the floor, then fumbled with the buttons on my shirt. The door opened, and the girls toted in more water, then left.

"Turn around," Panita said. She helped me get my shirt off, then unwound the cloth strap I had used to bind my breasts. I hugged my chest, trying to keep myself covered. Panita untied my boots, and I toed them off.

"Scrub." Panita pointed to the tub, kicked my dirty clothes and boots into the corner, then took her leave. I stuck my toe in the bath and shivered; the water must've come straight from the well. I knelt down in the basin, splashed water over myself, and clenched my jaw to keep my teeth from chattering. The smaller of the girls returned with a blanket, a sea sponge, and a cake of soap, then left me alone. The water turned murky as dirt loosened from my skin and hair. As the layers of dirt lifted from my body, I saw my skin again. I felt like a blossom opening to the sun.

I stepped from the tub and wrapped the blanket around me. It was warm, like it had just been taken from the oven. This small kindness made me think of Phillip, and the way he spread out his jacket for me to sit on in the root cellar under the church. Pressure started to build behind my eyes, but it wasn't the time for tears. What I needed was strength, so I dropped to my knees and started to pray, just like Mama Jane would have.

Lord, I know I only pray when I want something, and I'm sorry about that. I am in dire need of your grace. Please, please let Phillip be all right, Lord. Please keep him safe and lead him to me. I don't think I'll be able to find Amaranth without him, and I can't fight Rex by myself. Amen.

I opened my eyes, then bowed my head again and added: Please watch over Mama Jane, Ruth, Abel, Noah, and Elodie. Amen.

The door behind me swung open. I quickly stood and tightened my hold on the blanket that was covering me. Panita entered carrying a honey-colored gown with lace trim and starched undergarments. She unfolded a bodice with little stays running up and down. I held back a smile; Mama Jane had always said I was too young for a corset.

Panita helped me into the undergarment and laced it so tight that I could barely breathe. I stepped into the gown, and she buttoned the back as I fingered the delicate lace on the puffed sleeves. I'd never dreamed of a dress as pretty as this one. Panita dabbed my hair dry as best she could with the blanket, then brushed it out and braided a ribbon into a longer strand. She stood back to admire her handiwork, then reached up and pinched my cheeks like she was trying to draw blood.

"Stop it," I slapped her away.

"Bite your lip," she said.

"What?"

"Bite your lip." She pressed her upper teeth on her lower lip until it reddened. I did as she commanded, mainly because I was afraid of what she'd do if I didn't. I wouldn't have put it past her to pinch my lips.

I picked up my muddy boots.

"No," Panita said, and slapped them out of my hands.

My first instinct was to shrink away, but I was getting annoyed with her rudeness. I pointed to the boots and spoke slowly and surely: "Muddy or not, I'm not leaving these." The boots made me sure-footed, allowed me to walk on jagged rocks, and kept my feet dry.

Panita gave a huff, but I suppose she wasn't in the mood to argue. She grabbed the blanket, picked up the boots, and bundled them up.

"Come."

Barefoot, I followed her to the end of the hall to a set of double doors. She set the bundle on the floor of the hallway, knocked lightly on the door, and pinched my cheeks once more.

"Enter," Rex called.

Panita pushed both doors open and stepped aside so that I stood alone in the doorway. Rex sat at a table set for two. A feast was laid out before him. His eyes widened, and he gave a low whistle as he stood, dropping his napkin by his plate and extending his hand for me to join him. His face was clean-shaven, his damp hair slicked back. The suit he wore fit him well. In truth, he was handsome in a menacing sort of way.

I crossed the room in two strides, grabbed a buttered roll and a leg of roast chicken, and then plopped down in a chair. The taste of warm bread and butter was glorious. I inhaled deeply, taking in the yeasty aroma. I took the first precious bite, letting the butter coat my tongue. The juice of the chicken coated my fingers as I wolfed down the meat.

"Slow down," Rex said. "You'll make yourself sick." He stood to fetch a crystal pitcher, and I grabbed another piece of bread. "When was the last time you ate?" He filled my glass.

I didn't bother answering him. I had an animal need to fill myself with as much food as possible. Potatoes covered in gravy, green beans slathered in butter, and sliced chicken crowded my plate. Rex kept his eyes on me while I ate, but I ignored him.

"There's a clipper leaving tonight for Rotterdam."

I barely heard him over the sound of my own chewing.

"There won't be much in the way of comforts, but it will offer speed."

"Where's Rotterdam?" I asked between bites of chicken.

"Holland," Rex said. "From there we'll travel south to Bavaria, where our sept is."

"My sept is at Amaranth," I murmured. I had to remind myself of this fact. Then I turned to face the room. I have no idea if Rex had heard what I said, or if he was just choosing to ignore me because he was too deep in thought. Either way, he said nothing.

On the far end, between two windows, stood a bed with four carved posts rising up from each corner. A full-length mirror stood between the bed and a fancy cupboard. The room was twice the size of our cabin back on Cusabo.

Rex was silent, his eyes trained on the bed in such a way that made the tiny hairs on the back of my neck stand on end. I thought about what Phillip had said—that the women in the samurai sept did not have a voice in who they mated with. I needed to somehow take control of the situation.

"Tell me about Valen," I blurted. "Am I to be his wife?"

"Yes." Rex wore a blank expression.

I wanted to slink under the table, but I sensed he would pounce on any sign of fear. "What's he like?" I picked up my glass and dipped my finger in the water, then ran my fingertip around the rim, making a high-pitched squeak.

"Powerful." Fear and respect mingled in Rex's tone. He pushed his chair back and extended his good hand to me. "I have a gift for you in the armoire."

Rex took my elbow and guided me toward the bed, then turned to fumble with the latch of the cupboard. My mouth fell open when I saw my reflection in the mirror. Fine lacework edged my scooped neckline. The dress hugged every curve of my body, and I swayed from side to side, admiring the way the dress fell and swung. I was every inch a lady.

"Ah, here we are." Rex held out a pair of slippers. "They are Moroccan."

"Thank you," I murmured, running my fingers over the delicate beading. I slid them on my feet. They had a small heel that pushed my toes forward into the silk lining. Rex stepped aside, allowing me to admire myself in the mirror. My boots were bound to be more useful, but the slippers matched my dress beautifully. Before I could work out in my mind whether I should accept such a gift, there were two short raps at the door, then it creaked open.

Panita raised an eyebrow and gave a sly smile as she took in my form. "Carriage here," she announced.

35

The coach smelled of new leather. Rex slung his traveling bag on the floor and climbed in beside me. He drew the curtains on the windows, then rapped on the ceiling with his knuckles, and the carriage rocked forward.

"That dress certainly suits you." Rex took my wrist and placed my hand on his leather glove, like we were just another couple out for a ride. I pulled my hand away to fan myself.

My corset was so tight that I was forced to sit up straight, and I could only manage the shortest of breaths. Perhaps I shouldn't have eaten so much. The carriage bounced along, and the slit in the curtains flitted open and closed, revealing flickers of the comings and goings of people in the street. If I could have stood, I would have been pacing like a bobcat trapped in a cage.

"I require a degree of trust from you." Rex wore a tall black hat with a ribbon around the crown. His traveling coat was black wool with shiny brass buttons. Dressed so fine, he easily passed for a gentleman.

I imagined shoving the carriage door open and shouting for help. Surely a passerby on the street would offer assistance. Rex was speaking, but my thoughts drowned him out. Calm, I must remain calm. I inched my free hand to my knee and shifted my body toward the door. I met his eyes, felt my lips curl up, and gave a slight nod at whatever he was saying as my fingers slid to the door latch.

The carriage shook as it came to a halt. There was a rap on the roof, and the driver jumped down.

"We've arrived," Rex announced, and his door swung open. He shoved his traveling case into the arms of the driver. "Allow me to assist you out." He offered his hand. The air tasted salty, and tall ship masts swayed in the breeze. Colorful triangular flags flapped on posts on the back of a boat, as if they were waving to get my attention. There were so many new sights and smells, I hardly knew where to look.

However, I hardly had time to take it all in as my future bore down on me. Boarding a boat was the worst route I could take. A ship would take me further away from Phillip and Cusabo, and closer to Valen.

Rex released my hand and instructed the driver as he counted out coins.

"Goodness." I let my eyes go wide at the sights that surrounded me, but in reality, I was searching for an escape. I thought about what Elodie had said about it being best to run when there was a commotion.

Carts and carriages lined the street. Two men shouted at each other near us. Rex and the driver turned to see what the matter was, and suddenly I realized that this was the commotion I needed. My heart gave a leap, and I dashed forward, darting between the quarreling men and elbowing my way past a huddle of dockworkers.

"Hey!" The driver yelled.

A boy rolled a handcart into my path, but I dodged him and rounded a corner onto a crowded lane. I fell into the swell of people and let myself be swept up by the throng.

My toes gripped the silk lining of my slippers, and the heels of my shoes dug in the mud- and hay-strewn street. The heels were slowing me down; if only I'd insisted on wearing my boots, I could've run twice as fast. Lifting my skirt, I charged forward and resisted the urge to glance behind me. Don't look back, don't look back, I chanted to myself. Something heavy landed on my shoulder. I let out a high-pitched yelp as my head snapped back. A hand closed around my arm and pressed me into an embrace. Rex's brass buttons mashed my nose flat.

"Darling, there you are!" Rex bellowed cheerfully. He added in a low, dangerous whisper, "Run again and I will take your head." His breath was like fire in my ear. "And when I am done with you, I will make my way back to Charleston and devote myself to finding where you came from and who raised you. Then, I will take their head as well."

"You wouldn't dare!" I tried to wiggle free.

Rex crushed me against his chest. "I swear to you, everyone you have ever loved will suffer for your mistakes."

A shiver ran down my backbone. There was no doubt he'd be true to his word. We were buffeted by a wave of people. They passed us by like we were no more than an overturned crate of cabbages in the street.

Rex held me tightly, so I had no choice but to stop struggling. In truth, I could barely breathe.

"I don't want to go on any boat," I said through gritted teeth.

"I don't care." He wrapped his arm through mine and guided me toward the harbor. My bottom lip and chin were quivering.

The driver, clutching Rex's traveling case, waited for us on a walkway of wooden planks.

"Help me," I said to the driver in a shrill voice. "This man is kidnapping me." My heart was hammering in my chest.

The driver stared over my head at Rex. "Will that be all sir?" he asked.

"Yes." Rex placed several gold coins in the driver's open palm. "Come," he ordered, gripping my upper arm and ushering me toward a dock. Things were happening too quickly.

"You're hurting me." I squirmed and wriggled, trying to get loose of his grasp, but he only gripped me tighter. Something wet was running down my leg and pooling in my slipper. I was peeing on myself. Shame gushed from my core and my neck and chest prickled hot. I pulled at the skirt of my dress trying to hide what I'd done. It would be humiliating for Rex to see proof of how much he scared me.

"Stop it," Rex growled, and bear-hugged me to his chest. "Make one wrong move, and I will choke you until you pass out. Then, once we are on board, I will chain you up and let any sailor with a tuppence have his way with you."

"You need me pure for Valen," I said through gritted teeth.

"Valen will take you, virgin or not," Rex said. "I'll get paid either way."

We climbed the steep gangway of a three-masted clipper ship. A young boy carrying a tabby cat brushed by me. Men were working on the wide deck, yelling to each other, hauling ropes, and rigging sails.

A sturdy man with a leathery face caught sight of us and marched our way.

"Captain." Rex gave a nod.

"The Echo is a cargo ship, she's no place for a lady." The captain's accent sounded like Lugus's, except deeper and thicker.

Rex dug in his pocket, pulled out a leather pouch as big as my fist, and handed it to the Englishman, who weighed it in his palm. "The other half when we dock in Rotterdam," Rex promised.

"I assume she's your sister." The captain dipped his chin to me.

"She is." Rex pulled me close. "My dear mute sister."

"We don't have proper accommodations." The captain slid the leather pouch into his coat pocket.

"We'll make our way," Rex said. He led me below deck and nudged me down a ladder. The cavernous room was gloomy.

Sunlight streamed in through a single round porthole big enough to fit a hogshead barrel through. Hammocks had been strung between iron posts and crates stacked up against the walls.

Rex guided me away from the light. I tightened my undercarriage and refused to cry. I stumbled and stretched out my hands in front of me so I wouldn't run into anything. The air was musty with the odor of cut wood, strange spices, and fur.

Rex lifted a hatch. "Here's another ladder; go down." He cupped my shoulder, crowding me, as I felt my way down the rungs.

My eyes adjusted so I could make out shadows set against pitch-blackness. Rex steered me between crates and barrels to the back corner of the ship. I heard him drop his case and undo the rope that held it shut. Metal chinked as he lifted something from the bag.

"What's that?" The tiny hairs on my arms and neck stood on end.

"Hold out your hand," Rex commanded.

"No." I tucked my arms behind my back. "I'll be good. I won't run. I'll do what you ask." My breath came in spurts.

"It's too late for that." He felt around for my arms, but I twisted away. He grabbed my neck and pressed his thumb against my windpipe. I reached up to scratch him, and he twisted my wrist, then pressed it against a cold metal ring and clinked it shut. I heard the turn of a lock and felt a heaviness, then ran my fingers down a thick chain that attached to a clasp encircling a metal pole. Heat flushed through my body, and sweat beaded on my upper lip.

"Do I need to shackle your foot as well?" Rex asked.

I couldn't speak. My whole body sagged. He had won.

"Do I?" He pinched the tender flesh on my arm, and I squealed in pain.

"No." I gritted my teeth.

"Shrews who can't be trusted end up in chains." Rex

rummaged through the duffle and tossed something on the floor. "Sit," he demanded.

I didn't want to sit. I wanted to yank against the post as hard as I could and free myself, but I knew that was impossible. I dropped to the wadded blanket, tucked my legs under me, and hung my head as Rex moved things about. How had I let this happen? I stared down at the floor even though all I could see was darkness. I was stuck; shackled in a pit. Phillip would never find me here.

"I'll be up on deck." Rex walked away, then stopped. He shuffled, then came back. The blanket tugged as he crouched next to me.

"You may be thinking that once we are under sail you can free yourself and swim to shore, or just sink to the depths and walk across the seabed to dry land." His voice was soft, almost kind. "After all, you cannot drown, but even we immortals are no match for the vast sea." He ran his finger along the inside of my arm. "Do you remember what happens to our kind on the ocean floor?"

I didn't.

"The sleep of the deep," Rex said. "You see, the sun's rays can't penetrate the depths of the ocean, so it's biting cold down there. You will only be able to swim for so long before you become exhausted and sink to the bottom, where you will freeze. Tangled in seaweed, you'll drift with the currents until you wash ashore, half eaten by crabs and the like. It's a gruesome existence." He stood, and I heard him climb the rungs of the ladder. A painful lump rose in my throat.

"I wish I'd never left Cusabo." I buried my head in my hands and sobbed until my eyes were swollen and my face tight.

The sleep of the deep. Rex's words rang in my ears.

36

When I was just a child on Cusabo, a young man from the settlement stole a laying hen from a farmer. There was a big to-do about it, with a trial and everything. The Cusabo elders decided the thief should be punished, and since there wasn't any jail on the island, they stuck him in an abandoned well. The elders gave him food and water once a day but forbade anyone to speak to him. At night you could hear that man's wails clear out to our farm. Mama Jane said that was what happened to folks when they didn't have nobody to talk to; they ended up gnashing their teeth and going out of their mind. Thinking on it now, I considered that man lucky; at least he had been watered and fed.

It was pitch black in the cargo hold, so I had no way of knowing how many days had passed. It seemed like forever. At first, I frittered away the time trying to break loose from the shackles around my wrists, but it was no use. Then I took to talking to myself until my mouth went dry, and since I didn't have any water, I thought it best to stay quiet. Mostly, I just slept and thought about Phillip. I prayed he was safe and tried not to imagine the worst.

A slow, burning ache settled in my chest when I recalled how Phillip had attempted to protect me in the wagon. If only I'd moved faster when he'd been shot. There had been such a commotion after the gunshot, but I should've pressed past everyone and laid my hands on him as quick as I could. I should've fought harder against Rex when he pulled me from the wagon.

"Phillip." My voice rasped against the darkness. "Come for me." I pictured him making his way to Norfolk and somehow meeting up with Ram-An, Marie-Hélène, and our sept's ship. He'd be searching for me now. He'd never give up. I was his weakness. I was the healer of Amaranth. I was Bello's wife.

Bello. Why hadn't Phillip told me about Bello? I dug the edge of the shackle into my thigh. Maybe Bello was the true reason Phillip would never give up searching for me. He wanted whatever treasure and honor was waiting for him once he returned me to Amaranth. In my mind's eye, I saw Phillip surrounded by sacks of gold.

My throat spasmed, and I gave a great sob, then I couldn't stop. How could I have been so thickheaded as to imagine Phillip fancied me? He was just seeing me to Amaranth for the reward. I only recalled bits and pieces about Bello, but I did remember the loyalty he inspired in the men he led.

I cried until my face was tight and my eyes puffy, then I bit the fleshy inside of my cheek until I tasted blood. What if Phillip can't find me? What if he never made it to Norfolk, but is lying in a ditch somewhere with a festering wound? Ram-An and Marie-Hélène would think I was with Phillip, and that we were still on our way to Norfolk, so they would be waiting on the boat instead of searching for Phillip or me. The whole situation was hopeless. Nobody was coming to save me. I was something I'd never been: on my own.

Rex said it was important that I stay pure for Valen. He meant chaste. Did Valen want to marry me or just take me to his bed? The idea of Valen touching me was revolting; it made my stomach churn. I couldn't let Rex hand me over to Valen. The sobs came in hiccups, and I clenched my fists until my nails dug into my palms.

Bit by bit, between tears, a notion started to take hold. Mama Jane always said that only a fool depended wholly on the hands of others, and that the able-bodied must rise up.

Rise up. Rise up. Rise up. The thought echoed in my head.

I decided right then and there that I couldn't let Rex win. He may have brute strength, but I was fast, and my wits were sharp. I may not get to Amaranth, but I'd rather freeze on the seabed than let Rex decide my fate.

After I sniffled for a bit and wiped my nose, I sat up straight and made a declaration: "I'll grapple Rex tooth and nail all the way to hell if I have to, but I will not be handed over to Valen."

37

A cat padded back and forth, mewing and scratching at the hatch to my cargo hold.

My lips were cracked and my tongue swollen. The skin on my wrist was raw from the constant chafing of iron against it. I tore at the hem of my dress, ripped off a piece of cotton, and worked it in between my wrist and the metal.

The hatch to the cargo hold creaked open, letting in a faint shaft of light. I sat upright at the sound of a cat's mewl and a child's voice.

"You want to go down there?" asked the child. "Is it a rat?" The cat scratched against wood. "D'you smell a rat, girl?"

I smell a rat, I thought. His name is Rex. My heart skipped at the groan of the hatch lifting. The shaft of light widened.

"Go on, then," the child said.

The cat's paws hit the rungs of the ladder. Soon, it brushed up against my leg and mewed softly. I scratched her ear with my free hand.

"C'mon, puss," the child called from above. "C'mon, Boots."

Boots' purr reminded me of the low howl of the wind. She nuzzled her body close to mine, then pawed her way into my lap. Bending my head low, I rubbed my nose between her ears.

"Here, girl," the child called. There was a tremor in its voice, then the scrape of shoe leather on the ladder. "Boots? Kitty?"

Boots was curled up in my lap, kneading the pleats of my skirt. The child huffed and closed the hatch.

"Someone has given up on you," I whispered as I ran the tips of my fingers through Boots' short fur. For the first time in what seemed like months, my heart felt light. The cat stretched its neck, and I tickled under its chin.

"Who knew a little kitty could make me smile?" I spoke in a sing-song voice. "Is your name Boots?" The kitty mewed at her name. I started to hum a little ditty, and Boots batted at the piece of cloth wedged under my shackle.

Later, the child's footsteps returned, and the hatch squeaked open. Light sank into the darkness, giving the cargo hold a hazy glow. Crates and boxes were stacked on top of each other, and barrels were chained together and penned into corners. I was shackled with an ancient-looking cuff to an iron post that ran from the floor to the ceiling.

The tabby cat twitched her ears.

"Boots?" The boy wore worn leather shoes, and the hems of his pants were frayed. He held his candle high and twisted his head from side to side.

I lifted Boots up, and she yowled in protest. The boy swung around, wide-eyed, jabbing his candle like a dagger.

"She's here." My voice was a hoarse whisper.

The boy stood stock-still, then let out his breath. "I'm sorry, miss."

I raised my shackled arm as high as I could and licked my lips. "Can you bring me some water? Please?" My throat was bone dry. "I'll give your cat back."

The boy considered Boots, who had settled in my lap, then inched back until his heel hit the ladder. He pivoted around and scrambled up the rungs.

My shoulders sagged as I ran my fingertips over my face. My

cheeks felt hollow and my skin flaky. I had no way of knowing what kind of ghoul I looked like.

The boy returned with a wooden bucket, which he placed on the floor. He used the toe of his boot to slide it to me. A tin mug floated in the lukewarm water.

"You don't look like a witch." He backed up two full arms' lengths.

"I'm not," I said between gulps, but he didn't seem convinced. "Is that what Rex is saying?"

The boy nodded. "He told the captain you have the pox and are infective."

"I'm not sick." The water had a musty smell, but I didn't care. I splashed some on my face.

"I don't like him," the boy said.

I wanted to tell him not to fret, that Rex wouldn't harm a child, but that could very well have been a lie. "Just stay clear of him," I said, then lifted Boots up. She wiggled in protest.

The boy laid the candle on a crate, stepped forward, and cradled the twisting cat in his arms.

"I'll bet she's a good mouser." I tried to smile.

"The best." The boy grinned. He was missing his front teeth and had a splash of freckles across his nose. He was maybe ten years old. He eyed my iron bracelet. "What'd you do?"

"Tried to run away." I smoothed the cotton separating my skin from the metal ring. "Didn't make it too far."

"I ran away." He seemed proud to share this fact.

"Really?" I asked. "Where from?"

"Home."

"Where's home?"

I tried not to smile as he cocked his head to the side. "A pig farm," he said. "I never would have left if my dear mother hadn't died of the Yellow Jack fever." He blurted this out fast, but his eyes welled up anyway.

"I'm sorry for that," I said. "You must be very brave to be such a young sailor."

The boy gave a shrug.

"I thank you for the water," I said. "Can I ask you a question?"

"I suppose."

"How many days has it been since we left New York City?"

"Three."

"How many more days until we get to Rotterdam?"

"Depends on the wind," he said.

I wanted to ask the boy if he would help me, but he was already taking a chance by just bringing me water. If Rex thought this boy had given me any assistance, he'd snap his neck and throw him overboard. "You'd better get back on deck. You don't want Rex to catch you down here."

The boy gathered the bucket, mug, and candle, then turned to go.

"You should take Boots with you," I said.

"No, she needs to stay down here and get the mice. They like to burrow in the buffalo hides."

"Ah, so that explains that funny smell." I sniffed. It was a musty fur smell mixed with dried leather.

I watched the boy make his way between the crates. He paused for a moment halfway up the ladder. I wondered if he had changed his mind about his cat.

"My name's Rory," he called in a low voice. Then he scurried away, leaving me and my new companion in darkness.

38

If it hadn't been for Rory, I would have shriveled to skin and bone. Every night, while the other sailors slept, he smuggled water and food down to me and emptied my waste bucket. Best of all, he talked to me and reminded me I was flesh and blood.

"Gerald says I shouldn't be coming down here. He says if Mr. Watts or the captain finds out—" He gave a shudder at the thought.

Using my fingers, I scooped horsebeans from a tin cup. "He's right," I said, as much as I hated to admit it. It was selfish to ask Rory to risk his hide for me. Besides, how much help could someone so young be anyway? "Who is Mr. Watts again?" The constant hunger had made me weak and dulled my ability to hold onto a thought for very long.

"The first mate. Gerald says he's like a dog that's been poked one too many times with a stick. You never know when he'll turn on you."

"What does Rex do all day?" I asked.

"Reads in his cabin mostly. At night he dines with the captain; they play cards or chess into the wee hours."

The muscles in my shoulders tensed. "Of course." The notion that Rex was passing his days in leisure made my skin prickly hot. I supposed he thought he was teaching me a lesson. He wanted me to believe that hope had forsaken me. I swigged the last of the water and gave the bottle to Rory, who slipped it in his britches pocket.

"I'd better get back." He turned to leave.

"Can't you stay a bit longer?" I knew I sounded pitiful, but I was past caring about appearances. I spread my blanket out to give him room to sit. "How'd you come to be on the Echo?"

Rory plopped himself beside me, and Boots stretched out between us. "After my mother died, I hopped a train, and it took me to Norfolk."

"Really," I said. "That took some pluck."

"I found work at the docks helping to load the ships, then one day I met a sailor, Gerald. He said his captain was looking for a ship's boy and did I know anybody who would fit the bill. I told him I knew all about being a ship's boy."

"You lied." I nudged him.

"A little." Dimples dented his cheeks when he smiled. "I did know how to load a ship and how to tie off a line, and the rest I learned. Gerald says if I keep at it, I can make it all the way up to first mate."

"That's impressive," I said.

"Where are you from?" Rory asked.

That was a question I had been asking myself for a good while, even before I met Phillip. "I'm not sure." Back on Cusabo, I used to have dreams of a mountain that spewed fire. I always woke thinking how familiar it was, although I wasn't sure if that was because it was from a dream I kept having or because I had seen it for real.

Rory gave me a nod.

"I'm searching for my sister," I said. "It's been a real long time since I've seen her. I'm hoping she'll be able to explain things to me."

"Where is she?"

"A place called Amaranth."

"Tell me about it."

"I don't know much," I said. "It's an island off the coast of France. During high tide it's surrounded by the ocean, but during low tide there's a land bridge, and you can walk right across to Amaranth."

Rory leaned closer and cocked his head to me.

"It's wide and rocky at the bottom and gets narrower at the top, like a wedding cake. At the top is a castle-fortress. It has a spire that, at night, looks like it touches the moon." In my mind's eye, I could imagine Amaranth just how Phillip had described it. Even though I'd never seen it for myself, gooseflesh spread across my arms as I talked about it.

"I know this place." Rory grabbed my arm. "I know this Amaranth."

"Where?" I asked.

"It's just north of the port of Saint-Malo. Gerald says it's a sacred place built by the ancients."

I felt my pulse quicken. It seemed impossible that this boy could help me, but there he sat, wide-eyed and pure-hearted.

"What's wrong?" Rory asked. "Are you ill?"

"I'm fine." Fate was shining on me. "Do you think you could bring me a file or something so I can saw through this chain?"

"That will take you forever and a day." Rory examined the thick metal links.

"I don't care," I said. "I've got to try."

39

On the fifth day under sail, Rex came calling. Boots' ears twitched when the hatch opened, and she padded off to hide among the crates.

Rex's shadow floated on the ceiling as he approached where I sat, chained. He set his lantern down and regarded me for a long moment. His shoulders were broader than I remembered, and his nose and cheeks were bronzed from the sun.

"I would have brought you something to eat, but I understand that the ship's boy has taken it upon himself to do so." His words roared in my ears, but I couldn't let myself react. He hadn't come down here to kindly check on me; he'd come down here to poke me with a stick.

I backed myself against the wall and hung my head. I was going to be calm and tough. He was not going to get the best of me. I am as serene as a meadow at sunset, I told myself.

Rex knelt in front of me and took my chin in his hand to examine my face. "He isn't feeding you too well." He pinched my waist. "Your skin is sallow, and you've gotten scrawny." He pulled something out of his coat pocket. "Thirsty?" He shook the bag, and it made a splashing sound.

I grabbed the container, popped the cork, and drank until it was empty.

Rex held up a ship's biscuit. "How long has the boy been tending to you?" I reached out for the biscuit, but before I could grab it, he jerked it away. "Answer me," he said.

All I had left was instinct, which told me to be quiet on the subject of Rory. I wasn't about to give Rex any particulars if I could help it. Somewhere in the darkness, Boots hissed.

"I think the cat should go missing before young Rory, don't you?" Rex cocked his head to the side as he stood and took a step toward the crates. "It's only fitting that the cat's demise serves as an omen for the boy's passing."

The idea of Rex harming the only person who had shown me any kindness on this boat made me madder than a red wasp. I hurled the soft canteen at his feet.

"What's the matter?" Rex toed my slippers with his boot. "You don't approve of my plan? There are tales of whole ships' crews disappearing mid-voyage. I don't think one less ship's boy will make a difference to the world."

Instead of lashing out at him, I laid down and rested my cheek against the wood floor; there was no use in jabbering on with a madman. It was best to save my strength. Rex tousled my hair and pressed the back of his hand to my forehead while I fought the urge to shudder.

"Are you ill?" Rex's voice was cool, but there was a trace of concern in his eyes.

For a moment it occurred to me to speak the truth. The longer Rex kept me out of the sun and fresh air, the worse I was going to feel, but I couldn't bring myself to open my heart to him.

"Perhaps you'll think twice before defying me again." Rex straightened himself.

"I won't do you or Valen any good sick," I muttered.

"Heal thyself!" A crate scraped against the floor as he leaned against it. "Or can't you?" He was toying with me the way a tomcat bats a stunned field mouse between its paws.

Without warning, Rex changed subjects. "Have you ever broken a wild horse?" There was a faraway look in his eyes.

My mind floated back to Cusabo, where gentle island ponies roamed the marshland.

"Centuries ago, there were thousands of wild horses across the plains of Europe." Rex rubbed the wrist of his afflicted hand. "They were easy enough to capture; run them into a canyon, or get close to one and slip a noose around its neck." He turned his gaze to me. "It takes patience to break a spirited animal. Occasionally, a beast can be won with kindness, but for the most part, they must be crushed before they can be made obedient." He made a fist with his good hand and pounded it into the palm of his glove. "In my experience, a crushed soul, soft and malleable, is well worth the effort." The floorboards creaked as he walked away. "Take care," he said as his boot hit the ladder. "There is talk of a storm brewing." He climbed the ladder and closed the hatch behind him.

A swell of hatred surged through me. I kicked out hard and stubbed my toes against the wall. The pain felt comforting somehow. I jabbed the air with my chained wrist, and the iron cuff tore at my skin. My fingers ran down the metal links.

I had to get free. I didn't care if I rotted at the bottom of the ocean; anything was better than this.

I tried to pull the cuff over my hand, but it was no use. Even though I had lost weight, the cuff still wouldn't fit over my hand. I yanked at each metal ring, thinking, There must be a weak link. The wheels in my head were whirling with a plan for if I successfully freed myself. I had no idea how close to land we were, or if there were any other ships around, and I doubted I could swim to shore without tiring out and drowning. Maybe I could reveal myself to the sailors and ask for their help. Would they hide me? Rory had said they had no fondness for Rex, and surely once they saw I didn't have the pox . . .

Two links in the middle of the chain were coarse; perhaps they were rusty. I rubbed the links against the iron pole. A raspy echo filled the cargo hold. I wrapped my shackle in my skirt so only the sharper edge was exposed and rubbed that edge against the rusty link. This was quieter.

I scraped the link against the cuff until my fingers were sore, then took a break to check my progress. A teensy groove had been worn in the metal, so I continued to saw at the chain.

Didn't ships have rowboats? Maybe when I freed myself, and after everyone was asleep, I could lower the rowboat and drift with the currents until I was picked up by another ship or washed ashore somewhere.

I sawed with the edge of my shackle across the rusty chain until it became hot. Sore, I rested for a while before setting myself back to work. Hopefully, Rory had found me a file and would bring it soon.

The dip and rise of the hull lessened to a gentle roll. If a storm is coming, wouldn't the waves be higher? I continued to saw a groove into the iron link.

After some time, the hatch squeaked open and light filtered through the crates. Boots crept to the bottom stair as Rory tip-toed into the cargo hold.

"Here." Rory set down the lantern and handed me a thick biscuit, tough as an oyster's shell. My teeth barely made a dent when I bit it. "It's best to suck on it first, to soften it." He reached into his pocket and pulled out first a flask of water, and then a rasp as long as a fresh quill.

"Rex knows you've been helping me." I snatched the rasp and began to furiously file at the groove I'd worn in the metal.

Rory's face turned ashen.

"Is there somewhere you can hide?" I asked.

"On a ship?" Rory glanced over his shoulder. I supposed he expected Rex to appear out of the darkness.

"I'm so sorry."

"What's done is done." Rory fingered the links of my chain. "It'll take you forever and a day to whittle through this. Have you tried to pull your hand out?"

"Of course," I said, filing as fast as I could.

Rory leaned forward and grasped my iron bracelet between his hands. "Pull." He leaned away from me, bracing his feet against the floor and using his weight as ballast so I wouldn't heave him forward.

I leaned back and pulled with all my weight at the wrist. It didn't work; I winced as the metal dug into the fleshy pad under my thumb.

"Let me try." Rory took the rasp and set to sawing at the metal cuff. His lips pursed in concentration.

"Is a storm coming?" I asked.

"Yup." Rory didn't slow down or glance up.

"It doesn't seem like it." The wind had died, and the ship felt stock-still.

"The sea gets quiet as a millpond before a gale blows in. The calmer the waves, the bigger the squall."

"What does it look like up there?" I asked.

"Like glass." Rory's hand was a blur.

The fingers of my free hand drummed against the wall. Rory stopped to check his progress. He had worn a crease in the chain. He tugged at my wrist again, trying to pull it through the shackle. Boards squeaked overhead, and rain pattered against the deck.

"What are they doing up there?" I asked.

"Tying sails and battening hatches."

A rushing sound filled my ears, and the wall creaked as the ship listed sideways. The lantern tipped on its side, and I caught it with my free hand. "Ouch!" I shook my hand and blew on my fingers, trying to get the hot oil off my skin. The ship's boards groaned as it bobbed upright.

Rory glanced up and his face went slack as he examined the ceiling.

"All hands topside!" someone called up on deck.

"Blast!" Rory continued to file with his brow furrowed and his mouth set in a hard line.

A whooshing preceded another wave. The ship tilted to its side and groaned as it righted itself. I held the lantern steady, and Rory braced himself against the iron pole I was chained to.

Above us, sailors shouted and swore. A noise picked up that sounded like pebbles being hurled against a board.

Hail.

Rory tugged at the chain.

"All hands on deck!" a sailor hollered as he stomped a floor above us.

"This isn't working." Rory threw his hands up and pushed himself to his feet. "I've got to go." He took the lantern and made his way to the stairs, the pitch of the waves making him sway side to side like a drunkard.

My whole body ached like I had been beaten. Rory had given up. I was never going to escape this dungeon, and if I did, I doubted that I had enough strength to climb the stairs. Rex had gotten what he wanted; he had broken me.

The crates slid back and forth, scuffing against the floor, and I rolled with them as far as my tether would allow, then I hung there until another wave rolled me back. I had a gnawing feeling that something bad was about to happen. This ship was going to sink, and I'd spend the rest of my days chained to this post, frozen in time on the seabed.

Rory returned with a tall, thin bottle of brown liquid, which sloshed back and forth as he grinned down at me. I couldn't help but smile back at him, he seemed so happy with himself. I was also grateful he'd returned at all.

"Hold this." He passed me the lantern as he squatted beside me. He lifted the bottle to his mouth, and popped the cork out with his teeth, then doused my wrist with thick oil until the bottle ran empty. The grease oozed down my arm to my elbow and dripped on my skirt.

"What is this?"

"Whale oil." Rory drew a rag out of his pocket, wrapped it around the shackle, and started tugging.

I bent my thumb inward to make my hand as narrow as possible. Rory sucked in his breath and yanked hard. I yelped as the iron bit into my skin and crushed the bones of my hand. The cuff slid off.

Rory rolled on his back, the empty shackle tangled in the rag. I winced and laughed as I clutched my palm and fingers with my other hand. The oil was thick, and both my hands were slimy with it, but I was free.

"C'mon!" Rory tugged on my skirt. We scurried toward the ladder with Boots at our heels.

40

I struggled up the ladder, using my elbows to steady myself on the rungs—but it was no use. I kept slipping. Whale oil coated my hands and forearms like a second skin. Rory shoved his shoulder against my backside, heaving me upward. My legs were wobbly, but the promise of fresh air kept me lifting one foot above the other until I was topside.

Salt rain stung my skin and the wind whipped my hair, but I didn't care. I took a breath and felt lighter.

Thunder boomed, and lightning cracked open the sky. It took a moment for my eyes to adjust.

The deck was in a full-blown ruckus. A sailor shoved me aside as he plunged below deck. Men slid across the planks as the ship rolled to its side. I skidded out onto the deck, smacked into the mast, and hugged it like an old friend. A wave of water sloshed over me, and my slippers washed from my feet.

"This way!" Rory grabbed my hand, but his fingers slipped through mine, and he tumbled to the deck. "Blasted oil!" He wiped his palms on his shirt, then rose, got behind me, and heaved me up three stairs.

The rain was coming down in sheets, blurring everything. We were on the back deck of the ship. I threw my arms out as I skated over hailstones to the balustrade. The ship heaved and pitched me across the deck to the opposite railing.

"It's too rough!" Rory hollered. "Get below!"

"No!" I wove my arms between the railings. Nothing could make me go back to the bowels of that ship. Lightning streaked across the sky, and I saw a clear view of the boiling sea. Three giant spouts of water that looked like sea tornados were twisting in the distance. I glanced back just in time to catch sight of a wave, big as a barn, coming right at us.

"Hold on!" I shouted. Rory laced his arms through the railings.

I took a deep breath. The ship hung on the wave, then dropped with a horrible creak. Water poured over the sides of the boat. I slid over to Rory and shielded him with my body as best I could. Shivering, he spat out water and clung to my waist. The clouds glowed purple from the constant sparks of lightning.

"You get below!" I yelled over the howling wind.

"Not without you!" Rory hollered back.

Fat raindrops mixed with hailstones splattered all around us. It felt like the Devil himself was dumping buckets of frozen rocks on our heads.

A line broke free from the back sail and lashed across my shoulders. Rory caught it, and I managed to help him loop it around his waist, then knot it to the balustrade, securing him to the ship.

A heaviness weighed on my back, as if a steamy blanket had been hung on my shoulders. The sky lit up, and I whirled around.

Rex stood on the other side of the deck, his face twisted in rage. He lifted his arms and clenched his fists. Instinctively, I knew he was going to choke me, so I lifted my greasy hands to my neck and slathered my chest and neck in oil.

Rex looked determined as a bull as he charged toward me with his head down. A layer of hailstones covered the deck between us. His mouth and eyes gaped wide in disbelief as his feet skidded on the hailstones. In an attempt to regain his balance, his arms flailed in wide circles, but it was no use. He fell flat on his back and slid along the floorboards as the ship climbed another wave.

Rory and I held onto each other. The ship plunged with a groan, and the salt water stung as it poured over us.

"Don't let go of the railing!" I screamed.

A branch of lightning flashed, and Rex's eyes, crazed and full of fury, bore into Rory. The notion hit me that Rex wasn't going to kill me, I was too important, but he would kill Rory and let the captain and crew assume the boy had gone over in the storm. I had to stop him.

The ship pitched portside. Before I could think about consequences, I threw myself with it and slid across the deck directly at Rex. His nostrils flared when he saw me barreling toward him. He caught me by the leg, but I slipped away and rammed into the far balustrades. I may have shrieked in pain; my eyes watered, and everything went blurry and slowed down.

Rex grabbed my arm, jerked me up, and spun me around. My first instinct was to start scratching and kicking, but then I remembered what Phillip had taught me. I raised my leg and kneed Rex between his legs. Immediately his face went slack, and his shoulders slumped.

Seeing that I had gotten Rex good emboldened me to hit him again. His hands were covering his groin, and his eyes were bulging. I pressed my index and middle fingers together and jabbed his eye hard. My fingers sank into what felt like gritty oyster meat.

Rex let out a roar. His breathing was heavy, and his legs planted wide as if to steady himself. Blood streamed down the side of his face. He bared his teeth like a cornered wild animal.

A fist came out of the darkness. My teeth gnashed, then cracked. Blood poured into my mouth. Another wave pitched us against the balustrade. I grabbed hold of the pommel of Rex's sword, but my hands slipped over the metal, and I tumbled back against the ship's rails and felt the wood crack against my weight.

Instinctively, my arms flailed, and my torso lurched forward as if to fold my body in half. The spray of the water was freezing, and the ocean seemed to be rising up to welcome me. Rex grabbed my skirt, jerked me forward, and threw me against the deck.

I couldn't breathe. The wind had been knocked clear out of me. The heel of Rex's boot pressed against my face, crunching my nose flat. He stepped over me. My chest burned as I choked on the air. Lightning snapped, and I lifted my head in time to see Rex run his sword through Rory's stomach.

I opened my mouth to scream, but I was too dizzy, and my mouth was full of blood and bile. Rory's body slumped forward, but the rope I'd tied him with held him in place.

"No!" I wailed. My muscles were seizing. I clawed at the wooden planks. Rory needed me; I had to get to him. If I hadn't tied him to the balustrade, he could have run. I was so stupid! I should have insisted he get below.

Rex crossed the deck to me. The side of his face was bloody, and his eyeball was bulging out of its socket.

A searing white fire of hate flared inside of me. As soon as Rex was close enough, I kicked his shin with all the strength I had.

"It's over!" Rex jerked me up by my hair. He pulled me to my knees before him.

Rearing back, I butted my forehead against his thigh. I scratched at his legs. It is not over! Not over! I chanted in my mind. The hilt of his sword came down on my head. Stars burst behind my eyes, and warmth seeped from my scalp. Not over!

"Stop fighting me!" Rex braided his hand into my hair, yanking me to my feet. He lifted me higher and my toes dangled against the deck. He coughed and hacked, then spit in my face. I tried to smile as his warm saliva dripped down my cheek. I would not show defeat. He started to drag me to the steps.

Every one of my muscles burned. I refused let him haul me below deck. If he got me back down there, I was done for.

I pawed at his jacket. Out of nowhere, Phillip's voice filled my head: Use your wits! I could see Phillip clear as day, hunkered over in Brewster's tobacco barn, teaching me to fight. Use your wits! The wind whistled as a twisting spout of water churned up the ocean and blasted the ship. Shards of wooden balustrades broke apart and blew against us. Thousands of arrows, in the form of wood chips and splinters, darted our way.

Rex released me to shield his eyes. I squatted and covered my face.

It dawned on me that this waterspout was the commotion I needed: Rex was hunkered over, set on saving himself. Now was my time to strike. Peeking through the cracks of my fingers, I saw that we were an arm-length away from the side of the ship.

I lowered my head, squared my shoulders and plowed into Rex's side with all my might. He teetered sideways into the waterspout, his arms swinging like windmill blades. His eyes were wide, and he grimaced. Seeing his fear, the look of sheer horror on his face, triggered an instinct deep in me to reach out to him. I extended my arms. The fingers of my right hand caught his gold necklace.

Rex clasped my left hand. For an instant, we gripped each other tight. I moved to pull him to me, but his fingers slid through my slippery ones. Rex plummeted back over the edge of the ship. My heart jumped in my chest, like it was me who was falling. The necklace snapped, and I closed my fist around it. Rex howled as he was sucked into the swirling whirlpool of water.

The clouds seemed to catch fire. I shook my head in denial. My brain couldn't make sense of what my eyes were seeing. The sea spout folded over on itself and collapsed. Rex bobbed in the waves beside the ship. Breathing heavily, I held on to what was left of the remaining balustrades.

Rex's lips moved, but I couldn't hear what he said. Then, slowly, he sank into the deep. Our eyes held on to each other the entire time.

"Did that just happen?" I don't know if I said this aloud or to myself. Realizing that I was holding the necklace, I glanced around for somewhere to hide it. I stuffed it down the front of my dress, hoping it would lodge in my corset.

Rory was slumped over on the opposite side of the deck. I stumbled over to him and wrapped my arms around his shoulders. His breath came in shallow gurgles. I wasn't sure if I was capable of healing anyone at that moment, but I had to try. I pressed my cheek against his and let my hand fall to his stomach. His belly was warm and sticky.

I closed my eyes and waited for that inner connection. That inner essence that latches on to the beginning of my heartbeat; the initial ka- of the ka-thunk. When it didn't come, I pressed against Rory's stomach harder. Clotted blood gushed between my fingers.

"Please God, help me heal him." Soon as I said this, a thought crossed my mind: God was punishing me for shoving Rex off the ship.

I took a deep breath and thought only about healing Rory. A searing pain cut through my middle, like I had been slashed in half. My pneuma had caught the ka-thunk of my heart.

Rain pelted my body, which felt heavy as an anchor. Rory stirred, then coughed and took a jagged breath. I hung onto him, drifting in and out of awareness of what was going on around me. My legs and arms shivered, but I was too tired to care. One of my teeth wiggled in its socket where Rex had punched me.

The sea had calmed from a rolling boil to rough waves. It was no longer hailing, but hailstones clattered over the deck as the waves crested and fell.

Rory's heartbeat grew stronger in his chest, which was sooth-ing. Phillip would have been proud of me. Wherever he was now, I hoped he was okay.

My mind drifted back to all those hollow-eyed folks in the wagon. I prayed that they'd made it safely to freedom. The woman in the yellow kerchief had clearly already taken a shine to Elodie; I pictured them both in an open field on the Quaker settlement in Delaware. Rex had killed Tug and Bo, so they wouldn't have had anyone chasing them. Ruth would have liked Elodie, and Mama would have taken her in like she was one of her own, just like she did with me. Some people are just born generous.

"Anne." Rory squirmed above me. "Anne! Wake up!"

It took all my gumption to open my eyes. Rory fumbled with the knots of the rope that held him to the side of the ship.

"Anne!" He gulped in air. He shook me by the shoulder and reached his other hand under his shirt to examine his midsection. His eyes were big as portholes, and his face was confused as he patted his healed wound. Then the tears came.

"How?" he sobbed, pressing his face into my hair.

Gratitude and love washed over me and lit me up as if I had swallowed a piece of the sun. Rory's love seemed to pass into me, or perhaps my healing had passed through him and back to me. I don't know. I was too worn out to consider these notions as the wind and water swept over us.

"Where's Rex?" Rory yelled. He hooked his arms under mine and helped me to my feet.

"Shoved him over." I felt no remorse or joy for what I had done. It just was. Rory took my elbow, and we wobbled down the steps and toward the ladder that led below deck.

41

Rory hobbled down the ladder, and I limped after him. Grizzled faces gawked at us. Soaked sailors huddled together, riding out the storm. Rory held his arms out protectively and pressed me back against the ladder's rungs. A map was pinned to the wall next to pegs that held coils of rope, hooks, and clothing. Sleeping hammocks swayed, and Boots mewed from somewhere in the throng. The smell of brine, stale tobacco, and spilled rum was overpowered by the musk of men who had labored hard and not washed for days.

"Here ye go, lass." An old man held out a blanket, and Rory grabbed it.

"That's Gerald," Rory whispered as he wrapped the cloak around me.

The sailors pressed closer, gaping at me as if it had been years since they'd seen a lady.

"Rex tried to kill us." Rory's voice shook as he wiped his eyes.

Several sailors grumbled.

"What happened?" Gerald examined Rory's ripped and blood-soaked shirt. "Are ye hurt?"

"It's just a flesh wound." Rory shrugged, but Gerald raised his eyebrows. "This is Anne." Rory stood firmly in front of me. "She's not a witch, and she's not sick either. Rex had her shackled in the cargo hold as his prisoner. On the aft deck, he tried to—to—but then, she fought him—and pushed him over. He was swallowed by the sea."

Several gasps rose up. A few sailors mumbled low, "Aye."

"You can see she fought hard." Rory pointed to my face. The sailors closest to me furrowed their brows. One muttered that Rex got what he deserved.

"How'd she get free of her shackle?" the first mate asked.

"Whale oil," Rory said.

"Did she now?" The men parted for the captain. His leathery face was more sunburned that I remembered it being when I'd first boarded the ship. His clothes were rumpled and his beard shaggy. "And where'd she come by whale oil?"

"Lantern," I said. "Rex left it with me."

The captain raised his palm. "A ship's no place for a woman." He turned to his men. "'Tis bad luck to bring a lass aboard. Rex promised me she'd do no harm, but he was mistaken, and now he's paid the cost with his life."

The captain swung around, and I half-expected him to order me to walk the plank. An inkling crossed his face.

"Murderess!" the captain shouted. His breath was sour. "Mr. Watts, lock her in the brig. We'll turn her over to the constable in Plymouth." He took a step back and glared at Rory. "Lock the lad up with her, for mutiny."

"Mutiny?" Rory grumbled with confusion.

"Come on with you," Mr. Watts said as he twisted my arm with his calloused hands. He walked too close behind me, taking wheezy breaths and seizing every opportunity to brush against my backside with his thick waist.

I held my shoulders back and chin up. There was no way I was going to let the captain or Mr. Watts think they could get me riled. But deep inside, I was panicked. Was I doomed to be chained in the dark pit of the cargo hold?

My eyes darted around the passage, taking in every cask, chest, and porthole. The muscles in my legs and back twitched. Mr. Watts led Rory and me to the back of the ship and past the hatch of the cargo hold. We stepped between stacks of wooden crates to an iron cell that was half the size of a horse's stall.

Mr. Watts jangled some keys and unlocked the metal door, then shoved us inside. The floor was covered with straw. Wind blew through a tiny porthole. Mr. Watts clanged the cell door shut, twisting the key in the lock.

I brought my hand to my heart as I turned away from Mr. Watts and lifted my face to the porthole. A salt breeze ruffled my hair. Compared to the dank dungeon of the cargo hold, the brig was the promised land. My tongue pressed against the back of my teeth, and one wiggled. Rex had knocked my tooth loose when he punched me. I shuddered, remembering the crack of his fist against my mouth.

Rory hunched over, clutched the bars, and pressed his forehead against the iron. I shrugged off the blanket and wrapped it around Rory's shoulders. He didn't respond; he just stared straight ahead with his mouth agape.

"It's going to be all right," I said. There was no way of knowing if what I said was true, but I felt better for saying it. Rory just shook his head in disbelief. A black rat with a tail twice as long as its body skittered along the base of a crate, then disappeared into the dimness.

"Plymouth?" I asked after a long silence.

Rory stood silent for a moment before he answered. "England."

Boots' paws padded against the wood, and her shadow squeezed between the bars of our cell. She rubbed her body against my ankle, then moved to Rory. He bent down and picked her up.

"The captain's cousin is constable in Plymouth." His voice cracked. He held Boots against his chest, stroking her neck with his free hand.

"I'm so sorry I pulled you into this muddle." It was the honest truth. What had Ruth said? "If you sow the wind, you reap a whirlwind." Seemed like anyone I got close to suffered just because they knew me: Phillip, Elodie, everyone in the wagon, the slave catchers. Even Mama Jane, Ruth, Abel, and Noah had been run off our farm.

"I'd do it again in a thunderclap." Rory sniffled. He sat down with his back against the ship's wall, with Boots nestled in his lap. He examined the bloodstains and rips of his shirt and stuck his finger to his belly where Rex had plunged his sword.

"Rex ran me through." His eyebrows furrowed as he searched my face for answers.

Half-truths and right-out lies swirled in my head. Rex hadn't stabbed him; it had all been a dream. He only thought Rex ran him through; Rex had really missed him and speared the balustrade.

"Rex only . . ." I shut my mouth, then tried again, "Rex's sword . . ." I stammered over my words as I met Rory's eyes. He trusted me. He deserved the truth, even if that meant he could turn on me.

I knelt next to him and spoke in a low voice. "Have you ever seen anything that couldn't be explained?"

"O'course." He kept his eyes on Boots, rhythmically running his finger along her spine.

"Sometimes—well, all the time, really . . ." I decided to stick with the whole truth. "When people or animals are sick or hurt, I can lay hands on them and make them well again." I turned my palms over.

"Like a doctor?" His lips pressed together in a grimace.

"I suppose," I said.

"Gerald's brother had his leg sawed off by a doctor." Rory glared at the iron bars.

"I'd never do that," I assured him. "Give me your hand."

I held my palm out, and he took it. I placed my other hand on top of his and took a breath, and my shoulders relaxed. A kind of peace passed between us. Rory closed his eyes, and his face softened.

"Feel that?" I asked, and he nodded.

"What is it?" His voice was a whisper.

"Love? Mercy?" I gave a sigh. "I'm not sure. But I can feel your heart pumping and the blood rushing through your veins. I sense that you have a strong constitution." Our bond was deepening.

"I feel good when I'm near you." Rory angled his body to mine. "Safer. Stronger."

He yawned as I tucked the blanket under his chin. His breathing became even and slow. It didn't matter what it took; I had to protect him. He would not be made to suffer just because he had helped me.

Loose sails snapped overhead. Boards creaked under the solid steps of the captain as he approached. My jaw clenched. I leaned against Rory and pretended to be asleep. Surely the captain wouldn't bother us if we were sleeping. Through the slits of my eyes, I could see light flickering across the ceiling. I heard him set a lantern down, then listened to him puff on a pipe for a long time. My nerves began to fray with each passing moment, wondering what he could be planning for us.

Some sort of tiny creature, perhaps a gnat, nipped at my ankles. The gnat had a painful bite for such a tiny fly. Try as I might, I couldn't ignore the maddening pest. My feet flinched of their own accord with every bite until I gave in to swatting at my legs.

"Ye cost me a fair bit of gold," the captain said.

My lips pursed at the memory of Rex handing the captain a bag of gold and promising him the other half when we got to Rotterdam. Rex would have kept something as precious as gold close to him. He probably had it in his pocket when he went overboard. I pictured Rex curled up on the ocean floor, his lips blue and his skin pasty white. His body processes would shut down while he was cast about by the ocean currents.

"Stand up," the captain said.

I pretended that I didn't hear him. If I didn't speak to him, maybe he would just go away.

"Stand," he commanded.

I steeled myself as I slowly stood. The captain was cut from a similar cloth as Rex, and I sensed that he would feed on my fear if I let him.

"Come closer," he said in a low voice. He waved for me to approach him.

Rory was slumped over on his side, gently snoring. Calmly, I stepped closer to the metal bars, but not so close that the captain could have reached in and grabbed me.

"I'm supposing ye've heard I've relations in Plymouth." He rubbed his chin with his thumb and forefinger. His lips pulled back, showing a gap between his front teeth. He grabbed the bars quite suddenly. I winced and shrank back. The corners of his lips curled up at my reaction. "Scared little field mouse," he said.

The only thing keeping him from me was those bars, and he could unlock them anytime he wanted. I had to show him that I wasn't afraid. My nostrils flared, and I pushed my sleeves up. "What do you want?"

He cocked his head to the side. "Lift yer skirt."

"I beg your pardon?" My voice cracked, and I took a step back.

"Lift yer skirt." He stressed each word.

The tiny hairs on the back on my neck stood on end. If I had been able to run, I would have been off like a jackrabbit. I bit the inside of my cheek. I quickly lifted my skirt so he could see my ankles.

"Dainty," he said admiringly.

Bile rose in the back of my throat, and I dropped my skirt. "Have you searched Rex's quarters?" I asked. "Maybe the rest of your gold is in his duffle."

"It isn't there." The captain blew a perfect ring of smoke into the cell. It floated toward me, then dissolved in the breeze from the porthole.

"I suppose I could make back yer passage by selling ye into servitude." His eyes lingered on my feet. "You'll need to be hobbled, o'course, so ye can't run."

I winced and turned away from him. I couldn't let him see that he upset me. "Rory didn't help me escape," I blurted.

"The boy'll be hanged," the captain said without a trace of sadness. "Can't have my men thinking they can go against me." He picked up the lantern and walked away.

I ran my hands up and down the iron bars, pulling at them to test for any loose or rusted areas. There were none. I stuffed my hand down into the front of my dress and dug out the gold necklace I had ripped from Rex's neck. I considered putting my ring back on my finger, but knew if the captain saw it, he would take it from me. Weighing the necklace in my palm, I wondered if it was valuable enough to buy our freedom. What if I offered the necklace to the captain, but he sold me and hanged Rory anyway? The captain wasn't to be trusted. I slipped the necklace back down in my corset; I would use it as a last resort.

The image of Rex thrashing about in the waves ran through my mind. I tried not to think of his necklace next to my bosom. As I paced, I wondered if I was going crazy. I considered what would have happened if Rex's hand hadn't slipped through mine; I would be on the sea floor, asleep and yet not. Tossing with the current. The sleep of the deep.

I wrung my hands over and over. The charms on Rex's necklace were heavy against my skin, nagging me. A reminder of what

I was capable of. What had Rex been trying to tell me before he went under the water? Had he cursed me? Was I going to be sold into servitude for what I had done to him?

I was pacing in circles, winding myself up like a string around a top. When the string is pulled, the top spins and spins until it runs out of steam. What would Phillip do if he were in my place? What would Rowan do? It didn't matter. What did matter was what I was going to do, but my thoughts kept returning to the feel of Rex's hand slipping through mine.

Sunlight began to seep through the ceiling boards and porthole. I heard the men rouse and set to their chores.

Rory sat up and scratched his head, then brushed the hay out of his hair.

"Morning," I said. As uncomfortable as the brig was, it was a far cry better than being shackled in the cargo hold.

Rory shook himself off and took stock of the cell. His eyes lit on the waste bucket in the corner, half-covered with straw. I turned my back and hummed softly as he relieved himself.

Footsteps approached, and shadows danced across the ceiling. Gerald poked his head out from around a barrel.

"Gerald!" Rory sprang forward and slipped his hands through the bars.

As Gerald walked up to the cell, he shushed Rory, then passed over two hardtack biscuits. "How ye holding up?"

"All right," Rory said.

The old man's hand trembled as he passed me a glass bottle filled with water. "Captain has unsavory plans fer ye."

"How long till we make land?" I changed the subject.

"A day or two till Plymouth, if the wind holds," Gerald said.

Rory tapped his forehead against the flat bars.

"Don't be knocking the good sense our Lord gave ye out yer head," Gerald said. "Use that noggin of yers to make a plan."

Rory stepped back and nibbled at the biscuit. "It's weevily."

His face pinched in disgust.

"It's all I've got," Gerald said to Rory, then turned to me. "Captain was making a pretty pence to ferry you and Rex to Rotterdam." Gerald lowered his voice to a grim murmur. "Now with Rex gone, he wouldn't know where to take you or who would be waiting to receive ye."

A lump rose in my throat, and I swallowed it down. I tugged on my skirt to keep myself from wringing my hands.

"Ah, lass, not to worry. We will think of some way to get you out of this jangle."

I managed a smile, but deep down I thought it unlikely that we could make a stand against the captain and his crew.

42

"**H**ow long d'you think the captain will keep us locked up?" Rory asked.

I opened my mouth, then closed it. I couldn't bring myself to tell him of the captain's plans for us when we reached Plymouth. "Until we've learned our lesson, I suppose." I brushed back his hair and a few sprigs of straw fell to his shoulder.

"Tell me the one about the trickster rabbit again," Rory begged.

"Why don't you tell me a story," I suggested.

"I don't know any." His whole face drooped.

"Of course you do," I said. "I'll bet you have lots of tales."

"Gerald is the storyteller. Just name a subject, and he can spin a yarn a fathom deep." Rory's eyes were round, and he sprang to his knees and bounced. "He has stories of electric eels, and the spice markets in Morocco, and sailing around Cape Horn."

"Does he have any about Amaranth?" I asked.

"Matter of fact, he does." Rory sat up tall and scratched his head for a moment. "Maybe I could try to tell it."

"Please do."

"It was the ancients that built their temple on Amaranth."

"The ancients?" I asked.

He nodded. "They wanted a special place to worship their

gods."

"They had many gods?" I asked.

"Like the Greeks," Rory said. "There was this high priestess who could talk to birds." Rory extended his arm as if he were drawing back the curtain of time. "She kept all kinds of birds: hawks, ravens, and little finches, but her favorite birds were golden eagles."

Bald eagles built their nests in the live oak trees on Cusabo and hunted in the marsh. Mama Jane called them the king of all birds.

"One day, the Roman army invaded. They burned villages and killed anyone who put up a fight."

"The Romans from the Bible?" I asked.

"I think so," Rory said. "One day, the high priestess was visiting a village on the mainland. Suddenly, Roman soldiers appeared on horseback to sack the town. The men of the village fought the soldiers, and the priestess led the women, children, and old folks into the woods. But the Romans chased after them. The priestess told the villagers to run to the sea, and she called her eagles to set upon the Romans. When the other birds in the sky saw the eagles attacking, they joined in. Soon seagulls, pelicans, and cormorants were swooping down on the army." He spread his fingers out and pretended his hands were birds laying into the bad men. "The villagers and the priestess got away. They were crossing the land bridge to Amaranth when some of the soldiers caught up with them. The priestess waited until all the villagers were on the island. Then, when the army was chasing them across the land bridge, she cast a spell! A great wind came, and the sea swelled. All the soldiers drowned."

"What happened to the priestess?" I asked.

"I dunno." Rory shrugged. "But Gerald says that anyone who tries to cross the land bridge to Amaranth without permission drowns."

Rowan had to be the priestess in Gerald's story. I knew enough to understand that tales either diminished or were exaggerated as they passed through the ages, but it was difficult to tell which. Still, most folktales had an inkling of truth to them.

"Have you ever been to Amaranth?" I asked.

"Ships don't sail there, if that's what you mean. The whole island is surrounded by a rocky shoal, but I've been to Saint-Malo a few times."

"How far is Amaranth from Saint-Malo?"

"A full day's walk, maybe."

"How would we get to Saint-Malo?" I wondered aloud.

"Boats leave Plymouth headed to Brittany every day. All we need to do is sneak off the Echo and stow away on a boat headed to Saint-Malo." Rory crossed his arms over his narrow chest and lifted his chin, like he jumped ships twice a day before supper.

"Do you think we could do it?" I bit my thumbnail.

"Gerald would help us," he said.

"It's a good plan," I said. The truth was—it was the only plan.

"So, I can go with you?" he asked.

"Would you rather stay here?" I gestured to our iron cell.

"No ma'am," he said.

That evening, I heard Gerald's footsteps, and Rory stood up straight when he saw the man's sunburned face.

"Can you get me the key for this lock?" Rory wiggled the tip of his pointer finger in the keyhole.

"Don't think so. Mr. Watts carries it on his belt." Gerald bent down and fiddled with the lock. "Perchance I can find you something that'll do the trick."

43

"**A**ll hands on deck!"

I rubbed the sleep out of my eyes and blinked at the blurry vision of Rory pressed up against the iron bars of our cell. Pink streaks of sunlight streamed through the porthole. Overhead, sails flapped and ropes thudded against the planks.

"S'happening?" My voice was thick.

"We're coming about in Plymouth," Rory said without looking up.

I heard a click-click-click. He was prodding the lock of our cell with two skinny, nail-like pieces of metal. The lock clacked, and the cell door squeaked open.

"C'mon," Rory whispered, and I scrambled to my feet.

Overhead, the captain stomped, and the first mate called out to drop the jib and luff up. We tiptoed past stacked crates to the crew's hammocks and pallets.

"Mind the waste buckets." Rory pointed down as we stepped over blankets and satchels to the large porthole at the back of the ship. He drew back the oiled leather that covered the opening.

The sight of rocky shoreline was the fairest sight I'd seen in a long while. Black and white birds with long yellow beaks gathered on the gray rocks, eyeing the water. If we could swim to the rocks, there was a strip of sand and oats, and beyond that, trees. Rory bounced from foot to foot. I understood just how he felt; if I had wings, I would have taken flight.

"Land," I said. "We can swim to shore."

Rory's grin dissolved. "You go." He shuffled back.

"What?" I grabbed his hand a little too tight, and he jerked it away. "See? It's right there." We were maybe two ships' lengths from the rocks.

"I can't." His chin was trembling, and he seemed to be looking right through me. "Boots can't swim."

"Gerald said he'd put Boots ashore at the dock," I reminded him. My hands clenched and unclenched. I fought the urge to pull at my hair.

"I'll sink." Rory's face went pale. He was breathing hard and rubbing his arms as if he was cold.

"No you won't," I said, then surveyed the room, searching for anything that might float. My eyes landed on a barrel with its top ajar. I rushed to it and grabbed the round lid. It was light. "This will keep you afloat," I promised. "Hold on to it and kick your legs."

Rory hugged the barrel top to his chest, and then released it. "I can't do it."

I grabbed him by both shoulders. "Yes, you can." I sounded as bossy as Ruth, so I added, "I'll be with you." I nudged him to the porthole and cupped my hands together to make a step. "C'mon, Rory, you can't stay here. The captain means to have you hanged."

The color drained from Rory's face. "How d'you know that?"

"He told me himself when you were sleeping," I said. "You have to come with me."

"Why didn't you tell me this before?" Rory's breath came fast.

"I didn't want to upset you."

"I'd rather you stab me with the truth than soothe me with a lie."

"I'll take care to bear that in mind."

I laced my fingers together and offered them as a foothold. Rory pressed his boot into my hands, and I boosted him up. He clutched the barrel top tightly to his chest, poking his head through the window. Behind us, Boots mewed.

"Boots!" Rory called.

I hoisted Rory forward, and he tipped out of the porthole. There was a splash. I leaned out the window but saw only the barrel lid bobbing alone amid the ripples.

"Blast!" I heaved myself up and dove out the opening.

Flying through the air was heavenly, and then it was over. I hit water so cold it stung with the force of a thousand bald-faced hornets. Arching my back, I came up for air. Rory was flailing two lengths away. I swam to him, and he wrapped himself around me like an octopus. He was in a panic, gasping for air as I kicked hard to keep us afloat.

The water was choppy, and the shore was a lot further than I'd reckoned. Rory clutched my neck with all his might, making it impossible to breathe. My legs kicked and my arms stroked until my shoulders and legs cramped up.

We weren't going to make it; I couldn't carry us both. My chest was on fire as I gulped mouthfuls of salt water.

"Work your legs!" I cried.

Instead of kicking out, Rory walloped me, beating me down. I was dizzy. It was hard to tell which side was up. The shoreline seemed to be drifting further away, and I could feel myself tiring out. I reached out one last time and slipped below the water. Rory climbed me, shoving me under, his legs squeezing my shoulders as I sank.

To my surprise, my feet hit bottom, and I realized that I was in just over my head. I bounded out of the water and gulped in fresh air, but Rory's weight forced me back down. My toes gripped the mire, and I pushed forward, back to the sunlight. Over and over, I repeated the movements until my head stayed above the waves. I trudged to shore.

"You can stand," I said, but Rory didn't let go. "You can touch the bottom now; I'll help you."

I swatted Rory off my shoulders, then wrapped my arm around his waist to buoy him up. His teeth were chattering so hard he couldn't talk. We waded the last little ways and crawled onto the slick black stones that jutted out along the shoreline. I lay on my side, catching my breath and spitting out the gritty water while Rory sobbed. I peered out at the channel. The Echo was a ways off, its sails flapping in the breeze. The men on deck were tiny as beetles. It seemed a miracle that the sailors had not heard our splashes; perhaps they were too busy in their work.

Crabs darted sideways across the rocks, and I cast my head back to greet the sun. "We did it!" I let out a whoop. If I'd had the strength, I would have danced a jig.

Rory was on his side, whimpering and coughing.

"You made it, Rory; you swam to shore." I patted his back. Warmth spread inside of my chest, making me feel that anything was possible. "Give me your hand." I wanted to share this victory with Rory.

Rory sputtered a bit, then threw up. When he was done, he lifted his face to mine and gave me an anguished grin as he wiped his mouth.

We picked our way through the sea grass and climbed up a craggy cliff.

"Where are we going?" Rory's feet sloshed in his boots.

"Away from here." My dress was sagging with water. The broken shells and pebbles that bit into my bare feet made me wince. It was funny: a month before, I wouldn't have given a hoot about going barefoot. Just a fortnight in shoes, and I had gone soft.

44

The wind blew at our backs as Rory and I dashed across fields teeming with prickly shrubs, rocks, and spotted mushrooms, headed for a thicket of woods just beyond. It was only a matter of minutes before the captain would realize we'd escaped; then there'd be no telling how many men would be out combing the shoreline for us.

"The captain really said he'd have me hanged for mutiny?" Rory asked when were finally under the cover of the trees.

"Yes," I said. "He told me he was going to sell me into servitude once we landed."

Rory's mouth formed a hard line, and his eyes narrowed. "He's vengeful." He picked up a stone and hurled it into a tangle of briars. "Last year, he ordered the ship's bosun, a good man, hanged for stealing a bottle of rum. In January we took on a sailor named Lin in Bridgetown. At night, Lin would play his charango, and we would all sing. He had all sorts of stories about snakes in the sugarcane fields and working in the rum distillery." Rory smiled at the memory of his friend. "Mr. Watts didn't like Lin. I'm not sure exactly why; maybe because the crew liked Lin so much. After Lin came aboard, the main sail ripped in a fierce wind. A week or so later, we got stuck in a storm, and lightning struck the mizzen mast, then the ship ran aground due east of Anegada. The first mate started whispering to anyone who'd listen that Lin was a Jonah."

"What's a Jonah?" I asked.

"Someone who brings bad luck to a ship."

"What happened then?"

"The men all liked Lin. They knew he wasn't a Jonah. But the captain and first mate took every chance to find fault with him, blaming every ill wind or spoiled tin of beans on him. Slowly, they turned much of the crew against him." Rory's face became hang-dog. "I should have helped Lin, but Gerald said to stay out of the quarrel, it was the captain's beef, and if I helped Lin, I'd be on the captain's bad side too." Rory hung his head, and his voice got soft. "They threw Lin overboard in the middle of the Caribbean Sea without a speck of land in sight." Tears dripped down his cheeks.

"I'm sorry." I put my arms around him and rested my chin on top of his head. His life had not been easy.

Rory's shoulders shook as he buried his head into my bosom. "They could've waited to put him off in the next port," he sobbed. "He'd be alive now if—if—"

I stroked Rory's back. It was impossible to say why some folks could be so mean and others tender-hearted. Clearly, the captain kept order by keeping his crew fearful of who he'd turn on next. I doubted he would rest easy knowing that he'd missed out on a chance to make examples out of Rory and me.

Rory took a jagged breath and let it out slowly, then blew his nose on his sleeve. "I'm glad I'm off that ship."

"I am too," I said. "There's no telling what would've become of you."

"You think I'll ever see Boots again?" Rory asked as we tramped through the woods.

"I hope so." It was important to stay positive, but also sensible. I had boosted Rory out of that porthole into goodness knows what. The least I owed him was hope, but I also didn't want to lie.

"We will do our best to find Gerald and find Boots." I wondered how long we would have to live in the woods, waiting for the Echo to sail to another port.

"She's all I got." The corners of his mouth turned down.

"That's not true," I said. "You've got me, and we're a team now. God don't give everybody brothers and sisters, but if you're lucky, you can find some on your own. Just 'cause we're not kin doesn't mean we can't be family."

"I suppose we've done a fair job of looking out for each other," Rory said.

"That's what kin does." I laid my hand on his shoulder. "From now on, you're my brother." A soft lump grew in my throat. Saying it out loud made it so. I hadn't realized until that moment how much I had missed having a brother—being present for someone and having them be present for me.

Rory grinned, and his whole face brightened. Seeing his smile did a world of good to lift me up and fortify my resolve to keep moving forward.

We continued to pick through the thorny underbrush. The woods ended at a low stone wall that enclosed a pasture where a herd of brown and white cows grazed. On the far side of the meadow stood a long wooden outbuilding. A young woman in an apron came out of the building, wrapped a rope around a cow's head, and led it into the shed.

"Must be a milking shed," Rory said.

"This is a dairy farm." I stood. My eyes followed the wall east, where I saw a stone chimney jut out from the trees. "The main house is that way."

We skirted the wall, and when we got near to the yard of the cottage, I heard humming. Rory motioned to a privy, and we ducked behind it.

I poked my head around the side of the outhouse to see a woman hanging wash on a line drawn between two wooden poles.

Skirts, blouses, kerchiefs, and aprons fluttered in the breeze.

We hid in the tall grass behind the outhouse and waited. After some time, a cowbell clanged. "Tea's ready!" the woman hollered, and soon four girls about my age came running to the house from the direction of the milking shed. They stopped at the door, toed off their boots, and entered the cottage.

"Stay here," I whispered to Rory. I tiptoed to the clothesline and snatched what I could. Then I slipped to the door and grabbed a pair of boots that appeared like they might fit me.

A pang of guilt flooded over me for stealing someone's boots. I understood how important a sturdy pair of shoes were, and I was taking them from their rightful owner. I skulked back to the privy with Mama Jane's voice chanting Thou shall not steal in my head. It was the eighth commandment, and I had been told my whole life to keep it holy.

When we were back in the woods, Rory scoffed at the skirt I'd given him. "I can't wear this."

I dropped my chin to my chest and let my hair fall in my face. If I could keep Rory from seeing my disgrace, it would be a miracle. "The captain and constable are going to be looking for a boy and a girl, not two milkmaids."

Rory dropped the clothes and stuck out his chest. "You said I was your brother, not your sister."

"Do you want to get to Saint-Malo?" I spoke through my teeth, trying to hide my frustration, both with him and myself.

"Yes," he mumbled.

"Then put that skirt on." I ducked behind a fallen oak tree to change.

Rory rolled up his britches' legs and yanked on his skirt. I slipped on the apron, then tied my kerchief around my head. Rory did the same, but with a scowl, daring me to comment on his appearance. My lips clamped together. I fought the urge to make a playful comment. With his hair pulled back and only his bangs showing, his rosy cheeks gave him the likeness of a young girl.

We took off through the forest heading east. After we walked a bit, the trees thinned, and black smoke swirled up into the sky in the distance.

"You think that's Plymouth?" I asked, and he nodded.

"That black smoke is from the smelter," he said.

"What's that?"

"Where they melt down the copper and tin they mine in these parts." He shifted his gaze to the south and pointed over the trees. "Gerald's house is closer to the port, behind the warehouses, just down from the Sheppard's Stile."

"What's that?"

"The pub."

I nodded slowly even though I had no idea what he was talking about, but he'd said it matter of fact, like I should know what he meant. "What's the pub?" I asked finally.

"Where folks go to drink and eat. Gerald's sister makes meat pies and sells them to the Sheppard's Stile."

"Meat pies?" I'd never heard of such a thing.

"It's like a meat stew in a crust." Rory licked his lower lip. "With carrots, potatoes, and peas."

"Let's not talk about food." I didn't need to be reminded of how empty my stomach was. I worried my loose tooth with my tongue, then stopped lest I wiggle it out of my mouth.

We hunkered down and waited until dusk to approach the outskirts of Plymouth.

Rory and I stole down alleyways, avoiding the main streets. Suppertime aromas floated from houses, and I made an effort to breathe through my mouth and not my nose so my stomach wouldn't gurgle. We turned a corner and bumped into a law man with a bushy mustache.

"Pardon me." The officer touched the brim of his hat with his short, thick club.

Rory gave a nervous giggle and bobbed a curtsy, then hooked his arm through mine and pulled me into another dingy passageway. We stopped at a stoop at the end of a long alleyway. Rory picked up an empty flour sack and shook it out before using it as a cushion against the ash covered stair. Split wood, spent ashes, and flour sacks littered the cramped space.

"What are we doing here?" I asked. Gray clouds were rolling in, and the air was heavy with soot.

"It's Mrs. Thackary's place," Rory said, as if it was plain as day who Mrs. Thackary was. "Gerald's sister," he added.

"Oh." I peered up at the darkening sky, wondering if the clouds would break. Rory rested his elbows on his knees. The door above him flew open, and a stout woman gave a screech. She shared Gerald's wide forehead and graying reddish hair.

Rory hopped up, ripped the kerchief from his head, and flapped it in the air like it was a flag of surrender.

"It's me, Mrs. Thackery," he said. "It's Rory."

Mrs. Thackery lowered the bucket and gave a throaty wheeze. "Blimey, child! I nearly doused you with dishwater." She glanced up the alley, set her bucket on the stoop, and ushered us inside a warm kitchen that smelled of pie crust. "The constable has been here searching for you both. Gerald's worried sick. The captain offered a sovereign to whoever finds ye, and the whole of the ship's crew is scouring the town." She wiped her hands on her apron.

A loud banging erupted from the front of the house.

"The constable!" Mrs. Thackery turned on her heels, her eyes darting about until they landed on a door. "In the cupboard with you both."

Mop and broom handles clattered against Rory as he opened the door. I shoved the wooden handles back and joined him in the closet under the stairs.

"Not a whisper." Mrs. Thackery shut us in and turned the latch.

The darkness smelled of vinegar and lye soap. Rory was breathing hard, his back pressed against my chest. I tried to calm myself by taking slow, deep breaths. No matter what happened, I couldn't let Rory be hanged.

Heavy footsteps came into the kitchen, and a cat mewed. The door swung open, and Gerald's ruddy face stared back at us. Rory's cat, Boots, brushed against our ankles. Rory plucked her up and hugged her to his face, and I scratched her ears.

"Glad to have ye back among the living, my boy," Gerald said as he looked Rory up and down.

"We're in disguise," Rory said.

"Wise." Gerald gave a nod. He was doing a fine job of holding his laughter in. "You both need to stay hidden, at least while the hunt is on."

"How much longer?" I asked.

"The men are tired, and it will take more than a sovereign to keep sailors out of the taverns come nightfall. The lawmen will follow suit." Gerald gave us a wink. "Tessa will make ye some supper. I gotta go back out and join in the chase for ye dastardly mutineers."

"Can you find when the next steamer leaves for Saint-Malo?" Rory asked. "We need to book two passages soon as we can."

"Aye," Gerald said, then shut us back in and latched the door.

45

Mrs. Thackery fed us meat pies, which were as delicious as Rory had described. I bit into one, and thick brown gravy, tender meat, and plump peas burst in my mouth. After supper, I sipped tea—real tea with honey—and marveled at how much better I felt.

Rory chatted with Mrs. Thackery as she mixed flour, butter, and sugar in a bowl. The kitchen was warm and lively. With a dusting of flour on her apron, Mrs. Thackery refilled my teacup and let Rory scrape the mixing bowl with his fingers. She rolled out shortbread and insisted Rory have a second cup of milk. She even poured Boots a bowl of milk. When at last Mrs. Thackery took a seat for herself, Boots crawled in her lap and purred.

"It's good luck to have a kitchen cat," Mrs. Thackery said.

"Boots has been a ship's cat for so long," Rory said. "Do you think she could be a kitchen cat?"

"Of course she could," Mrs. Thackery said. "She was born to it." Boots curled in her lap.

It was well past midnight when Gerald finally returned home. Mrs. Thackery met him at the door.

"You reek of tobacco and whiskey," Mrs. Thackery said as their footsteps came into the kitchen.

"I had a wee dram, so as not to arouse suspicion among the men that I was aiding anyone in particular." Gerald shut the kitchen door behind him. He looked at Rory and me. "I can't say as I blame ye to escape by sea," he said. "The constable is of the mind that ye are hiding in someone's hay loft."

Rory squeezed my hand. This was good news.

"Go to bed, Tessa," Gerald said to his sister. "I'll stay up with these two for a bit." He pulled out two stools from under the table and bade me and Rory to sit.

Mrs. Thackery kissed the top of Rory's head and touched my shoulder. "I put a few biscuits in yonder basket for you." She dipped her head toward the table next to the iron stove before she excused herself.

"Any word of steamers?" Rory asked Gerald.

"Aye. There's one bound for Saint-Malo at dawn. I secured two tickets in steerage."

"Thank you," Rory said. "But I got nothing to repay you with."

"I do." I stepped to the cupboard and fished out Rex's necklace from my corset, unthreaded my ring from the chain, and slid it on to my finger.

"Where's this from?" Gerald asked as he examined the silver cross, black pearl, and gold discs on the chain.

"Rex."

Gerald nodded. "Seems just that he should pay for your freedom."

"There's a dairy up the hill and to the west of here," I said. "If you get the chance, could you give them one of the gold coins? We took some clothes from them."

"I'll see to it when things settle down," he said.

"Thank you." I couldn't say it enough. "You've been so kind."

"That's what friends do, is it not?" Gerald leaned over and gave Rory's arm a playful pinch, then grinned. "Ye should have seen Mr. Watts when he found ye'd escaped. White as spring wool, he was!" The old man slapped his hand against his knee. "Captain tossed him off the ship, then ordered us crew to search stem to stern for ye."

Boots crawled into Rory's lap.

"Tessa's grown fond of the puss," Gerald said. "D'you want we should keep her for you?"

"No." Rory tightened his grip on Boots.

"It could be dangerous where we're going," I said to Rory. "Boots may fair better here. You may be safer here too."

"Do you not want me going with you?" Rory asked.

"Of course I do," I said. "It's just that I don't know what kind of danger lies ahead."

Rory mulled this over. "Maybe it is better if Boots stays with Mrs. Thackery. But I can't stay here with the captain casting about for my neck. I'm going to France with you."

"All right then." I forced a smile and smoothed my skirt, hoping I wasn't leading him to his death. I picked my teacup up and put it back down. Rory was old enough to know his own mind, I supposed.

"Would ye like some more tea?" Gerald asked.

"No thank you," I said.

Gerald went to the iron stove and brushed some ashes from the oven onto a saucer. "Rub this soot on yer face and neck. It'll add to yer disguise."

The soot was powdery black with gray flakes. Rory and I smeared it on our faces, necks, and the backs of our hands.

"Ye look more like chimney sweeps than milkmaids," Gerald said, then gave a yawn. "But ye don't resemble yer true selves."

Gerald and Rory eventually fell asleep at the kitchen table, but I stayed awake, too pent up with nerves that we would miss our boat. I wondered if Rory would be better off staying with Mrs. Thackery; the woman obviously cared for him. But I didn't see how that could work if the captain wanted him hanged. I tried to imagine what Phillip would do if he were in my place. The clear choice was to take Rory with me.

I woke him before dawn.

"May the good Saint Nicholas be at yer tiller," Gerald said. Rory threw his arms around the old man. "There now." Gerald patted Rory's back. "Yer on to a new adventure." The old man's eyes were shiny.

"Thank you." I placed my hand over my heart. Gerald opened his arms and pulled me into an embrace.

"Take care of each other," Gerald said, ushering us out the back door.

Torches cast a glow over the throng of travelers gathered at the harbor. A constable stood on a platform behind the ticket takers, eyeing the crowd.

"Keep your head down," I whispered. We huddled close behind a woman who was bouncing on her toes trying to soothe her crying baby.

The steamship's whistle gave me a start. For a moment, I was back in the boxcar with Rex. My knees wobbled. I pinched the flesh on the underside of my arm to show myself that I was really here in Plymouth. Shaking away all thoughts of Rex, I stepped forward and handed my ticket to the ship's man at the gangway.

"Steerage," he said, and tore the ticket in half. He waved his hand so I would move along, which I did. He didn't even glance at me.

Relief swept over me as I stepped on the steamer's lantern-lit deck. "We made it." I turned to Rory, but he'd gone pale as fresh cream. I followed his stare across the deck, and there, leaning against a pole and puffing on a pipe, was Mr. Watts, the Echo's first mate.

"Let's get below." I prodded Rory toward a doorway.

"D'you think he saw us?" Rory asked when we were on the stairs.

"I hope not," I said, hurrying him lower into the hull of the ship.

We wound our way down till we couldn't go any lower, then pressed into a room big as five train boxcars. Folks had spread blankets out on the floor, and others were sitting with their backs against the walls. We settled among the travelers.

The ship began to sway. Above us, the passengers who could afford it probably had chairs or beds to rest on. Down here, there wasn't even a bench, and folks took turns standing or sitting on the floor. Rory and I kept to ourselves, and the other passengers paid us no mind.

"Tomorrow we'll be in France," Rory whispered.

"God willing," I said. We had a long day and night ahead of us, and all I could do was hope that we could spend it hidden from Mr. Watts.

We passed the time making up stories about the other passengers, where they had come from, where they were headed, and what they were going to do when they got there.

My nerves were in a jangle. It was too much to believe that tomorrow I'd be in the same country as Rowan. I crossed and recrossed my legs, trying to find a comfortable position. In my mind I could hear Ruth telling me to stop fidgeting, and my mouth curled up in a smile. Ruth always thought she knew best, even when she didn't. I wondered who she was lording over now. Probably Noah and Abel. At least they could go fishing to get a little peace. Rory's head was heavy on my shoulder. He twitched in his sleep, and I wondered what he was dreaming about.

I closed my eyes. In my mind, Amaranth was a lot like Cusabo, except rockier. It would have a big house, like the one in Charleston, set atop a mountain. I recalled how Phillip had described it, and then all I could think about was Phillip. My heartbeat jumped to my throat when I thought about him twisting my ring and caressing my hand in the wagon. That really happened; it wasn't a dream, I told myself. I twisted my ring around my finger even though it didn't feel the same as when Phillip did it. Phillip's eyes lit up when he spoke about something that excited him. I longed to see him scratch at the golden stubble of his beard, and his lopsided smile. I pinched myself as a distraction, but then I did the only thing I knew to do, and that was to pray that one day I'd see him again.

46

"**A**nne." Rory jiggled my shoulder, and I jerked awake. "Can we go on deck?"

I yawned. "I suppose." He pulled me to my feet, and we picked our way through the sleeping bodies stretched out on the floor until we reached the empty staircase.

Topside, the wind tasted salty and clean. We leaned against the railing with a handful of other passengers, watching a speck of land come into view. A twang of sorrow nipped at me—I was supposed to be with Phillip when I saw France's the shoreline for the first time.

I whispered his name. An ache rose from my heart to my lips. Surely he would have made it to Amaranth by now. If he hadn't, Rowan and I would go searching for him. We'd never stop searching until we found him.

"That's it." Rory pointed. "Saint-Malo."

"Mercy." I stood on my tiptoes.

"Yep." Rory beamed. A towering church spire soared over the other buildings, and a high stone wall separated the town from the beach. A man and a child stood on the sea wall, watching our ship navigate the channel.

"Look at those turrets." I pointed to the wide, circular towers at the corners of the city wall.

"They remind me of a rook chess piece," Rory said.

"Where's Amaranth?" I craned my neck.

"Up the coast. We're making our approach from the south." Rory's kerchief whipped about his head. He reached up to tug it off, but I grabbed his hand.

"Not now. When we get ashore you can change." Our eyes met, and he gave a scowl. He was not fond of being dressed as a girl.

Side by side, we watched the fortified city come into view. Buildings and houses, some with fancy squared-off roofs, stood side by side with wide streets cutting paths between more buildings. Beyond the town were fields, and beyond that, trees. I looked to the north, toward Amaranth.

"Does that wall go all the way around the town?" I asked.

"Yes." Rory bounced from one foot to the other.

The beach was wide and looked to be made from the same muddy sand that surrounded Cusabo. Fishermen floated in flat-bottomed boats, casting nets. They raised their hands as we passed by, and Rory and I waved back.

"That's a Norwegian ship." Rory pointed to a vessel moored in the harbor that flew a red flag with a white and blue cross. "And that one's samurai." An oblong red flag fluttered atop a five-mast ship, and gold stitching glimmered in the sun in the shape of what looked like a horned lizard.

"Samurai?" My throat went dry as if I had swallowed sawdust.

"See the three-headed dragon on their flag?" Rory said, and I gave a nod. "Regular Japanese ships have a white flag with a red dot." He pointed to another boat and chattered on, but my eyes were rooted to the deck of the samurai ship. The entire crew had black hair and wore dark blue tunics with wide-legged pants. I counted twelve of them. One by one, they stopped their work to watch our steamer as we passed. One man stepped to the railing and stared directly at me. It was Hattori.

Another sailor came to his side, and when she lifted her head, I recognized Momo. Hattori took her hand in his, then pointed to our ship. Momo's jaw tensed, but she turned away from Hattori and arched her eyebrows. She gave a quick wink—or maybe it was an involuntary twitch, I couldn't be sure.

I rubbed my eyes and wondered if I was just over tired.

"They know I'm here." I rubbed the back of my neck. A prickle spiraled out from my stork bite and made my entire body tingle, as if a hive of honeybees had been trapped under my skin and chose that exact moment to try to escape.

"Huh?" Rory's shoulder brushed my elbow.

"Urchin!" a familiar voice barked.

Rory's head snapped back, his hair flying every which way. I spun around, startled by the ruckus.

Mr. Watts loomed over Rory with the milkmaid's kerchief clenched in his fist. "I knew it was you, you little scamp." Mr. Watts leered at me with bloodshot eyes. "And what do we have here?" His breath reeked with whisky and what smelled like spoiled meat. Perhaps an opossum had crawled in the back of his throat and died. "I wager the captain'll give me thirty pieces of silver for the likes of you." He cupped his hand under my arm and squeezed.

"Ouch!" I tried to wriggle away, but he was strong as an ox and quicker than I thought. "Soon as we make land, I'm booking passage on the first boat back to Plymouth, and if either of you makes a stink, I'll slit yer throats." A dagger's handle stuck out of his belt.

I glanced over my shoulder. The samurai sailors called to each other and gestured to our ship as we came about in the harbor.

"Stop yer squirming." Mr. Watts had released me, but Rory's neck was wedged in the crook of his arm. Rory's face was bright red, and spit dripped from his lower lip. Mr. Watts edged us away from the railing to the mid deck on the far side of the ship, where sailors were tossing ropes overboard and securing the gangway.

Mr. Watts unloosed the back of Rory's apron and wound the strings around his own hand so Rory couldn't run.

"Accept yer fate," Mr. Watts slurred. Sweat beaded on his forehead and neck.

"You're drunk." I flinched away from him.

"No." He leaned in too close to me. "I've had a little nip, but I am completely capable."

The cogs in my head were spinning like a mill wheel during a hard rain. We would fare better with Mr. Watts than with the samurai; of that I had no doubt. Mr. Watts may even prove to be a distraction, if he could keep himself upright and didn't vomit on his boots. If the samurai got me aboard their ship, I was done for. There were too many of them for Rory and me to take on. They'd sail me off to their islands, and I might never see Rowan or Phillip. God knows what they would do to Rory. They'd force me to be a part of their tribe, and that was something that I couldn't let happen.

Mr. Watts jerked Rory's apron strings, and Rory stumbled back and landed at his feet. Mr. Watts hauled off and kicked him in the stomach. "That's for making me look foolish with the captain."

Rory winced and curled in on himself to protect his belly.

"Stop hurting him," I said. "I'll do what you want; just let Rory be." I dropped down and slipped my hands under Rory's arms.

"Those samurai are here for me," I whispered in Rory's ear as I helped him to his feet.

Rory's forehead crinkled in confusion.

"Can't we just stay on this ship and take it back to Plymouth?" I asked.

"This ship's continuing south." Mr. Watts muttered. He drew his dagger and pressed against Rory's side, pulling him close. "Do as I say, or I'll gut this little heathen like a mackerel."

"Put that knife away," I said. "We'll go with you. Just don't hurt us."

Whether because the alcohol had made him persuadable or

he was afraid that the other passengers would notice, Mr. Watts slipped the dagger back in the scabbard on his belt.

"You'd better not run off," he said to me. One of his eyes was squinted and the other wide open. He wound Rory's apron strings around his fist and hooked his arms through my elbow then prodded us to the gangway.

47

The wharf was bustling with folks hauling all manner of sail-cloth and sack. Wisps of tobacco smoke mingled with sweat. Mr. Watts jostled Rory and me past men hoisting barrels onto a ship; his fingernails dug into the flesh of my arm. I ducked my head and used my free hand to shield the side of my face, hoping to avoid all samurai.

Mr. Watts stumbled on a loose cobblestone. Had he not been hanging on to me and Rory, he might have toppled face-first onto the street. He righted himself and swayed too close to me. "Stand up straight." I prodded him upright with my elbow, and he let out a belch.

"Lord, help us." That was something Mama Jane used to say when things seemed particularly bleak.

We stepped to the cobblestone street and waited for a man with a barrow full of oysters to pass. A child rushed past me, and I flinched. An awful, gut-clawing sense of dread had me casting my eyes down and dragging my feet. Truth be told, I was relieved to have Mr. Watts prodding me through the crowd.

From the corner of my eye, I caught a flash of blue. Before you could say "picaroon," we were surrounded by samurai. The hilts of their swords jutted out over their shoulders.

"Let us pass." Mr. Watts puffed out his chest.

Three samurai blocked our way forward, and three more closed the gap behind us. Momo stood a boot-length away from my right shoulder, staring me down like I had poisoned her best dog.

"Step aside," Mr. Watts persisted. "Who are you?"

Passengers from the steamship trudged by lugging their bags; a few of them stopped to gawk openly at the samurai.

"I am Hattori." He gave a polite dip of his head. A faint crimson glow hovered around him. "You have something that belongs to us." He ran his eyes from my brow to my boots.

Mr. Watts tightened his grip on my arm. "These two thieves escaped the brig on a British cargo ship. In accordance with maritime law, I'm returning them to England." His head was cocked to the side, and his chin jutted out.

Hattori proffered a gold coin. "How much for the girl?"

Mr. Watts let go of Rory and snatched at the gold piece, missing it. Hattori held it closer to him, and Mr. Watts managed to pluck it from his fingers. Rory took off running and quickly melded into the crowd. Mr. Watts held the coin up to study the etching, squinted at me, then back at the coin. "Fifty of these."

Hattori spoke something to his people, who all turned out their pockets and placed any gold they had into his cupped hands. He shook his head and barked an order. Straightaway, one of his men dashed back toward their ship.

My gullet tightened like I had swallowed a big piece of turnip that wouldn't go down. "I'm worth more than that," I managed to say.

"One hundred coins." Hattori inched closer.

Mr. Watts wrapped his arm around my waist and pressed his mouth to my ear. "What makes you so dear?"

I had no answer. Hattori's eyes were pools of darkness that beckoned me closer, as if in them I might discover secrets of unknown worlds. The corners of his mouth turned up like a fox that was ready to pounce on a chipmunk. I blinked and dropped my gaze.

"Two hundred coins," Hattori said to Mr. Watts, "and I'll let you walk away unscathed."

"My sister will pay you more." I'd found my voice. "She'll pay you triple whatever he offers."

"And where might your sister be?" Mr. Watts' breath tickled my neck.

"Amaranth." How could a single word strengthen me? I raised my eyes to Hattori's and said in a clear tone: "Rowan is my sister's name."

A tiny muscle under Hattori's eye flinched, and I could feel his uncertainty. His lips curved up.

"Rowan, the oracle of Amaranth." My voice was bold as I stressed each word.

Mr. Watts' eye twitched, whether in fear or excitement I couldn't tell. He licked his lips. "This girl is not for sale."

Hattori barked an order that sounded like "Ima."

The samurai sprang on us. Mr. Watts released me and drew his dagger. I moved to run, but someone grabbed me from behind and wrenched my elbows high behind me. A spray of blood hit my face, and I screamed, which was a mistake. Blood coated my tongue. I spit like mad to get the taste out of my mouth. A woman screamed. The handle of Mr. Watts' dagger protruded from his throat. He gurgled and collapsed. A swarm of onlookers had formed around us, and several samurai shoved people back.

"Help!" I hollered, loud as I could.

A hand mashed against my mouth and nose. I bit the hand's index finger and tasted a new flavor of blood. Somewhere, a child shrieked. The crowd was a whirling mass of faces. A steam whistle blew. Momo lifted my feet, while someone else hooked their arms under my shoulders.

"No!" I screamed. This couldn't be happening. I wiggled and writhed to get away. I kicked out as hard as I could and struck Momo in the jaw.

At that moment, facing upward, I had a clear view of the sky. The sun was peeking through the clouds. Seagulls scattered, and what looked like a brown blur was dropping out of the heavens. I could only watch as the blur spread its vast wings. The bird plunged its talons into the head of the samurai whose arms were hooked under mine. Arms, elbows, and feathers erupted in a frenzy. I toppled onto Mr. Watts' body; my cheek pressed against his nose. I pushed myself up and recoiled. Mr. Watts had a far-off gaze, and blood trickled from the corner of his mouth. A shudder swept through my body. I scuttled away from him and into the chaos of legs.

"Get her!" Hattori shouted.

The heel of a boot crushed my hand, but it didn't matter that I was being trampled. I crawled out of the free-for-all and took off running up the street, away from the docks. Two constables on horseback trotted past me, but they barely glanced my way. Their focus was on the ruckus.

Footsteps pounded the cobbles behind me; they sounded close, but I didn't dare turn around. I wasn't about to waste an ounce of energy looking back. A screech echoed off the buildings, then a shadow passed overhead. A golden eagle soared just above the rooftops; its wings appeared to span as wide as the street. It peered right at me, then climbed higher, as if it wanted me to sprout wings and fly too.

"Anne!" Rory bounded down the steps of a church. He had taken off his skirt, apron, and kerchief, and now resembled his old self.

I stumbled to him, breathing hard, my heartbeat drumming in my chest.

"Quick! That samurai is behind you!" Rory took my hand and tugged me up the street. "The city gate is this way." We let go of each other to weave in and out of wagons and people going about their business.

My chest was burning, but the sight of the eagle perched atop the arch of the gate spurred me on. It was Rowan's eagle! She had sent me an eagle! The great bird took flight as we ran under the arch, past wagons, and out into a grassy field.

I only slowed my pace because I heard Rory gasp. In the distance, a cloud of gray dust was rising off the road. My body trembled, and my mouth dropped open. An ancient instinct rooted deep inside me had taken over, and something pulled at my core.

At first I was flabbergasted, unable to comprehend what my eyes were seeing. The golden eagle flew to the approaching riders, swooped down over their heads, then glided to the front of their formation. A woman led the charge, her long, dark hair billowing as her horse galloped.

"It's a militia!" Rory's eyes were wide as wagon wheels.

"It's Rowan!" I shouted to the heavens. Pure joy took hold of me as I jumped up and down, waving my arms over my head to show her I was here.

In my excitement I had forgotten myself. The razor-sharp edge of a blade pressing against my neck brought me back to real life.

"Don't make a move," Hattori said behind me.

48

My legs became treasonous, quivering under me, but I locked my knees before they buckled. "Now look here—" I started.

"Silence." Hattori's curved, scythe-like blade bit into my skin.

"Let her be!" Rory came swatting at the samurai.

Hattori kicked out, and Rory hit the dirt, hard.

"Rory!" I called as he lay twitching, his eyes rolling around in his head. "You hurt me, and Rowan will take your head." Invoking her name buoyed my strength. Horse hooves rumbled on the road ahead of us, but they were still too far off to do me any good. My body began to shake, whether from fear or anger I couldn't tell. I could've spit venom, as helpless and boiling mad as I was. I shouldn't have stopped running. Hattori had caught me, and there was no one to blame but myself.

Hattori's blade dug into my neck. "I would gladly die to keep you from reaching Amaranth." I remembered Rex's words, that he would kill me himself rather than allow me to step foot on Amaranth's domain.

I am not giving up the ghost in sight of my sister, I thought.

"Do it," I said through gritted teeth. My mouth had betrayed me. I'd meant to plead for my life, to stall Hattori, but a deeper animal instinct had won out. Or was God speaking through me? Courage had been summoned, and it had its own strategy.

"As you please." Hattori drew back his blade.

"Know this: Rowan will hunt you down and take your head."

"I will die a hero to my people," Hattori said. "They will sing songs about me." He would be immortalized.

"Hattori!" Momo's voice came from behind us. Her tone was panicked, like she had an urgent message.

Hattori loosened his grip on me. I steeled myself, then rammed my head backward against his face. There was a nauseating crack against my skull, like an eggshell breaking.

Hattori stammered and released me. I sprang forward. A swoosh cut the air and a gut-wrenching burn sliced through my shoulder blade.

Arms out, I skidded across the ground and rolled over. My teeth gnashed against the grit in my mouth. Warmth oozed from my shoulder, which I was sure had been set on fire.

"Hattori!" Momo shrieked. She was closer now. I couldn't fight off two samurai. Rowan was too far away; she wouldn't be able to get to me in time. I was going to die. Black spots blotted my vision, and I wheezed. Breathing took all my effort. It felt like I was sucking in air through a hollow reed. I forced myself to roll over.

Hattori swayed. His nostrils flared, and he bared his teeth like a wild animal. Bloody snot gushed from his nose.

Somehow, he had split in two. I blinked and realized I was seeing double. "Broke your nose," I muttered, then spit the dirt out of my mouth.

I looked out to the road. Rowan's black hair flew behind her. She was so close, yet too far away to save me.

Hattori raised his sword over his head and glared down at me.

"No!" Momo hollered and jumped on his back. Hattori teetered and fell. I quickly rolled to the side. They tumbled an arm's length away from me. Hattori's curved sword thudded in the grass.

Run away, every instinct screamed, but I didn't listen. I

crawled to Hattori's sword, then pushed myself up and wobbled on my feet. The sword was heavier than I'd supposed. I held it low. Warm rivulets streamed down the right side of my back. I was bleeding, though how much, I had no way of knowing.

Hattori grunted and shoved Momo off of him. He stood, spit at her, then stumbled toward me.

"Get back!" It took all my strength to steady the hefty blade. My right arm was weak and prickled with an awful stinging from where he had sliced my shoulder. I wasn't strong enough to actually lift the sword, so I balanced the pommel against my pelvis and waved it around by swaying my hips.

Hattori pulled a dagger from his belt and jabbed the air between us. Rowan's golden eagle circled overhead.

I swayed, and the blade swung with me. Hattori lunged at me. His dagger hit my sword. A clang resounded, and a painful vibration shot up my arm. I struggled to keep from dropping it.

Hattori's grin stretched across his whole face. A clump of hair had come loose from his braid. Blood coated his upper lip, giving him a terrifying yet comical appearance. He had the stance of a swordsman, the same stance Phillip had taught me.

Hattori clanked his dagger against my sword again, and my sword lurched down to the left. A sickening, sharp pain ripped through my shoulder, radiating down my right arm, which trembled uncontrollably.

I sprang forward, jabbing my blade in his direction, but he easily moved out of harm's way. I couldn't win. I knew this. My only hope was to stay alive.

Hattori pounced at me, hammering my blade again and again, like it had personally wronged him. With every strike, spasms ripped at my arm and shoulder blade. The muscles in my left arm and shoulder quivered from exhaustion. Hattori grunted as his blade slashed against mine. The sword fell from my hands and thunked in the dirt, and my heart fell with it.

Hattori was out of breath. So was I. I held up my empty palms in surrender and stepped back.

"I've won." Hattori sheathed his dagger and heaved up his sword.

"It's over," I panted. Past him, I could see Rowan growing near. Her eyes focused, and her lips pressed into a hard line.

Hattori didn't take the time to glance over his shoulder. He hoisted his sword. His eyes bulged wide with the frenzied look of a rabid animal as he charged at me.

I staggered to the side. His sword came down with a swish, an inch away from my boot, then clunked as it bit into the dirt. The eagle circled us overhead.

I supported my right arm with my left. My head reeled, and my legs quaked.

Hattori planted his feet and lifted his sword once more. He stared directly at me, gave a curt nod, and heaved his sword back. A grunt came from behind him. His eye twitched, and his mouth flew open. He dropped his blade and started to paw at his arched back.

I shook my head in confusion. Hattori fell to his knees.

Momo stood right behind him, her eyes and mouth slack. Hattori toppled forward; a jeweled dagger handle stuck out of his lower back.

I blinked, trying to comprehend what had happened. Momo stared blankly at Hattori's back.

"Why?" I asked.

Momo inhaled sharply. A single tear clung to her eyelash. "Kinship," she said. "For you. For me. For all of us."

49

Horse hooves kicked up billowy clouds of dust. Stirrups jangled as horses surrounded us. Momo raised her hands and backed away.

A woman slid out of her saddle and faced me. A sword with a simple cross-tie hilt hung at her hip. Her beauty was fierce. Black curls cascaded over her shoulders, and her eyes were bluer than the finest indigo dye. Slowly, her lips turned up, and then her whole face broke into a smile as she held my gaze. My heart throbbed in time with hers; I could feel it. We were selfsame, two lodestones drawing one another close.

I swayed on my feet. "I'm Anne." It was all I could think to say.

"Sister," Rowan said.

I'd been longing for this moment, picturing and re-picturing it in my mind. Now that it was here, I was dumbstruck.

"You're safe now." Rowan stepped closer, and I fell into her arms. "Anne." Her voice was the sweetest sound I'd ever heard. The people who circled us seemed far away. She cupped my face in her hand. "I was afraid that I'd never find you." Tears welled in her eyes. We rested our foreheads together and stood there, lolling in each other's shine.

"Rowan." She smelled like fresh linen and warm fires. "Is it really you?" A shroud of numbness covered me, like I was waking from a deep sleep.

"Yes," Rowan said, wiping her shiny cheeks. She pressed her hand on my shoulder. I winced and recoiled. Her hand was blotted with blood from where she'd touched me. "Let's see to your wound."

"Hattori." I pointed to his figure, which lay completely still on the ground. "He tried to—"

"Don't concern yourself with him," Rowan said. She eased me away from the commotion and walked me toward her horse, who was grazing on a patch of grass.

"Momo." I searched for her in the commotion, but too much was happening. "She stabbed him."

"Who is the boy?" Rowan asked. Rory was rubbing his head, standing amongst and speaking with several men.

"That's Rory. He helped me get here. Who are all these folks?" At least fifteen people had fanned out around us.

"My guards." Rowan threw her cape on the ground and bade me to sit. She dug in her saddlebag, drew out a lambskin satchel, and opened it, revealing cotton squares, balm, several sticks, and a flask.

"Here." She uncorked the flask and offered it to me. "It's Armagnac. Drink it. It will calm your nerves."

The Armagnac stung my mouth and coated my tongue. It was harsh to swallow and set my throat on fire. Rowan used her dagger to cut the back of my blouse open.

"This is a deep laceration." She dabbed at my wound. "Take another sip of Armagnac. This cut must be cleaned before it festers."

Momo shrugged off her jacket as she approached us and held it up as a privacy barrier between me and the guards. The Armagnac went down easier now that I was used to the burn. The pear brandy was sweet against my lips and made me feel as if I could float.

"Thank you for helping Anne," Rowan said. Momo dipped her head.

"Why did you?" I asked Momo. My lips tingled as I sipped the brandy.

"You belong with your sister, not the samurai." Momo cast her eyes down.

"Bite on this." Rowan handed me a stick the size of a paintbrush stem. She splashed liquid on my open wound. The alcohol burned like a firestorm. My whole body jerked, and my teeth sank into the wood. I clenched my fists and held my breath.

Rowan let my skin dry, then dabbed balm on my shoulder. "I'm going to pack your wound to try and stop the bleeding. Are you all right?"

I nodded, unable to speak.

"Momo, what is your plan?" Rowan asked. I focused on their conversation.

"To join with you, if you'll have me." Momo leaned closer. If she was disturbed by what Rowan was doing, I could not tell.

Rowan pressed bandages against my shoulder. "Anne and I are both in your debt." She wound a long piece of linen around my chest and neck, covering my right shoulder. When she was finished, she packed her bag.

"Take my jacket." Momo helped me slip my arms in the sleeves and cinch the belt. She took a few steps back and watched the guards that stood over Hattori.

"I can't believe this is all happening." I blinked and rubbed my eyes.

"You've had a shock," Rowan said.

"I suppose." My head swirled.

"You are just as I remember," Rowan said, then dropped her head. "You must find me old."

"You're beyond anything I ever dreamed."

Rowan's face flushed. "I understand that you and Phillip have formed an attachment."

"Is that what he said?" I asked. Rowan nodded. My chest felt like it might burst. Then I remembered what Rex had said to me. "Do I still have a husband?" I couldn't bring myself to mention him by name.

"No," Rowan said. I let out a sigh and let my head fall back. "Bello stopped being your husband long ago. He has been free to marry for many years."

"Did he?" I asked hopefully.

"No." Her lips pressed together in a tight line; I felt mine do the same.

"Why not?"

"He has no need." Rowan shrugged. "Ladies flock to powerful men."

"Oh." Heat rose from my chest to my cheeks, not from jealousy, but because I wasn't sure how to react. I thought it best to talk of something else. "Why didn't Phillip come with you?"

"He is not well." Rowan spoke slowly, carefully. "His wound where he was shot festers. Ram-An removed the bullet, but he's delirious with fever."

I had no words. All the joy that had been somersaulting inside of me turned hollow.

"It's a miracle he was able to make his way to Norfolk in his condition. Marie-Hélène is with him now."

"I need to go to him." I shuffled my feet, wanting to take action but not sure what to do. "How long will it take to get there?"

"A few hours."

I groaned. "That long?"

"We'll make haste." She took my hand.

A gaggle of townsfolk gawked at us under the city gate. Five samurai stood apart from them, staring at Hattori, who lay facedown on the ground surrounded by Rowan's guards and Rory.

"Ram-An," Rowan called. One of the guards turned. "We

must leave here before we draw too much attention."

"Ram-An," I half-whispered. He was thinner than he had been in Charleston.

Ram-An tapped Rory's shoulder and pointed to me. Rory ran to my side, and Ram-An followed closely behind.

"Are you all right?" I asked.

"Think so." He rubbed his head.

"This is my sister, Rowan," I said.

Rowan bent so she could meet Rory eye-to-eye and extended her hand, which he took in his own. "I am honored to meet you," she said. "You are a hero."

For once, Rory was speechless.

Ram-An dipped his head toward me. "I am pleased to find you safe."

"It's good to see you," I said. "But Phillip . . ."

"I know." His lips curved down.

"Ram-An, assemble the guards," Rowan ordered. "We must leave now."

"What shall we do with Hattori?" Ram-An asked.

"Leave him," Rowan said. "Let him return to his sept, beaten. Momo is coming with us."

"Very well," Ram-An said. He called for the guards, and they all gathered around us.

"My sister, Anne, healer of Amaranth, has returned," Rowan said to her guards.

The guards, including Momo, bowed to me.

"Hello." I raised my hand. My mouth pursed. It flustered me to meet so many people at once. I'd never remember them all.

Rowan continued: "Anne is accompanied by Rory, and by Momo, formerly of the samurai sept." The guards nodded.

Rowan turned to Ram-An. "Can you take Rory and lead the charge?" One of the guards led Rowan's horse to her. She took the reins.

"Of course," Ram-An said, then turned to the guards. "The sisters will ride in the middle. I want an even flank on both sides and behind for their protection. Momo can ride with the rear flank. Keep a tight formation," he called to the guards, then lifted Rory onto his horse and climbed on behind him.

Rowan climbed on her horse and scooted close to the horn of the saddle. A guard lifted me behind her. There was room in the saddle for us both.

I rested the side of my face against Rowan's back and wrapped my arms around her waist in a hug.

"Do you feel that?" Rowan glanced at me over her shoulder.

"Yes." I squeezed her tighter. It was impossible to put into words. The certainty that I was complete. A rush of feeling that I'd inhaled the stars and had become part of them. In fact, I was now part of every living thing that had ever and would ever exist. I was at one with the entire world.

50

The golden eagle flew high above us, its wings spread protectivly. We rode as a group in formation across the countryside, through fields, forests, and orchards, until our path merged with a coastal trail.

A salt breeze blew. There was a time, not too long ago, when I'd taken salty air for granted; it had just always been there, like the moon and water. Now it brought a shower of memories: Cusabo, Mama Jane, Ruth, Abel and Noah, Phillip face-down in the waves, crab traps, the Echo, the captain, Mr. Watts, and the three-headed dragon on the samurai flag.

I forced myself to think cheery thoughts about Phillip, but I'd seen grown men writhe in agony from a festering wound, and it was impossible not to fret. It was as if my mind and body had been torn in two: one half perfectly contented and brimming with joyful elation over finding Rowan, and the other anxious with fear over Phillip. The image of him being trampled in the wagon, hay flying every which way, kept turning over and over in my mind. I gritted my teeth as I recalled reaching out to him, then dragging his boot with me out of the wagon. I'd taken his boot! I bit the inside of my cheek. He only had one shoe when he made it to Norfolk, just like when he lost his boot to the water moccasin in the marsh when we first left Cusabo. Fate had a curious sense of humor.

How was it possible that Phillip had made it to Amaranth and was waiting for me there? Too much had happened in such a short time, and I couldn't make sense of all that had come to pass. It was as if a burlap sack had been placed over my head and I'd been spun around and around, then told to walk in a straight line.

Time dragged on. It was almost more than my flesh and blood could bear. Gray clouds rolled in from the sea, some taking the shape of galloping horses, hooded monks, yoked oxen, and tobacco plants.

Being with Rowan had made my heart swell a hundred times its normal size. She didn't say much, other than to point out the occasional deer or stone pyre. She leaned forward in the saddle, and I with her; our intent was on Amaranth.

"How much farther?" I asked after we galloped by a walled farmhouse and village. It felt like we'd been riding forever.

"Just beyond that rise." Rowan nodded to a ridge. Ram-An and Rory bounded up the hill, and we followed.

The sun broke through the clouds and shone down on a marsh; a brilliant blue-green ocean gleamed in the distance. A jagged fortress rose out of the sea, its spire rising to the sky. Walls towered out of the craggy base, making it seem that the fortifications had been carved by the hand of God. Seagulls floated, then dove into the water surrounding the island. A fear struck me that I was having a fevered dream, and if I didn't hurry, the whole citadel would disappear in a cloud of mist.

A flock of white sheep with black faces and feet bleated as we galloped past them into the marshy lowlands and along a tidal creek that led to the sea. Waves lapped the shore, then shushed as they receded. The golden eagle called out a soft cry, and birds flew from the tallest tower of the castle. Hawks, eagles, ospreys, and owls clouded the sky. I felt my mouth go slack and my body stiffen. Had I not been with Rowan, I would have been frightened by the sight. The throng of birds seemed joyful as they soared high and dove around one another in a graceful sky-dance.

Ram-An maneuvered his horse next to ours. "The tide is high," he said. "Shall we wait to cross or swim the horses?"

"Swim!" I blurted. I sat up straight, my eyes narrowed on the island.

Rowan's horse edged to the water.

"I'll sink!" Rory cried.

"You'll be safe," Ram-An assured him.

Rowan's horse plowed into the waves like it had swum the channel a thousand times before. Water splashed and soaked my skirt to my legs. My bottom lifted off the saddle, and I squeezed my sister's waist as hard as I could. She reached her arm back and grabbed my leg.

"I've got you," I hollered. She glanced back at me, her lips curled up and her eye crinkled. I hugged her tighter and cupped my chin into the crook of her neck. We were two forces, healing and prophesy, joined together. The ocean was colder than well water, cramping my muscles as we fought against the current. Swimming in the choppy surf, the horse gave snorts but plowed ahead.

It seemed like we'd been swimming for an hour when the horse grabbed a foothold and climbed onto the island.

A man sporting a metal helmet and grasping a spear was waiting for us on Amaranth. "Madame!" He bowed.

The horse shook itself off, and I held on tight.

"Let's go!" I squeezed my legs.

Rowan leaned forward. The cobbled street snaked up and across the island. The aroma of wood smoke and old straw hung in the air. Townsfolk cleared our path and gawked as we raced past. A child darted after us with his goat on a leash. The goat wore a bell that clanged as it trotted along. The street narrowed as we zigzagged our way to the top, where we passed under an archway and clopped over a wooden bridge.

"It's Rowan!" a man's voice called.

"Raise the portcullis!" someone shouted. Chains rattled, and an iron gate lifted.

51

A fountain gurgled in the center of the courtyard. Wind whistled through cracks in the stone. Sliding out of the saddle, I turned in a circle, gazing up at the ancient walls that surrounded the cloister. I shook out my tired legs. My eyes darted from the narrow slits in the high walls to the lanterns that glowed in arched windows. I tried not to blink for fear that I would miss something that demanded to be seen.

Ram-An and Rory rode through the gate, followed by the other guards. The courtyard broke into a lively gathering of snorting horses and folks calling to one another.

"Where is Phillip?" I asked Rowan.

"The infirmary."

Rowan pushed open a heavy wooden door, and we entered a room bigger than ten Cusabo cabins. Lamps hung from rods along the walls, and the curved ceiling sparkled with tiny gold tiles. I caught a whiff of beeswax. At the far end of the room was a wide staircase.

"This way," she said.

I took the stairs two at a time, but stopped when I got to the top. The room went on forever. I blinked and squinted. The walls were made of mirrors. The ceiling rose up like an upside-down bowl, painted dark blue with stars. Somewhere, harp strings were plucked.

"Come." Rowan led me through the room. Several people pushed back their chairs as they stood, gaping at us.

Bells rang out. "What's that?" I asked.

"Chimes, to announce a guest." Rowan took my hand, and we walked quickly. The castle was a like a rabbit's warren, with hallways, alcoves, and stairwells leading every which way. We followed a corridor until we reached a stairwell that had been cut out of stone and circled around itself. Winding down the stairs, my heart lifted in my chest, and I could sense that Phillip was close.

Five iron beds lined both side walls of the room. Shelves filled with bottled tonics and powders crowded the back wall. Mama Jane should've been there to see all the herbs and potions.

In the far corner, a woman huddled over a bed, dabbing a sponge at a lump of blankets. She lifted her face, and I drew in my breath sharp. Marie-Hélène was a ghost of herself; dark half-moons hung under her eyes, and her hair was a mess of tangles. She looked as if she'd been wearing the same wrinkled clothes for a month.

"Thank the gods." Marie-Hélène wobbled to stand when she saw me.

My legs went stiff. The stale air tasted like vinegar. I swallowed, then pushed my shoulders back and pressed forward, past the empty beds to the bundled-up patient in the far corner.

Even in his sickly condition, Phillip was a welcome sight. A blanket was bunched around his head for warmth. His eyes were shut, and his skin so pale it was almost see-through. A brownish-gold beard covered his chin and mouth, and his hair was matted to his forehead.

"He's been calling for you." Marie-Hélène moved to the foot of the bed to make room for me to pass. "Take my seat." She held her hand out for me to rest on the stool.

"Hey," I whispered as I brushed Phillip's hair away from his face. His linen shirt was halfway unbuttoned, and underneath it, a bandage was wrapped around his middle.

Marie-Hélène sniffled. "Cure him." It was a feeble command.

"Come with me." Rowan wrapped an arm around Marie-Hélène's shoulder and led her toward the door. "Go find Ram-An. He has a boy with him, Rory. I need you to make sure he is fed and has clean clothes."

"But I should stay," Marie-Hélène protested.

"We also brought a samurai with us. Her name is Momo. I need you to see to her and Rory, and make sure they feel welcome." Rowan gently nudged Marie-Hélène from the room, then turned back to me after she had shut the door.

Carefully, I undid the rest of the buttons on Phillip's shirt. He grimaced as I pulled away the pieces of gauze that stuck to his belly.

"Oh, Phillip." I pushed the stool aside and sat on the edge of his bed. I needed to be as close to him as possible. Memories of what he and I had done bubbled up: the way his pulse had bounded against the hollow of his neck when he faced me in the tunnel under Charleston; the horrified look on his face after he'd cut my hair in the stable; him teaching me to defend myself in Brewster's tobacco barn; and the way he gently caressed my face as his tongue darted against mine when we kissed in the root cellar under the church.

Droplets of sweat formed at Phillip's temples as I tugged off the last bandage, this one drenched in blood. I chewed on my lower lip. His belly looked like it had been turned inside out. A layer of pus was all that was holding his insides in place. I'd never seen the like. I took a deep breath, blew it out, and arranged my face into what I hoped appeared to be the picture of calm.

My breaths came in little bursts, like I was wearing a tight corset. Without thinking, I pressed my palm into his belly. Stickiness mushed between my fingers. Heat gripped my innards, and I doubled over and gagged. A thimbleful of Armagnac and bile landed on the sheets beside him. My heart stopped, then gave a heavy tha-thunk. Blood rushed in my ears. Tingles rose up my arm, then spiraled through my whole body. A blessing washed over me like my soul had bloomed fresh.

Rowan gasped.

Phillip's body was hovering above the mattress. A wobbly feeling came over me, like I was far out to sea, bobbing weightless in salty water. The hazy realization that I was floating with him occurred to me. I breathed out, and we both sank into the mattress. A thin layer of baby-flesh now covered his belly. The skin on my right shoulder blade prickled, like I'd scratched my back with a fig leaf.

My head was sloshy. I lay my ear on Phillip's chest, listening to his heartbeat, which lulled me into a dream. Clouds hung all around me. Tiny water droplets meshed together to form a web that layered over and over and over itself. Phillip's breath became steady, then he strained to lift his head.

"Be still," I whispered. I wanted to stay adrift in the clouds.

"Anne." His voice was dry. "You came."

I raised my head and rubbed my eyes. Our noses were inches apart. Part of me wanted to dance a jig, and the other part wanted to break down sobbing.

Phillip took a shallow breath. "Knew you'd make it." His lips were cracked.

Without taking my eyes off him, I held my arm out to Rowan. "Water," I said. Rowan placed a copper mug in my hand, and I lifted it to Phillip's mouth.

"Second time." Water dribbled from his lips.

"Second what?" I ran the fleshy pad of my thumb over his scarred eyebrow.

"You saved me." Phillip tried to grin, but winced instead.

"Shh." I thought back to the morning that he'd washed up on Cusabo. It felt like I'd lived a whole lifetime since then.

"Did Rex hurt you?" he asked.

"He tried." A small bit of pride gushed through me. "I bested him."

"Of course you did." Phillip reached his hands to his middle and touched the fresh skin. He craned his neck to look at his stomach. "Only a fool would rise up against you." He lifted the back of my hand to his lips.

"Rex told me about Bello." I tried to keep my voice steady, but it betrayed me by shaking. Would I ever learn to control my feelings?

"Oh." Phillip's head fell back against the pillow, and I pretended to examine his midsection.

"I wanted to explain that to you," Phillip said, gazing up at me. "I was afraid if you knew about Bello, you wouldn't have come with me."

He was right. If I thought I might have a three-thousand-year-old husband waiting for me, I'd probably have rooted myself to Cusabo.

"I'm sorry." Phillip dropped his eyes.

I wrapped my fingers around his wrist to feel for the thump of his heart. "I forgive you." At that moment I would have given him anything.

Phillip braided his fingers into mine, then pressed the palm of my hand to his cheek. His skin had a soft flush.

There was a rustling at the doorway, and the air in the room shifted. A figure caught my eye.

A man in a belted tunic and leather britches entered the room. A sword hung low at his hip. His dark hair was duller than I remembered, a few strands of silver sparkling when they caught the lantern light. His face was perfectly formed, with the exception of the slight bend on the bridge of his nose. To my surprise, my heart sputtered in recognition; I wondered if his did too.

Bello. I felt my lips move. His smile was smooth as glass, like he knew he was in command over all that he saw. His lips parted then puckered as if he wanted to say something, but then stopped himself. He pushed his sleeves up his arms, showing well-defined forearms.

Bello lifted his hand to me. Without even thinking about it, I stood, answering his silent command. His grin widened, and I could almost read his thoughts, the sheer pleasure that I still responded to his whims without question. An icy shudder ran through me as I hesitated, then my eyes rested on Phillip. My heart broke a little at how defeated he seemed.

"It's okay," Phillip mumbled. "Go to him." His hand formed a fist, then went limp.

I parted my lips but couldn't form any words. The person standing before me was no longer the husband I had known. Time had smoothed Bello's rough edges, making him confident, controlled. Not a hair out of place. The tilt of his chin signaled that he was agitated; I wasn't rushing to his side. It was strange that after all this time I could still read his gestures and mood.

I was no longer the same person I'd been when I'd known him. My history with Bello was just that: ancient, an entire lifetime ago. It seemed only natural that I would feel something for him, but those feelings were faded, like a linen kerchief that had been washed and rewashed and hung out in the sun. I had been reborn with a different name and new desires. I needed Bello to understand that I was no longer bound to him.

The bed squeaked as I sat back down beside Phillip. "I'd rather stay here with you, if that's all right." I lifted his hand and softly kissed his knuckles. I couldn't imagine what the future held, but the one thing I was certain of was I wanted Phillip to be a part of it.

Bello cleared his throat, a reminder that he was still waiting, but I kept my head down, hoping that if I just ignored him, he'd go away.

Rowan walked up the center aisle and positioned herself between Bello and me. "My sister's name is now Anne," she said.

Gratitude washed over me. Rowan seemed to know exactly what I wanted.

"I must speak to her." Bello tried to side-step past Rowan, but she was too quick for him. She stood tall, with her arms out to block his path. They were having a tug-of-war, and I was the rope.

"Anne has had a long journey, she's been injured, and she has just healed Phillip. She needs time to recover," Rowan said. Her protective stance spurred a memory of a long-ago time, when she had risen up against Bello to argue in my favor. My sister had spent her whole life looking after me or looking for me.

Bello puffed out his chest like a cock of the walk. For a moment it seemed as if he would shove Rowan aside, but then he gathered himself. "As you see fit."

Bello's eyes met mine. "Until tomorrow," he said, sure to have the last word, then reluctantly backed out of the room. Rowan latched the door behind him and let out a sigh.

"Thank you," I said. Rowan came to me and kissed my cheek.

"I should stitch up your shoulder," she said. She motioned to the bed next to Phillip's, then stood between us and held up a sheet as a screen. I untied my jacket and lay face down on the mattress. Rowan covered me with the sheet, then stepped to the counter and returned with a set of shears that she used to cut away the bandage on my shoulder. She inhaled sharply. "This can't be."

"What?" I lifted my head.

Rowan pursed her lips as she met my eye. She rubbed her forehead, then grabbed my arm. "You've healed yourself."

"What?" She was teasing me, surely pulling my leg. I tried to wiggle my loose tooth, but it wouldn't move; it was rooted in my mouth.

Phillip swung his legs out of his bed and stood over me. He ran his fingers over the skin on my shoulder, which tickled in a heavenly manner. "Did you have an injury here?"

"Hattori slashed my shoulder." I gritted my teeth at the thought, then tried to think back to the last time it ached. "The last I remember it hurting was when I slid off the horse in the courtyard."

Phillip tucked a strand of hair behind my ear.

"Then my back prickled when I healed you," I said. Phillip glanced back to the rumpled sheets and blanket on his cot, then back to me.

"Anne," Rowan said, the pitch of her voice rising. "You healed yourself." She gave a hoot of laughter.

"That's never happened." I still didn't quite believe it. "What does it look like?"

"Like the skin on the underside of your arm," Phillip said. "There isn't a hint of a scar."

"I must've done it when I healed you." My whole face stretched into a grin. I fluttered my feet like I was swimming. It was an uncommon feeling, doing something that I'd never been able to do before. My chest puffed up. I had the rare notion that anything was possible.

Rowan went to the counter, opened a drawer, and returned with a folded-up nightdress, which I slipped over my head. "What are you planning for your next magic trick?" she asked.

"I don't know." I shrugged and twirled my ring. "Where's your ruby?" In every dream or vision that I had of Rowan, she always wore her necklace.

She reached down the collar of her robe and fished out a long leather rope. "When you gave this to me, you said it would keep me safe and healthy," she said, holding up the stone. "And so it has. But now I return this healing charm to you." She placed the leather loop over my head so the ruby rested in the hollow between my breasts. "May it shield you from all that is evil."

The stone was rough and dull, but when I rubbed it with my

thumb it glowed, much like an ember continues to give off heat after it has been removed from the fire.

Phillip sat on the edge of his bed, watching Rowan and me. "Where is my sword?" he asked.

"Under your bed," Rowan said.

He pulled out his scabbard. An ivory handle stuck out behind the thicker hilt of his blade.

"Soror." I reached out for it. Phillip drew my blade out and laid it beside me. "I thought I lost it in the wagon." My fingers curled around the hilt, then pressed it against my thigh.

"You named your sword Sister." Rowan's lips curved up, and the skin around her eyes crinkled.

"Of course," I said.

"Nothing should surprise me, yet you always do."

"I want to offer my sword to you as well." Phillip knelt beside my cot and held his blade out to me. "On my honor, and before the gods, I pledge myself and my sword to you, Anne of Amaranth." His deep brown eyes held mine.

"Thank you," I said. For the first time since being reunited with Rowan, I longed to be alone with Phillip, just like we were on the trail to Norfolk. Those days seemed far away; even though they'd been difficult, they were filled with purpose and discovery.

Rowan stood and busied herself at the wash basin on the counter.

Phillip laid his sword on the bed beside me and brushed his thumb against my cheek. "You are my weakness," he whispered into my ear.

"You are my weakness too," I said. He lifted my hand and kissed it.

Rowan dried her hands on a towel and turned to Phillip and me. "I can't remember when I've been so full of hope," she said.

"I think I was being led here all the time," I said as I reached my hand out to her. "I mean, I couldn't see that when I was in the thick of it, but now I see that every step I took was leading me to you."

I took Phillip's and Rowan's hands. A golden shine had settled around us. It was vibrating like a plucked harp string.

52

Phillip stood at the sound of knocking on the infirmary door. Rowan answered it and swung the door wide for Rory, Momo, and Marie-Hélène. Rory bounded down the aisle. He had bathed and was wearing a white tunic, leather pants, and new boots.

"This is how the men dress here," he said. His cheeks were rosy and his eyes bright.

"It suits you," I said, sitting up in my bed so I could see everyone.

"They fed me chicken and bread. I even had apple tart."

"All I've had is broth and bread," I told him. Rowan had promised that if I could keep down the broth, I could eat a normal supper. I was too tired to argue. She hadn't left my side since we'd found each other.

Marie-Hélène pulled up a stool next to my bed, sat, and slipped her hand in mine. "It is such a relief to have you here and have you safe."

"Thank you." I squeezed her hand.

Momo stood next to Rowan at the end of my bed. She curled her fingers around the brass foot rail.

"I owe you so much," I said to Momo. "Things would have gone differently had you told Hattori I was in the loft on Cusabo."

"I was miserable." She hung her head. "I couldn't bring myself to drag you into a life of misery as well."

"I thought misery loves company," Rory chirped.

"In my case, misery hated misery," Momo said.

There was a knock at the door. Rowan rushed to open it and let in Ram-An, who handed her a blue pouch. "We are all here," Rowan announced as she held up the velvet purse and gave it a shake.

Phillip cocked his head to the side as Rowan returned to the foot of my bed.

"Gather around, everyone," Rowan said. "Take a seat where you can."

I leaned forward in my bed, and Marie-Hélène fluffed up my pillows. Rory, Ram-An, and Momo sat on the edge of the cot to my left. Phillip sat on his bed. Rowan, who was clearly in charge, stood and cleared her throat.

"It is customary to honor those who have shown bravery in difficult times," Rowan said. "Normally, we have a banquet to celebrate, but in this case, I felt a more intimate ceremony was called for." She loosened the tie on the velvet pouch. "In honor of your valor, I have had gold rings forged." She pulled out a thick gold band and held it up. My eyes widened, and I licked my bottom lip.

"To Ram-An," Rowan continued. "When I first told you of my plan to find my sister, you volunteered to lead the charge. You've spent the last thirty years researching and plotting the best way to bring Anne to Amaranth. Through your diligence and intelligence, we have succeeded." Rowan looked at me and asked, "Do you have anything to add?"

"I do," I said. She passed the ring to me. It was thick and smooth on the outside, a plain gold band, but there were words etched on the inside. "Thank you for all you've done, Ram-An, and for your kindness to me."

Ram-An held out his hand, and I slipped it on his finger.

"A perfect fit," he said. "Thank you both."

"For Marie-Hélène." Rowan said, and Marie-Hélène stood with her head straight and shoulders back. "Who has been a faithful guard and companion. You are a master of details, large and small."

Rowan passed the ring to me.

"Thank you, Marie-Hélène, for everything," I said. My toes curled up under the bed covers. It seemed there had been a great deal of planning regarding me that I'd had no idea about. My chin dropped to my chest as I considered hiding under the bedclothes. This ceremony was certainly humbling.

"This is for Phillip," Rowan said, holding up a ring. "For your perseverance. For your faith in me." Rowan's voice cracked, and her eyes became shiny. "For finding Anne and risking your life to guide her home."

Rowan passed the ring to me. I turned it over in my palm, trying to grasp the breadth of all Phillip had done for me.

"You taught me so much: how to fight, how to be brave, how to walk like a boy." I smiled up at him. "I will never forget our journey."

Phillip held out his hand, and I slipped the ring on his finger. It was a perfect fit. Our fingers knitted together as if our bodies remembered each other's touch and wanted more. His eyes held mine, and for a moment, it seemed that everyone else had disappeared, and we were the only two people in the world. "We are bonded," I whispered.

"We are bonded." He kissed the tips of my fingers.

Marie-Hélène cleared her throat, and Rory snickered.

"For Rory." Rowan held up a gold band. "Who, at great risk to his own life and limb, aided Anne in her quest."

Rowan passed the ring to me.

"Rory, you are my brother. As soon as I'm allowed, I'm going to teach you how to swim."

Rory beamed as I slipped the ring on his finger, then held out his hand to admire it. "I've never had anything so nice," he said.

"For Momo," Rowan began. "Who, at great risk to herself, took action to renounce her sept, but gained a new family."

Rowan gave me her ring.

"I will never be able to thank you enough for what you've done for me," I said, sliding the ring over her knuckle.

"I did what I had to do," Momo said. "By saving you, I freed myself, which was not my intention, but I think was the gods' intent."

Rowan held up another gold band. "To Anne, whose bravery and kindness humbles me. I have you by my side once more, sister." Rowan gave me the ring, and I slipped it on my left hand.

"What does the inside say?" I asked.

"'Ad astra per aspera,'" Rowan said. "Through adversity to the stars."

"Where is yours?" I asked Rowan.

She pulled out one more ring. "Would you like to say something?" she asked me in a small voice.

"You deserve much more than a ring," I said.

"I will settle for having you by my side."

I held up the ring. "This symbolizes our bond. You never gave up on me. You sent your best people to risk their lives. I am grateful and proud to call you my sister." I pressed the ring to my lips and kissed it before I slipped it on her finger. "We are selfsame." Rowan sat on the edge of my bed, and we pressed our foreheads together. "We used to do this."

"Yes, we did." Teardrops clung to her eyelashes.

"Rowan," I said.

"Yes, sister?" she asked.

"I'm really hungry."

Rowan leaned back and laughed. "Ram-An, could you arrange for food for seven to be brought to the infirmary? I wish to dine with my favorite people."

While we waited for supper, Momo explained the samurai to Marie-Hélène. Rory entertained Rowan with his tale of how he and I had escaped the Echo. I scooted over so Phillip could climb into bed with me, and I rested my head on his shoulder.

"Are you happy?" he asked.

"Very," I said, holding out my hand against his to admire our matching rings. "I feel . . . confident." I stretched out my legs and sighed a long, comfortable sigh.

"You should. You've earned it."

"Do you want to hear about what happened with Rex?" I asked.

"When you're ready." Phillip used his nose and mouth to rub against the top of my head.

For the first time in what seemed like forever, I felt that I could truly breathe. No matter what tomorrow brought, I knew that I could face it. After all, hadn't I faced hard times before? Besides, I was with my people. Phillip's heart beat a steady rhythm under my ear. My sister glanced down to admire her ring, then smiled at me. I closed my eyes and thanked God for all his gifts.

Acknowledgements

I would like to thank the following people for their love, encouragement, and support:

Daniel Bonner, Wyatt Bonner, Tommy and Bernie Bonner, Tiffany Boozer, John and Rebecca Dempsey, Jerry and Jill Dennis, Kimberly Elkins, Starla Fitch, Christina Kann, Joe and Toni LePage, Leslie Muir, Brendan Murphy, Mike and Chris Murphy, Ryan and Melissa Murphy, Julianne Schaaf, Ginny Sloan, Carmen Toussaint, Rusty and Lisa Watts, Kelly Williams, all of my anesthesia and surgical friends, and the fine people at Brandylane.

Much of this book was written at Rockvale Writer's Colony in College Grove, TN, and at Rivendell Writer's Colony in Sewanee, TN.

About the Author

K. E. Bonner was always the first kid to sit down during a spelling bee. It wasn't until she was an adult that she was diagnosed with dyslexia, which explained why she always had to study three times harder than her peers. Being dyslexic taught her perseverance and kindness, her two favorite attributes. She lives in Georgia with her husband, two sons, and two dogs. When not writing, she loves to read, swim, explore new places, and meet fascinating people. If you have a dog, she would love to scratch behind its ears and tell it what a good pup it is.

9 781947 860926